# A Memory of Grief

Dale T. Phillips

To Jill,
Thanks for
being a reader.
Dale

### Try these other works by Dale T. Phillips

*Shadow of the Wendigo* (Supernatural Thriller)

**The Zack Taylor Mystery Series**
*A Memory of Grief*
*A Fall From Grace*
*A Shadow on the Wall*

**Story Collections**
*Fables and Fantasies* (Fantasy)
*Crooked Paths* (Mystery/Crime)
*Strange Tales* (Magic Realism, Paranormal)
*Apocalypse Tango* (Science Fiction)
*Halls of Horror* (Horror)
*Jumble Sale* (Mixed Genres)
*The Big Book of Genre Stories* (Different Genres)

**Non-fiction Career Help**
*How to Improve Your Interviewing Skills*

**With Other Authors**
*Insanity Tales*
*Rogue Wave: Best New England Crime Stories 2015*

Sign up for my newsletter to get special offers
http://www.daletphillips.com

# DEDICATION

*To Mindy, Bridget, and Erin, Always and Forever*

*Who showed me that family can be a wonderful and loving thing*

*And for Cherie, who always believes*

# ACKNOWLEDGMENTS

While the writing road is a lonely, solitary path, publication is a highway that requires the assistance of many. And so my thanks go out to the following folks, as well as those who have not been named, but have helped make this book possible:

First and foremost, my family, for putting up with me and my peculiar obsession of writing.

To my supportive "extended family" and friends, who nourished me with love along the way.

To Regina, who has listened to me yap about my dream of writing a novel since I was back taking classes from Stephen King, getting his feedback on my work.

To the critiquers and proofreaders, especially to the Tyngsboro Writer's Group, including but not limited to, the following: Joe Ross, Mike Johnson, Karen Johnson, Matt Lewin, Rick Cooper, Brian Hammar, Todd Savelle, and The Immortal Bernie Z. And to the staff of the Tyngsboro Public Library, who allowed us a space to meet for so long. Then to my later editors, who helped with reissuing the book.

To all those who taught me to write, and passed on the love and passion of the written word. And to all those giants who inspired me, older and modern. Too many to name, so just a few: Harlan Ellison, Stephen King, John D. MacDonald, Ray Bradbury, Robert Heinlein, Spider Robinson, Joe Haldeman.

Last, but certainly not least, YOU, dear reader, for having the wisdom and taste to read and appreciate this book. Zack has been a part of my life for a long time—I hope he'll be a part of yours.

*All that is left to one who grieves*
*Is convalescence. No change of heart or spiritual*
*Conversion, for the heart has changed*
*And the soul has been converted*
*To a thing that sees*
*How much it costs to lose a friend it loves*

— The Epic of Gilgamesh, Herbert Mason translation

# CHAPTER 1

Pain can be nature's way of telling you that you have done something really stupid. So I was getting quite a lecture. There was no way I could have won the fight, and sure, I'd known that going in. But I gave it my best. Then came the kick to my head, so fast that I had no time to block or duck. For the next hour, I'd simply tried to reassemble my thoughts.

Now I sat on a barstool, aching down to the bone with bruises and stiff limbs, holding an ice-filled bar towel against the cut over my eye. The coolness felt good. My head throbbed, but by some miracle I didn't seem to have a concussion, so I counted my blessings.

We were at a private nightclub near the edge of Miami's Little Havana. At Hernando's Hideaway, I was in charge of security, taking care of whatever trouble came up. Here in Miami, there was always trouble.

The mirror behind the bar showed the reflection of people around me. Hernando had permitted my rooting section to come in with me, even though the place didn't open for another few hours. The pain took all my focus for the moment, so I didn't want to talk to anyone. But I couldn't ignore Esteban, watching me from behind the bar.

"Your face looks hurted, Zack. Are you okay?"

I wasn't, but I didn't want to worry the kid.

"I'm fine."

"Want more ice?"

The water dripping down between my fingers had gone tepid.

"Sure."

He took the wrap from me, shook out a few slivers of ice, wrung the cloth out, and meticulously refilled it with cubes from behind the bar.

"Thanks," I said when he handed it back. I put it to my bruised flesh and sat very still. Snippets of conversation began to register.

"When Zack landed that kick in the second round, I thought he had him."

"Nah, man," said someone. "That just woke Gutierrez up, and he poured it on. Man, that guy's gonna be world champ someday."

"You did us all proud today, Zack," someone else said, slapping my back, which jolted me with fresh pain. "How about a drink?"

Esteban frowned and shook his head. "No, no, no. Zack don't drink. Zack never drinks."

The guy looked at Esteban and then at me. "Special Ed here for real? You work in a *bar.*"

I shrugged, sending another wave of hurt cascading through my injured cranium. I moaned softly, and my mind drifted away again. No one bothered me for a few minutes, and my head finally stopped hammering so hard.

Esteban placed an envelope on the bar in front of me.

"Zack, look. A letter came for you."

I looked at it, puzzled. Only my friend Ben knew where I was, and he always phoned, never wrote. He was supposed to call later to find out how I'd done. We'd have a good laugh when I explained how badly I'd got my butt whipped.

I put down the cloth and picked up the envelope. There was my name, in spiky handwriting, with no return address and a postmark from North Carolina.

Since my arms felt tired and heavy from the pounding I'd taken, it took a fumbling minute to pull out a newspaper clipping and a folded sheet of paper. The clipping fell, and fluttered to the floor. Somebody reached down to pick it up while I tried to read what looked like a letter. Moisture from the bar had mottled the paper with large, wet blots.

"You dropped this," someone said. I waved him off, trying to concentrate on making sense of the letter. He spoke again. "Don't you know a guy named Benjamin Sterling?"

"Yeah, Ben's my best friend," I said. I put down the letter and turned in the direction of the voice, my head pounding in protest. "Is he on the phone?"

There was no answer, just a sudden, strange silence. The guy looked away, and thrust the clipping at someone else. That guy frowned while reading it, then looked up at me.

"What is it?" I asked.

Neither of them spoke. The second guy put the piece of paper on the bar, and they both silently slipped back into the crowd. Wondering at their strange behavior, I picked up the clipping. It was from the Press-Herald in Portland, Maine. It said that Benjamin Sterling, a cook at the Pine Haven resort, had died from a self-inflicted gunshot wound, after a brief period in the Portland hospital for food poisoning.

No. It wasn't true, couldn't be true. No way. It was some other Ben Sterling. "No, no," I rasped. It was a joke, a sick joke.

Someone put a hand on my shoulder. I shrugged it away, angry. I grabbed the letter from the bar. My hands were shaking as I read it:

*Dear Zak,*

*We never got along but Ben always sed that we were the only two who mattered in his life. I rote to say how sorry I am about his dying. I still cant believe he done it. Shows you just never know. Thay called me*

11

*from Main and buryed him in the city cimatarry. I woulda called you but dint have no number, just this address.*

*Maureen*

*P.S. I did love him, but we was just too differnt.*

I felt cold inside, confused. I didn't believe it. What the hell was Ben's ex-wife up to? I read it again, and found myself trembling. My jaw was clenched so tight my teeth hurt. Killed himself? No damn way. I scanned the clipping again, trying to make sense of it, for Ben would never do that. Not ever.

I tried to stand, but dizziness forced me back onto the stool. People mumbled condolences, but their words slid off me like cold raindrops. I tuned them out. I needed a drink to push this away. My past came rushing back once more, after all the years of trying to forget. The floodwaters of memory swept in; I went under.

Some time later, the crowd was gone. Without people here, the room was too empty and still. It reminded me of the hollow ache inside.

Esteban stood staring at me, not moving. The pounding in my head had subsided to a dull ache, and the dizziness was gone. I wondered how long he and I had been like this.

I started breathing again. "Is Hernando upstairs?"

Esteban nodded, then shifted his eyes downward. "The bad man's with him."

"Raul?" I growled. "Did he push you again?"

"No. He only called me a stupid retard. It's okay."

"It's not okay!" I roared, slamming my hands to the bar and jumping up. The stool crashed to the floor, and Esteban backed away, looking terrified. I closed my eyes and ground my hands into my face. I couldn't stop shaking. I forced calm into my voice.

"I'm sorry, Esteban. I didn't mean to yell. Forget what he said. There's nothing wrong with you." I looked toward the back, to the stairs leading to Hernando's office. "He's just a bad man who enjoys hurting other people. And he has to stop."

I felt the old rage stir within me, a beast unchained and hungry. Something was going to happen. Something bad.

Dale T. Phillips

# CHAPTER 2

At the top of the stairs, I could hear Raul's loud voice coming through the thick office door. I barged right in without knocking.

Hernando sat behind his desk, looking fresh and elegant in his white suit, his black hair streaked with gray. The manicured right hand waved to make a point, and his gold ring winked in the office light.

Raul was a different story. Wrinkled, rumpled, and furiously sweaty, at six-foot -two and over four hundred pounds, he looked less like an accountant, and more like some monstrous baby. He applied a thoroughly wet handkerchief to his mottled red face, despite the cool office air. He glared at me for a moment and turned away as if I didn't matter.

"I'm telling you, you need to make some changes," Raul said to Hernando. "You'll bring in more money."

"I would rather lose everything than become like those South Beach clubs," Hernando replied. "Some are no better than crack houses."

"Yeah, well, you should have their cash flow. You know how much those places take in every night?"

"Excuse me," I interrupted. "Hernando, can I speak to you for a minute?"

Raul turned to me in a fury. "We're having a fucking *business* meeting here, dickhead."

"Sorry to interrupt, but this can't wait."

"It's gonna have to wait. You're as stupid as that retard downstairs."

I snapped out my right hand, seizing him by the windpipe. His mouth opened soundlessly, and his eyes bugged out.

"Zack," said Hernando. I looked at him. "Let him go."

I looked back at Raul, where it seemed like someone else's hand squeezed a human throat. I clicked back into the world and let go. Raul coughed and rubbed his injured trachea, while I wiped the greasy sweat from my hand onto my pants. It had been like grabbing a giant garden slug.

"I need five minutes," I said.

Raul started to speak, but I cut him off with a gesture. He shut his mouth and moved toward the door.

"Raul." He looked back. "If you ever talk to Esteban like that again, I will break your legs. You leave that kid alone or you'll get hurt. Got me?"

He left, shooting me a look of pure poison.

Hernando sighed and set aside a sheaf of papers. "You have something very important to tell me, I think. What is wrong?"

I pulled out the letter and the clipping and handed them to him. He read them through, frowning, and looked up.

"This Benjamin was your good friend, yes? The one you speak of."

My throat got thick as I spoke. "He saved my life."

Hernando nodded. "If someone is very lucky, he will have a friend such as this. But only once. I had such a friend, long ago in my country, before the bearded ones came with their guns and uniforms." He glanced back at the letter and shook his head. "Who is this person who sends you such news?"

"Ben's ex-wife Maureen. She and I never really got along. Ben got involved with her because she was getting beaten by her ex-con boyfriend."

"What happened?"

I shook my head. "He used a line from Bob Dylan."

*'I helped her out of a jam, I guess, but I used a little too much force'.*

"Ben felt so guilty about her getting hurt that he married her. When he did, I kept my mouth shut and never tried to come between them. Sometimes people you care for make mistakes, and you can't do anything about it.

"It didn't even last a year. Ben treated her well and tried hard to make it work, but she walked out on him. I helped him pick up the pieces, and haven't seen or heard from her since. And now this. She says she's sorry he shot himself. I know he didn't. That means someone killed him. I'm going up to Maine where he died, and find out what happened. I don't know how long I'll be gone. I'll stay until you find a replacement, but I'd like to go as soon as possible."

Hernando held up his hand. "A wrong has been done, and you must go. I will make arrangements for tonight." He smiled. "I think to replace you, I will need two men, large ones. Is there anything you need?" He produced a gold money clip that held a sheaf of bills.

"No, thank you." I waved it away.

"But you must at least take your wages. This will be easier than a check, yes?" He peeled off some hundreds and handed them to me. It was more than what he owed me, but I couldn't refuse the only help he could offer.

"Thank you. I hate to leave like this."

"And I am sorry you must leave, and sorry for your pain. I shall miss you."

Hernando looked over at the table where a chessboard was laid out, our casual game in progress.

"I shall miss our games as well. No one plays quite like you. Always attacking and sacrificing for more attacks."

I smiled and shrugged. "Sometimes it works."

"And all too often you pay the price for your foolishness. Ah, Zachary." He shook his head. "You have that great pain that you carry like a load of stones within you. And to hide it, you seek the darkness, and the people that live there. Even here in sunny Miami you hide in the shadows.

"You are missing a home, a family, love. You had one very good friend, and now he is gone, and you want to hurt someone to fill that hole. You are not bad, but you know the ways of criminals, and you may use those ways to strike out against others. You will have to lie, wear masks of deceit. But you must keep true to yourself, or this quest for revenge will destroy you and others. You will have to find something to fill that emptiness."

"I'll be fine."

"Only if you control your rage. Look what you did to Raul just now, without even thinking. If that anger is unleashed and unchecked, more people will be hurt."

Hernando sat back in his chair.

"I almost feel sorry for this man who killed your friend. He will be a lucky one to see the jail."

"I've never killed anyone," I said. "I just want to see him caught."

"Men like this are not easily caught. If he killed your friend, he is very, very dangerous. You must be careful."

"I will, Hernando."

"You will not. You will hurl yourself into this, not caring if you live or die, just like your attacks in chess."

I sat there, not knowing what to say.

"If you *should* live through this," he said, "come back when you are done, and tell me what happened."

"I'll do that. Good-bye. Take care of Esteban."

Hernando rose and extended his hand. We shook, and I was aware of yet more loss.

I went to the chessboard and tipped over my king, resigning. The game here was over, and a whole new one was beginning.

Downstairs, Esteban leaned on his mop as I told him I was going away for a while. His face screwed up like he was going to cry, until I told him I'd send him postcards and a T-shirt, and he lit up like it was Christmas.

Behind the bar, the liquor bottles stood like deadly chess pieces, calling me to play.

Dale T. Phillips

# CHAPTER 3

When I returned to my rented room, my landlady, Mrs. Harris, was watering her flowers in a tropical orange print dress. She smiled and waved, but as I got closer, she got a good look at me and her expression changed.

"Zack, what's wrong? You look like you lost your best friend."

"I have."

She pursed her lips and set down the watering can. "Come inside and tell me about it."

I followed her into the house, where the air conditioning had the interior chilled about thirty degrees cooler than outside. She left me on the couch while she went into the other room. There was a small painting by Salvador Dali on the wall. It was an original, not a copy, and I normally liked it, but now all I could do was stare blankly.

She returned with two glasses of iced tea, and handed me one. I took it and gripped it with both hands. She sat in the chair opposite, sipped from her glass, and studied me and my injured face.

"Were you fighting?"

I looked up. "Sparring match at the gym."

She nodded and said nothing. I held the cool glass up to the cut, against the swollen flesh.

"Want an ice bag for that?"

"No, thanks." I took a long drink, savoring the cool sweetness. Mrs. Harris sat and sipped, not speaking, letting me get it out at my own pace. I drained the glass, set it down, and brought out the letter with the clipping inside. She took it from me. She retrieved her glasses from the side table, slipped them on, and read the letter.

"That's the one who came to visit you, right?" I nodded, and she nodded back. "He was a nice young man. Funny, too."

"He didn't kill himself," I said. "Someone killed him."

"Oh." She flicked the letter with a fingernail and thought for a minute. She cocked her head as she looked at me. "So you're going to go see what really happened. You want to catch the one who killed him."

I nodded.

"Well, then." We were silent as she drank more tea.

"Don't worry about the room," she said. "It'll all be here when you get back."

"I don't know how long I'll be gone."

"Don't worry about that. You leaving tonight?"

"As soon as I can pack and clean out the refrigerator."

She waved her hand. "Leave it. I'll go in there tomorrow and take care of everything."

"That's a lot of trouble."

"Forget it." She made another brushing gesture with her hand. "You taking the books?"

I had three overflowing bookcases and a dozen stuffed boxes.

"No. I'll be traveling light."

"You'd never fit them all anyway. I never knew anyone who reads as much as you. You could be a teacher."

I shook my head at the thought.

"We'll miss you, kiddo." She looked sad. "I feel a lot safer with you here."

"You could get a dog." I smiled for the first time since hearing the news. She snorted a laugh. I rubbed my hands together, and she finished her tea.

"Forgive me for being curious," she said. "But how are you going to go about finding out what happened?"

"I don't really know," I replied. "Guess I'll just start with the place he worked. Talk to people there. And he would have found a martial arts school, or dojo, to work out at, so I'll check those."

"What will you say?"

"I'll just talk to them about how they got along with him, if he said anything that might have indicated trouble, stuff like that. From my security experience, I'm pretty good at reading people, and can tell if they're lying. If something isn't right, if I think they're not telling the truth, I'll follow them around, see who else they talk to, and so on."

She frowned. "And you might tip off the killer that way, before you know who it is. Sounds dangerous. Couldn't you just go to the police?"

"Ah, that could be problematic. Past history, you know."

She made a face of mock horror. "You mean I've been harboring a criminal under my roof?"

"Afraid so. Sort of. Former. Maybe I should have told you," I said.

"Well, it's not something you drop in casual conversation, for goodness sake. You're a good person, I know that about you. My guess is that you've hung out with some not-so-good people in the past. You've definitely got some kind of secret, something you feel guilty about. So I guess the police are out."

"They'd probably wind up investigating me instead."

"That doesn't leave you a lot to go on," she said, looking thoughtful. "What if it was some random thing? We have a lot of those here, you know."

"Maybe, but Ben was good at protecting himself. If they're calling it a suicide, he wouldn't have had any defensive wounds. Somebody got close to him with a gun, and that would be hard to do. He could have stopped most people at close range."

"Are you like that?"

"Somewhat."

"Good thing," she said. "Don't get hurt, 'cause then I couldn't move those weights out of the garage. Where are you going, anyway?"

"Maine."

"Ah. It's gotta be cooler there." She sounded wistful.

"That's a fact. And it'll be nice to see real hardwood trees again," I said. "And hills. But I'll miss you."

"Just my cooking, I'm sure."

"I don't have many friends, and you've been good to me."

She smiled and reached over to pat my knee.

"And if I was forty years younger, I'd have been a lot better to you, like that young lady I saw you skinny-dipping with in my pool that night." She laughed. "Oh, now I've embarrassed you. Good to see you can still blush. Well, maybe you'll meet someone nice up there." She paused. "You've just kind of drifted through life up until now, haven't you?"

I nodded.

"But you've got a mission now," she continued. "If it doesn't kill you, maybe it'll do you some good. So you go on, now, and do what you have to do."

We stood up, and I gave her a goodbye hug. In the garage that she'd let me convert into a gym, I put the weights and the bench against the wall. I went to take down the heavy canvas bag that hung from a rig in the ceiling. The bag was made for kicking and punching, and I sure as hell wanted to hit something, to make it hurt like I was hurting. I wanted it to be the person who had killed Ben. I started hammering on the bag, as the rage poured forth from me in a hot river. But the fight with Gutierrez had taken its toll, and I soon stopped, out of breath and more sore than I'd been before.

24

After a time I got myself under control, and took the bag down, though the size and weight made me think of a dead body. I pushed that thought away, and got the rest of my things packed. It didn't take long, with my Spartan quarters. Then I said goodbye to the palmetto bugs and the little scampering lizards, and went downtown.

Soon I was at my bank, trying to get money from my account, sitting before a fresh-cheeked kid, signing papers. He didn't look old enough to shave, but here he was, with a photograph of a wife and child on his desk. The woman in the picture was also young, and was tanned and pretty in that South Florida way. She looked happy in the photo, holding her child with obvious pride and love, and I felt an ache, as I was reminded of all I didn't have.

For someone who'd done what I had done, a family was not in the cards. I had run away from my past, but dragged it behind me everywhere I went. I could only press my nose to the glass for a glimpse of normal people enjoying life in the warmth and the light. The people I was close to lived in the night, in isolation, in the darkness of the human soul. People who hurt and got hurt, who understood suffering and dealt with it on a daily basis.

The lucky young man said something, breaking my reverie. I signed more papers, got a bank check and a sizable chunk of cash, and left.

At the post office, I signed more papers to have my mail forwarded in my name to General Delivery at the Portland Post Office. With all my affairs arranged, I drove out of town, headed north.

It was far too easy for me to leave. When you hide from the world, you don't make many attachments. I was gone so fast and with so little trace of my living here, it was as if I were a ghost.

Once past Fort Lauderdale, the traffic eased up a bit. I stopped and ate, then got back on Interstate 95, which ran all the way north to Maine. As the sun went down, leaving great, bloody streaks through the sky, the night bugs came out to die by the thousands on my windshield. Animals lay crushed and broken in the road.

The highway ran up past the horrid sprawl of Jacksonville, through Georgia, and on into the night. When my eyes were grainy, somewhere in the endless stretches of the Carolinas, I pulled over at a rest stop full of campers and minivans. I caught a little nap, but my long-dead brother Tim came by to disturb my dreams. This time, he had Ben with him for some tag-team haunting.

The dream scared me awake. Shaking, I got out and walked around, listening to the rumble of the late-night trucks and the hiss of tires on asphalt. Booze was the only thing that made the ghosts go away. I wanted a drink very badly.

But drinking and ghosts had to wait until I could deal with them. I had a killer to catch, and a thousand miles to drive before I was even close. I got back in the car, and started driving again, as the sun began to lighten the sky.

# CHAPTER 4

The address Maureen had given in her letter was in a little Carolina town at the end of nowhere, more than two hours off the highway. I got to the area around lunchtime, stopped for gas, and asked for directions.

The place where Maureen lived turned out to be a shabby mobile home park. Mobile home was really too grand a term, for these worn trailers sagged in uneven rows like defeated old soldiers. The vehicles parked in the postage-stamp yards ran to pickups, motorcycles, and dented old cars held together with Bondo, duct tape, and baling wire. Rusted junk was scattered about like an ancient giant's discarded armor. Castoffs of furniture and broken things lay baked and peeling in the sun.

Ben wouldn't have wanted this for Maureen, not even after what she'd done to him. I felt several kinds of uncomfortable and wanted to get out of here, but I needed to talk to her.

I found the trailer number and shut off the engine. My cool cocoon was gone as soon as I opened the door and the hot, stagnant air wrapped around me like a musty old coat. Miami's air could be a steam bath, but at least it had the ocean. Here there was no relief, no breeze, like being in Hell.

No one else was fool enough to be out in this weather. The only sound, apart from the ticking of my car's engine, was the hum of air conditioners from some of the trailers. I wondered how those without them survived.

The dust in the yard puffed up as I walked through it, and there was a sour odor of rotted food. Movement caught my eye as a peeper twitched a curtain in the window of the adjacent trailer. At the door of number twenty-seven, the heat of the sun reflected off the metal siding. The whole trailer shuddered like a living thing when I knocked.

The door opened to show a gray, tired-looking woman. It took me a few seconds to recognize Maureen, for she looked at least a decade older than her thirty years. She also had a nasty, purplish bruise high up on her cheek, just under the eye.

She recognized me, and her mouth made a little O of surprise. She shot a look over her shoulder, and turned back to me with eyes full of naked fear. Before I could say anything, a loud voice drawled from inside, a sound thick with ugly backwoods meanness.

"Who the hell is it?"

"Uh, just a salesman, honey," she said.

"Well, tell 'im to piss off. And close the goddamned door. You're lettin' in the hot air."

I knew where the hot air was coming from, but kept quiet. Maureen whispered quickly.

"There's a diner in town, the Rest E-Z. Kin you meet me there? About an hour?"

I nodded, just before Maureen was brushed aside like a curtain. The man was at least six -foot -five, and he filled the doorway. Beard stubble darkened his cheeks, and all he wore was a stained, sleeveless T-shirt and boxer shorts. He was losing his hair and gaining a gut, but his arms were beefy with muscle, the left one sporting a tattoo of a naked woman riding an anchor. Ex-Navy, then, and ex-boxer, I guessed, seeing the lumpy tissue around the eyes and ears, the broken nose, and the big scarred knuckles.

Since he was probably the source of Maureen's facial, part of me wanted to get him out in the hot, dirty yard and teach him a lesson. But I knew that whatever punishment I gave him, he'd later give back to her twice over.

It hurt me to do it, but I smiled my oh-gosh smile, doing my best to look sheepish and apologetic. He didn't smile back.

"Sorry to bother you." I almost said "sir", but couldn't bring myself to do it. "I was just leaving."

He scowled. Maybe I'd ruined his plans by not mouthing off, so he didn't have an excuse to punch me. He poked a finger at me like he was pronouncing sentence.

"Don't you come back heah no more, or I might have to teach you a lesson."

He slammed the door so hard that the whole trailer shook. I walked back to the car, trembling from the effort of keeping the anger in. Ben's death had cost me, and I wanted someone else to pay. If I was this close to the edge, it was just a matter of time before I exploded.

The four patrons of the Rest E-Z Diner looked up when I entered, studied me, and bobbed their heads back down. The interior was hot, but it was better than being outside. The ceiling fans revolved in lazy circles, nudging the sluggish air just enough to make it breathable. There was a smell of old grease.

The booths had red vinyl bench seats split in a number of places and patched with tape of a different hue. On the tabletops, black cracks ran like rivers on a map. A stale odor of sweat and cigarette smoke clung to the seats, and my shirt tried to cling as well.

This diner was a time machine from back in the days before air conditioning, and the only redeeming feature was that each booth had an old chrome jukebox on the wall where you could feed in quarters and play country music songs. They had the good old stuff, from back when the music was real and came from the heart, not manufactured to sound like every other pop song. For four quarters, I got

29

five tunes. Patsy Cline began falling to pieces, and I smiled and looked over the plastic-coated menu that felt sticky.

A large woman, wearing a brown polyester waitress uniform and a nametag that read "Shirley," smiled a big-hearted, big-woman smile as she came over. She reminded me of a friendly bear.

"Wakinagetcha?"

For a moment I thought she was speaking Cherokee, but then I realized what she was saying. She took out a pen from behind her ear and pulled a pad from the pocket of her apron.

"How about two hot dogs with onions and a bottle of root beer, please."

She leisurely wrote my order on the pad.

"Sure thing, honey," she said, slowly moving away from the table. If I had to be in this heat all the time, I'd probably move like that, too.

Marty Robbins was in trouble in old El Paso when Shirley returned with my root beer. With nothing to do but wait, I braved going outside, and bought a newspaper from the vending machine. On the way back to my seat, I pocketed one of the little matchbooks with the Rest E-Z logo on it and a phone number. Back at my seat, I read the paper and silently sang along with Hank Williams.

Shirley brought the hot dogs, two wrinkled things wrapped in soggy buns. The stale potato chips were definitely the crowning touch. I took my time, read every word in the paper twice through, and got almost half the second dog down before pushing it away. I did not think I would be returning to dine at this establishment. I declined the offer of dessert.

The other customers left, except for one old man. It was too quiet without the music. Every minute spent there made me itch to get away. Flies buzzed in the big front window, making lazy attempts to get through the glass. The fans overhead ticked their monotonous refrain. The old man got up and left, and I was alone.

Maureen finally showed up, wearing a brown uniform to match the one Shirley wore. She looked better than she had at the trailer, but even makeup and big sunglasses couldn't completely hide the bruise. She carefully looked around before coming over.

Shirley came from out back, holding a big glass pot of coffee.

"Maureen, honey, whatchu doing here? You're not on for another hour." Then she noticed Maureen's face. "Oh, honey, are you all right?" Shirley shot a hard look at me, the friendly woman all gone. "You one of Bobby Lee's buddies?"

"Who?"

"It's all right," said Maureen. "He's okay."

"He better be, or this coffee might get spilled by accident."

"Hey, I'm on her side," I said.

Shirley scowled at me like she didn't believe it.

Maureen spoke up. "I gotta talk to him, Shirl. Let me know if someone's coming? I don't want Bobby Lee finding out."

Shirley looked at the two of us and nodded. "Sure thing, hon. You let me know if you need anything." She replaced the coffee pot and stayed out of earshot, standing guard.

Maureen left her sunglasses on and stood fidgeting by the booth. Neither of us spoke right away. We were two embarrassed people who didn't know what to say, with only a ghost in common.

"Thanks for coming," Maureen said in her thick accent. Her eyes avoided mine. "I wadn't sure you would."

"Yeah, your friend doesn't seem to care for visitors. Sorry if I caused you any trouble. I tried to call ahead, but couldn't find any listing."

"The phone's in Bobby Lee's name."

"Ah." There was another silence. I really wished she'd sit down. It was awkward talking up to her, and the sunglasses didn't help.

31

"Thank you for sending me the news," I said. "It was good of you to let me know."

"Your address was in the box of stuff they sent."

"Did you go to the funeral?"

Her head dropped, as if she was embarrassed.

"I couldn't."

I guessed the reason and swallowed hard, thinking of how Ben had helped people all his life and wound up alone at the end of it.

"So how did you find out?"

"Some policeman called from up in Maine."

"What was his name?"

"I forget. He told me what happened, said he was sorry. He asked me some questions, and I told him about Ben and me breaking up, the divorce and all."

"Anything else?"

"Asked if I'd ever seen any sign of Ben wanting to kill hisself. I couldn't think of any."

"So what did you think when you heard that Ben had shot himself?"

"I'se real surprised and all. I thought it was kinda strange."

"He didn't do it," I said, feeling bitter. God, she'd been married to him. She should have known him better.

"But that's what the paper said."

"The paper's wrong. Ben didn't pull that trigger. Someone else did."

When that sank in, her eyes went wide.

"You mean someone kilt him? Why?"

"That's what I intend to find out. I'm going up there."

"Oh, Lord."

There was another silence while she digested this. She frowned.

"How come you know that, anyway?"

"That he didn't kill himself?" I looked off into the distance, pushing away painful memories. "It's a complicated story," I said at last. "Let's just say I've known him so well for so long, I know he wouldn't do that."

"Yeah, I guess you knew him even better'n me. Here, men will go huntin' or fishin' or drinkin' together, but they's just friends, like when Bobby Lee talks about his Navy buddies. But it weren't nothin' like the way Ben's eyes would light up when he talked about some of the places you boys used to go. I'se a little jealous, you know? He'd 'a died for you. I ain't never seen nothin' like that. Men ain't like that where I come from. Sometimes I even thought ..." She stopped abruptly, blushing furiously, unable to meet my eyes. I guessed where she was going.

I sighed. "It wasn't like that."

"I'm sorry. I didn't mean ..."

"Forget it."

She was quiet a moment before speaking, tracing one of the cracks in the tabletop with her fingernail.

"See, that's why I get confused and all about you two. Any other man I ever knew would'a smacked me for saying innythang like that. But you're like him. He never got mad when I thought he would. But I seen him mad, I seen him hit people."

She bit her lip before going on, as if some dark memory stirred within her. "But when I'd try to make him just a little bit mad sometimes, you know, just to know he cared, like when I'd flirt with a man and all, he dint do nothin'. He never even yelled at me. So I figured, I dunno ..."

The realization of what she was saying struck me. "Oh, my God. You left him because he didn't hit you, because you thought he didn't love you." I shook my head in disbelief. "Maureen, Ben loved you very much, and it hurt him when you left."

From beneath the sunglasses, a drop rolled down her cheek. From the other side came another drop. And she wasn't making a sound. She'd probably had lots of practice. Used to being hurt by the men in her life, she had come to expect it as her due. Now I knew why she lived with someone like Bobby Lee.

I also understood why Ben had married her. He wanted to save her. When we were kids, playing cowboys like the ones we saw on television, he wanted to be Paladin, journeying out like a knight of old to help the afflicted. Me, I wanted to be a bounty hunter like Steve McQueen, in Wanted: Dead or Alive.

I looked at Maureen with pity. I wasn't angry at her anymore. What was done, was done. The past couldn't be changed. If it could, my whole life would have been different.

"Honey!" Shirley's voice came out sharp and loud. Maureen looked out the window and gave a gasp of fright. She scurried out back, through the door to the kitchen.

The door jingled open and a man in dirty jeans and shirt, with a scraggly beard and a billed cap, looked around and saw me. He stared at me and made no pretense of not being rude.

"Something wrong?" I said.

He ignored me and sat at the counter and engaged Shirley in conversation, nodding toward me as he spoke. She shrugged and spoke back.

I'd found out about all I was going to. Leaving enough money for the lunch and a generous tip, I went back out into the stifling heat, as the dirty man's gaze bored into the back of my head.

# CHAPTER 5

If you can stay awake, nighttime is the best time to drive Interstate 95. There are no traffic snarls. It's uncrowded and cool and quiet, except when the big tractor-trailer trucks roar by you like the Roadrunner streaking by Wile E. Coyote. You find some faraway station on the radio that you can hear only at night, set the cruise control, and click off the miles.

The only trouble is, if you have painful memories, like I do, they'll come to visit you in the empty solitude of a night drive. I tried thinking of the good times with Ben, but the horror of his sudden death washed all else away. And Ben's death brought up the memory of Tim, as raw and hard as if it had happened yesterday.

Eventually, even my ghosts got sleepy. Somewhere in New Jersey, my eyes grew heavy, so I pulled in and napped for a few hours at the Molly Pitcher Rest Stop.

Next morning, I was crossing the long, high bridge over the Piscataqua River that divided Maine and New Hampshire. The early morning sun sparkled off the water far below, giving the bright promise of a lovely day, and burning off the black thoughts. Maine was an old friend that always welcomed you back.

The morning was cool and the sky was clear blue, without the haze of Miami. No need for the air conditioner here. I cranked down the window and breathed in clean, crisp air, which took the edge off my weariness.

I drove up the turnpike to the Maine Mall, and got off the highway to find a room. I wound up at the Gibson Motor Court, even though it sounded like a place for guitars and traffic violators. Five minutes after I got in, I shut the heavy drapes and lay down to sleep.

Waking in darkness in an unfamiliar place is a scary feeling, especially when you've been dreaming about ghosts. Disoriented, wondering if I was still dreaming, I stumbled to the drapes and pulled one open so the light flooded in. My body clock was completely out of whack. I was sore all over, a throbbing headache threatened to pop my forehead out, and my mouth tasted like used socks.

A long, long, hot shower helped on all counts. I did a few light stretches to work against the stiffness, and changed into some clean clothes. I stopped by the motel office, and took a handful of matchbooks with the motel name and number printed on them. My new business cards. The office had maps as well, so I got one of Portland, and another one of the surrounding area. Then I went in search of food, and found a place that looked respectable. After eating, I felt better, and my headache was mostly gone.

From a pay phone, I made a few calls to city offices to find out where Ben was buried. At the cemetery, I walked around until I found the marker for Ben's grave, a plain, flat stone, with only his name. A small tribute, lost in a sea of granite forget-me-nots. Nothing to say what he was like, how he'd helped people, how he'd made them smile.

Staring at the grave gave me an ache that was so bad I wanted to go back to the emotional numbness I'd cultivated for so long. The new pain revived the old, and memories came back, sharp as spikes. With the memories came the old siren's call to drown them, to drink them away with all my thoughts. People who haven't been there don't know what it's like to have that serpent whispering seductively in your ear, telling you how to stop the pain. For some of us, the tortures of destroying yourself by continually drinking to blackout are nothing compared to the nightmares we carry around in our heads.

"You're too young to be out here." The nearby voice startled me out of my thoughts. Few things make you jump like a voice in a cemetery when you think you're alone. A sad-faced old woman stood there, dressed in worn, dark clothes. She had thick glasses and a cane.

"This place should be for people like me," she said. "People who've lived until they're old and tired." She nodded her head in the direction of Ben's stone. "Not your wife, I hope?"

I really wasn't in any kind of talkative mood, but I spoke anyway. "No. My friend."

"Ah. That's bad, but not like losing your husband of forty-two years. That's my Henry, over there." She indicated another marker. "Yours pretty recent, I gather? Haven't seen you out here before."

"Yeah." Why wouldn't she go away and leave me alone?

"It's hard at first, but it gets better with time."

I wanted her gone, so I could wallow in my private misery.

She kept at it. "How did your friend die?"

Trying to shock her a little, to see if I could scare her off, I said, "He was murdered."

"Oh." She put a hand to her mouth. "Oh, my." That quieted her for a minute, but I couldn't focus while she stood there. I turned to go, but she piped up yet again.

"What are you going to do?"

I looked at her. "I'm going to find out who did it, and make them pay." I started walking away.

"Don't end up here," she called out. "Before your time, that is. We all end up here eventually."

What she said sent me over the edge. I turned back and almost spit the words at her. "So what the hell are we here for, then? If we're all just going to die? What's it all for, all this suffering, huh? What's the goddamned point?"

She recoiled, putting a hand up to protect herself. Ashamed of myself, and furious, I turned away once more.

"I wanted to kill myself," she said. "And I still do, some days."

That stopped me.

"When my Henry passed, I was crazy with grief. Father Mike was telling me he'd gone to a better place, so I asked him why shouldn't I join him, if I could be with him in a better place? He said that wasn't God's plan, that I should remember Henry and continue on down here until God was ready. He said it was what we did with our time that mattered. That if we had all the time in the world, we would never value anything. That our lives were all temporary was what made everything so precious."

To someone like me who had wasted so much, her words were an indictment. I had squandered years, running away from myself and my past. Maybe that was why I was so adamant about catching Ben's killer, so I could justify my existence.

I'd been thinking about it for a minute or two, and started to ask the old woman another question. But when I turned around, she wasn't there. I looked in all directions, and didn't see her. The back of my neck felt unnaturally cold, and I shivered in the August heat.

I all but ran out of there.

# CHAPTER 6

To me, hospitals were the place where people went to die, so I wasn't happy to be at one. The Maine Medical Center was a complex of fortress-like structures. I wondered if they meant to keep the diseases out, or keep the sickness bottled up behind the walls.

The woman at the information desk sent me to the ironically named Patient Services, where it took far too long to confirm that Ben had been a patient, and then only after I'd claimed to be a relative and offered to make a payment on his bill. As I'd suspected, he'd had no insurance and had been killed before the bill had been settled.

He'd been treated by a Dr. Rivard, and they directed me to the third floor room where Ben had stayed. The nurse behind the third floor desk station was all attitude, like Big Nurse from *One Flew Over the Cuckoo's Nest*. She eyed me like a schoolteacher sizing up a potential troublemaker.

"Hello," I said, trying to be my most winning. She didn't smile. "Could you please tell me where I can find Dr. Rivard?"

"Dr. Rivard is on vacation." She bit off the words.

"Do you know when he'll be back?"

"End of the month."

The sound I heard was my teeth grinding in frustration. "I wonder if you could help me then," I said, doubting it. I took out an old picture of Ben and me, arm in arm, laughing in front of a canoe.

"This man was here a while ago with food poisoning. Do you remember him?"

"I wouldn't know. I just transferred up here last week."

Probably here for her winning personality.

The next two nurses I asked didn't even break stride as they answered in the negative. I was about ready to tackle one just to get her to stop moving.

"Excuse me," I said, waving the picture at yet one more quickly moving figure. "Do you remember this man? He had food poisoning?"

She stopped to look.

"Allison."

"Excuse me?"

"Allison Chambers. I think she was on duty then."

"Do you know where I might find her?"

She gestured vaguely down the corridor and strode away. Further down the hall I saw a black-haired nurse come out of a room.

"Nurse Chambers?"

"Yes?" She stopped and turned, flashing a lovely pair of blue eyes. But they looked impatient, and I was tired of impatient people. Other than myself, that is.

"This man was in here not too long ago." I thrust the picture at her before she could run away. "Ben Sterling. He had food poisoning."

"Mushrooms." She looked up from the picture to me, the long eyelashes making a graceful sweep.

"Beg pardon?"

"He ate poison mushrooms."

"Oh," I said. "Could you take a minute and tell me about him?"

"We're pretty busy right now."

"I know. Everyone's made that quite clear." Even to myself, I sounded peeved.

"We have patients to take care of."

"If I jump out the window and break my leg, will you talk to me then?"

"You could try it." She was certainly a cool one.

"Look, I've been here for an hour trying to get some information. All I've got so far is a runaround."

"We have to get medications to people. They come before you."

"I only want a few minutes of your time. I just came from the cemetery where my friend is buried." Then I shamelessly piled it on. "Did you ever lose someone that mattered?"

That made her pause. "This is really the wrong time."

"So when would be a good time?"

"An hour from now, when things quiet down. I usually get a break around then."

"Where should I meet you?"

"Downstairs in the cafeteria."

"Thank you."

She walked away, leaving behind a clean, faintly powdery scent that I liked.

I went back out to my car for the maps, and brought them back to the cafeteria. I paid for a cup of coffee and took a seat where I could watch the door. I studied the maps to learn the area until Nurse Chambers came in. She bought a coffee and came over to where I sat. She hadn't lost a bit of loveliness in the last sixty minutes. I stood up, feeling an odd flutter.

Starched white uniforms were not what I considered flattering, but she made hers look good, with a trim, solid frame that moved well. Short black hair framed those luminous blue eyes that seemed dangerously attractive. Her nose had a rather appealing slight upward tilt, and her lips were full without being thick. She wore very little makeup, and needed none. As she added two sugars to her coffee, I sneaked a peek at her finger and saw no telltale ring of entanglement.

"I'd like to apologize for before," I said. "I was pushy and rude." I managed get it out without tripping over my tongue.

She looked at me, her lip cocked in a half smirk.

"Yes, you were. Maybe I was, too, a little."

"I guess nobody has any patience."

She winced at my pun. "Well, you're not a comedian, so who are you?"

I showed her the photo. She put down her cup and looked closely at it.

"Ben and I grew up together," I explained. "We went to school together, worked at some of the same jobs, went on trips with each other. He even saved my life once. This was taken about four years ago. Did you know he died shortly after being released from here?"

"Yes, I heard. I'm very sorry."

"So am I. I'm trying to find out what happened to him."

She wrinkled her brow. Even that was nice. "You mean why he …?"

"He didn't kill himself." I said it quickly. "Yes, I know, they said it was suicide, but it wasn't. Ben … Ben wasn't like that. We both hated guns, never used them. He would never kill himself, so somebody shot him. I wonder if you could tell me anything about when he was here. Under the circumstances, I don't think you'll be violating any patient confidentiality."

"He had traces of amanita mushroom in his system. Deathcaps. He was here for three days, with a high fever and frequent vomiting. We gave him fluids, and kept him hydrated. He was getting better, but he should have stayed here another two or three days."

"He left early?"

"Yes, he was very weak. We were amazed to see him stand, let alone walk. His face was white, but he did it, even though the doctor told him not to. If a patient wants to

A Memory of Grief

check out, we can't really stop them. I heard they told him he'd have to return to his job or they'd replace him."

I swore under my breath.

"Your friend was nice," she said. "Even though he was sick, he was polite to all of us nurses. He'd be racked with cramps and still cracking jokes."

"That's Ben."

"Did he have a family?"

"Some very distant relatives he hasn't seen in twenty years."

"He was so young." She shook her head. "What a shame."

"Could he have seen anything, maybe something illegal, while he was here?"

She thought for a minute, and shook her head.

"I can't think of anything. We didn't have any obvious criminals, at least that I know of. He was in his room the whole time. He had a roommate for one night, awaiting gallbladder surgery. But Mr. Decker is sixty-seven and not much of a threat."

"Did the police come by?"

"Yes, they spoke with Dr. Rivard. He's away on vacation now. He couldn't tell them very much."

"I don't have much to go on myself."

"Do you really think someone killed him?"

"Someone pulled that trigger, someone who could get close enough. Ben was pretty good at taking care of himself. But for the life of me, I can't think of why this happened."

"Are you some kind of ..." She smiled, looking embarrassed. "Private eye?"

"No, just someone trying to find out what happened to a friend."

"What about the police?"

"Unless there's something to go on, they can't do much. I have more time to ask around, and as you found out, I don't mind bothering people to get answers. Maybe if I bother the right people, something will turn up."

She looked at me as a frown creased that lovely forehead. "If your friend was murdered, isn't that dangerous?"

"Yes."

"That doesn't frighten you? It sounds kind of like poking bears with a stick." She was watching me closely. "And if they use guns and you don't—"

"People who carry guns rely on that advantage. A lot of them don't even know how to use one properly. They wave it around like in the movies, and you're more likely to get shot by accident than on purpose. If you know what you're doing, sometimes you stand a good chance against them."

She looked at me with a sideways glance, one corner of her mouth turned up. "You're full of it."

"Hey, Ben and I took years of martial arts. I'm not bullshitting you."

"I hate to point out the obvious ..." I knew what she was getting at.

"He wasn't expecting trouble, and I am. If he was as sick as you say, he might have been too weak to stop them or he might have been surprised. They won't have that now."

She swallowed the last of her coffee. "Well, I have to get back to work."

"You don't believe me."

She shrugged. "Anyway, good luck."

"Thank you for your help."

I watched her walk out. Maybe she hadn't helped my search much, but I thought how nice it would be to see her again.

# CHAPTER 7

The next morning found me at a pay-phone outside a
Cumberland Farms convenience store with a handful of
change, looking for the man who had been in the hospital
room with Ben. I'd invented a cover story so I could ask
questions. I'd be Dave Johnson, insurance agent.

There were ten Deckers listed in the phone book. On the
fifth try, Mrs. Decker told me that yes, her husband Arnold
had gone in for gallbladder surgery, and she supposed I
could come see them. The address was in Buxton, just
outside of Portland. The missus gave me directions.

A change into a respectable-looking dark suit and tie
made me look more like Dave the insurance agent. I checked
my map and headed out of town, following the route I'd
been given. The farther I went, the farther apart were the
houses. They got older, too, as did the cars, some aged
enough to be approaching classic status. If I went far
enough, maybe I'd see a log cabin and a Model T.

The Decker home was small, almost a cottage, stuck on a
lonely side road. The place needed exterior work, and the
grass in the yard was overly long. A 1978 dark green Ford sat
in the driveway, patterned with primer paint and a fair

amount of rust. From a field across the road, grazing cows looked at me with bovine serenity as I got out.

The door was answered by a woman who looked like a taller version of Dr. Ruth. She eyed me sharply.

"Dave Johnson, ma'am." I smiled. "I called earlier."

She grunted, stepping back to let me through the door.

"Come on in, then. Thought you might be one of them damned Jehovah's Witlesses. Mind the cats now," she said. The place reeked of stale cat urine, almost as strong as the lion cage at the zoo. A Siamese and a calico came out and looked me over. The Siamese turned up her nose, but the calico came over and rubbed up against my legs.

"Nice cats," I said.

"That's Constance, the friendliest. She's shameless. The other one's Mitzi. Mrs. Beal you won't see. She's under the couch. Doesn't much like visitors. Not that we get many these days." She seemed angry at me for something.

The place was small and depressing, the habitat of folks at the end of both their lives and their money. Everything looked old and worn. I suddenly felt very uncomfortable coming to their home under false pretenses.

"You ahn't from heah, ah you?" I realized her accent was pure Downeast, hardly an 'r' to be found. I also realized the way she said 'here' reminded me of Bobby Lee.

"No, ma'am. They sent me up from Boston."

"Boston, eh?" she sniffed. "Nevah had much use for the place."

"Me either, to tell the truth," I smiled. She didn't smile back.

"I suppose this is about the money." Her tone was sharp.

"Money?"

"The four hundred dollars. What they told us the insurance wouldn't cover. I told them, we don't have it."

She was trying to be strong and defiant, but I sensed it was pretty much a front, and tears were not far away.

"Oh, no, ma'am. I'm here about something else."

"Oh." She was obviously relieved. "Oh. Would you like a cup of tea? Or coffee?"

"No, thank you, ma'am."

"So if it isn't the money, then, what is it?"

"Well, ma'am, there was another man in the hospital room when your husband was there."

"What do you mean?"

"When your husband was awaiting his surgery, he was put in a room with another man. I just have a few questions."

"Well, I don't know nothing about that. You'll have to ask Arnie. Come on in. Mind the cat there."

She led me out of the tiny kitchen to the tiny living room. I had to step carefully to avoid Constance, who wrapped herself around my ankles like a new pair of socks.

"Don't mind the mess," the woman said. "It's been hahd for me, with Arnie in the hospital and my arthuritis." I could barely understand the word, because she gave it about four and a half syllables.

Arnie sat on the couch, and there wasn't a lot of him. His skin was an unhealthy yellow and hung on him loosely, like a character in a Gahan Wilson cartoon. The television was on, the volume turned up high, and he didn't glance up from it as we came in. The woman walked over and turned the set off.

"Hey," he squawked. "I was watchin' my show."

"Arnie, this man here is from the insurance company. He wants to talk to you."

He peered at me suspiciously. "We already talked to you people. We told you we ain't got the goddamned money. What the hell do you want from us? You want the house? Take it. Take the goddamned thing. Just leave us the Christ alone."

"I'm not here about the money, Mr. Decker. I just wanted to ask you a few questions."

"Not here for the money?"

"No sir."

47

"Well that's a goddamned miracle. Every other bastahd in a suit and tie has been after us like we stole somethin' from them. You'd think they'd go out of business if they didn't get money from us. We're goddamned sick of it. Filled out about a thousand forms, then they come back and tell us we got to give them four hundred dollars more. Now where the hell we supposed to get that, huh?"

"I don't know, sir. I'm not here for that."

"Well, what the hell are you here for, then?"

"Mr. Decker, while you were awaiting surgery, you were in a room with another man. Do you remember him?"

"Course I do. I ain't senile, for Christ's sake. What you think, I'm too old, my minds' goin'?"

"Just routine, sir. Do you know what he was in for?"

"He was a young fella. They said something about food poisoning. He was awful sick, even puked a couple of times. I wanted a private room, but your damn company wouldn't pay for it. So I hadda listen to this fella getting sick."

"Did you speak to him at all?"

"No."

"You were in a room with someone and didn't speak to them?"

"Well, weren't neither of us in a social mood, if you know what I mean. We had that curtain thing pulled between us, so we couldn't see each other. He was awful sick, and I was thinking about them cuttin' me open. Wasn't sure I'd come through. Wasn't sure he would either, the way he was spewin'."

"So you didn't hear him speak?"

"Well, he got a phone call, the night before he left."

"Do you know from who?"

"No, he talked real low. After he hung up, though, he kinda groaned and said, 'That bastahd'."

"That bastard?"

"That's right."

"Do you know who he was referring to?"

"No. Like I said, it wadn't like we was chewin' the fat togethuh."

"Was there anything else?"

"He cussed a little."

"Like he was mad at the person he just talked to?"

"Yessah, just like that. He was too sick to talk much, and I was too worried to listen."

"Mr. Decker, is there anything else you can think of that went on there? Anything out of the ordinary?"

"He didn't sleep much that night. Thrashed like a trout, groanin' away. I was awake a lot myself. They took me in early next morning."

I stood up. "Well, thank you for your time. You've been very helpful."

"Time we got, money we ain't. You didn't ask much."

"Like you said, you were just there for the one night."

"He's not in any trouble is he? That young fella?"

I swallowed. "No, he's not in any trouble."

"Well, that's good. I don't want to get nobody in trouble. Now can I go back to my show?"

The wife turned on the television and led me back out, looking embarrassed. Her eyes were wet. "I'm sorry about Arnie." Why were so many women always apologizing for men?

"He's been in a lot of pain for so long. The surgery helped some, but he's still hurting. And we've been so worried ..." She turned away, unable to hold it in any longer. Her shoulders shook as the dam broke. I stood there like an idiot, not knowing what to do. I looked at Constance the calico, who was also watching the woman. She didn't seem to know what to do, either.

"Thank you for your time, ma'am. I'll be going."

"Oh, please, I'm so sorry." She snuffed a bit and had control again. "It's just that you don't seem like any insurance man." She made it sound like a compliment.

"What do I seem like, ma'am?"

"Well, you're nice. The others were such ... you know. They told us they were going to take us to court, all kinds of things. With what we get to live on, there's nothing left. The medicines cost so much. We just don't know what to do anymore."

"They're *threatening* you over four hundred dollars?"

"Yes, sir, they want their money, that's for sure."

"Well, let me see what I can do about it."

As I drove away, I found it strange that I had agreed to get involved in someone else's problem. What was I doing? But the plight of these folks just didn't seem right. They had nothing but a little bit of time left. They should have it in peace.

Then I thought that maybe something of Ben was speaking to me.

Now there was a thought.

# CHAPTER 8

When I returned to Portland, I kept my suit on, hoping people would mistake me for someone respectable as I tried the local martial arts studios.

The telephone directory listed fifteen different dojos in the metro area. Six of them were near each other downtown. While driving there, I passed a statue of a seated man with bushy hair and a beard. As I drove around the area looking for a parking place, he seemed to be laughing at my foolish efforts. After the third loop around the one-way streets, I headed farther out, finally finding a place about five blocks away from where I was going.

Walking back, I checked out the statue. Henry Wadsworth Longfellow. The poet who immortalized Hiawatha, Evangeline, and the very brief ride of Paul Revere. Figures that Revere got the history credit, and Dawes and Prescott became footnotes because their names were harder to rhyme. So it goes.

The front of the dojo sported a flashy logo on big glass windows that had been covered up on the inside with paper sheets to above eye level. The door was unlocked, so I walked in.

The morning sun sent amber rays of light through the tops of the windows, illuminating huge trophy display cases. The biggest trophy was a ball-busting six-footer, in its own glass cabinet.

The center of the room contained a wide wrestling-type mat. Mirrors on the walls allowed you to see yourself from every spot in the room. If there was a space that didn't have a mirror, it had framed photographs showing the owner, one Danny Thibodeaux, in fighting poses, accepting trophies, and shaking hands with C-list celebrities. Even in the photos of his students, he was in every shot. This wasn't a dojo, it was a shrine to ego.

I read the inscription on the big-ass trophy:

*Danny Thibodeaux*
*New England Championships*
*First Place*

"Pretty impressive, isn't it?"

I turned to look at the speaker, trying to change the expression on my face so it didn't look as if I'd bitten into a lemon. The kid looked about twenty, and stood about five foot seven, with sandy-colored hair. When he gazed at the trophy, he seemed to be worshiping a holy relic.

"He got that last year. And he'll get another one at this year's tourney."

"Maybe you'll need a bigger place to store them all."

"Yeah, pretty soon." He'd totally missed my sarcasm. "So, are you interested in signing up for some lessons?"

"I'm sorry. I didn't catch your name."

"Call me Chip. I work for Danny. I help take care of the place, you know, even teach a few classes. Had my black belt for two years now."

"Any of your trophies here?" I nodded to indicate the display cases.

"Uh, no, you know, it's Danny's studio and all. There wouldn't be room if all his students put up their trophies. We win a lot, you know."

"Is that the emphasis here? Winning trophies?"

"Oh, no, I was just saying. We do it all, you know? It's just that we kick ass in all the tournaments. We're kinda proud of that, being the best and all. Working with Danny motivates us to win."

*I'll just bet*, I thought.

"So, you interested in some classes?" He certainly was a tenacious salesman.

"Actually, I was wondering if someone had come by here. You recognize him?"

I showed the picture. The kid's smile evaporated and was replaced by a look of fury. He looked up at me with his mouth all scrunched up and walked away to yell into the back of the studio. A voice came from within, and someone poked their head out. The kid jerked his head toward me and crossed his arms, like a boy who's called his dad to come beat someone up.

The guy who came out was the same one from all the pictures. At about six foot four, Danny Thibodeaux towered over me by a good six inches, taller than even his big shiny trophy. He had maybe thirty pounds on me too, and not a bit of it fat. His fitted muscle shirt and tight jeans carefully emphasized his build. He moved fluidly, like a powerful jungle cat, and had a smug look that said he knew how well he moved.

But there was a problem with the whole package. His face looked like it was put together wrong, with misshapen ears stuck out like little wings from the side of his head. His eyes didn't line up, and his upper lip, which sported a small mustache, stuck out past his bad teeth. The weak little chin didn't help much, either. I guessed the mirrors and pictures were highly developed overcompensation for his lack of looks.

"What's the problem here?" He had a crooked smile on his face. Ah, the great god descends to bring order.

"I was wondering if this guy had ever come by." I showed him the photograph.

He looked at it for a long moment, the smile fading briefly. It was back when he looked up.

"Friend of yours, huh? Yeah, he was here." He looked me up and down, measuring me in an instant. He reached out and squeezed my bicep through the suit, and saw I didn't like it. His eyes grew hot and bright.

"You fight, too." He smiled wider, like a crocodile sensing fresh meat. "Yeah, that's how that eye of yours got messed up, isn't it? How about a little match, you and me, just a couple of rounds of light contact?"

"No thanks." I wanted no part of what was coming.

"Hey, don't be afraid, I'll go easy. We'll make it real friendly. I know this is pretty intimidating." He waved his hand to indicate the cases.

"You wouldn't get a trophy for beating me."

His face darkened as he realized what I thought of him and that I wasn't afraid at all. It was a dumb move on my part. Now he wouldn't stop until he got what he wanted.

"Your friend didn't want a match, either. He wanted a place to work out, but I said he'd have to spar with me first, you know, try out. Had to really talk him into it."

"Must've taken some doing," I said.

"When we finally got down to it, I kicked his ass, and he left here with his tail between his legs. Never came back. Went over to the nice soft-style school where he wouldn't get hurt. Isn't that right, Chip?" He called loudly over his shoulder without looking.

"Sure is, Danny," Chip piped up, all but wagging his tail.

"Really," I said, my face wooden. I doubted the outcome was as Danny-boy had boasted. Ben was good, smooth and fast, and he fought without anger, something I couldn't always do. Even now I felt that hot, angry spark within me start to glow. This guy was a pro at pushing buttons.

"Yeah, he went off to do that barnyard animal stuff. You know, chicken wing, ruptured duck, that crap. You wouldn't be a 'chicken' wing guy, would you?" He put heavy emphasis on the word, and I was glad. As long as he kept it on this third-grade level, I could laugh it off and keep control. I turned to go.

"Thought so." He waited until I was almost at the door and fired his last shot. "That's why he killed himself," he said loudly. "Because he was a loser."

I turned back, shaking with rage. He grinned in triumph, and I wanted to pound that grin off his face.

"Yeah, I can tell you something about him," he said.

I stopped, but one more smartass remark and I'd let loose.

"But for me to help you, you gotta help me. One little practice, three rounds. And I'll tell you what I know. Only way."

"Okay, hotshot. You got your match," I said, without thinking.

"Cool. Six o'clock tonight, then. Right here."

Of course. He wanted an audience.

I left the place cursing myself for an idiot. I'd let him get my goat and hustle me. Getting mad and losing control means you make mistakes. I wondered just how bad this one would be.

Dale T. Phillips

# CHAPTER 9

Ben had worked at an oceanside resort hotel complex called Pine Haven. The road to the resort wound a lazy path through salt marshes, and gave teasing glimpses of water through gaps in the trees. The air was tangy with the scent of the surrounding tidal pools, but the breeze off the ocean blew in cool and light. I needed this to calm down, especially after talking to Thibodeaux the Jerk.

The tall trees standing guard duty by the roadside were more spruce and fir than pine, so the resort name of Pine Haven on the huge wooden sign was probably artistic license.

Once around the last curve, the hotel loomed before you. It was all white, and impressively huge, one of those wooden monstrosities built in another era. It perched in regal majesty there on the high ground, with acres of windows providing a view of the manicured flower gardens and paths that sloped gently down to the seaside. But brute nature would not be denied, and outcroppings of rock erupted like crooked teeth at various points of the landscape, contrasting sharply with the soft comfort to be had inside the hotel.

The shore itself was mostly jumbled slabs of rock, but there was a small stretch of sandy beach, probably artificially made by the resort owners. The breeze put whitecaps on the waves and it looked a bit rough for boating, but there were still a few sails bobbing out on the water.

The hotel interior decor was ancient, dark wood, polished over time to give an aura of the comfortable solidity of established Old Money. Oil paintings in mammoth gilded frames anchored the place to the past, as did the photographs along the walls that showed the resort's history and the famous people who had been guests. It seemed a self-congratulatory club of those born to wealth, who thought this meant they were God's anointed.

Once I'd checked out the inside, I went back out into the fresh air and continued exploring. The ramshackle quarters for the hired help were behind a bank of trees, discreetly hidden from the main hotel. Wouldn't want the paying guests getting upset by viewing the private life of the sweaty peasants who served them. The setup reminded me of an antebellum plantation.

A young guy walked by dressed in a white cook's jacket with baggy black-and-white checked pants.

"Excuse me," I said. He stopped and looked at me, not offering a greeting or a challenge. "I'm trying to find out where Ben Sterling stayed. Would you know which room that was, and if someone's there I could talk to?"

He was a strong-looking kid with glasses and a pockmarked face. "Through there," he pointed. "Down the hall, third door on the right. Mike's still there. They roomed together."

Music blared from several of the rooms, but the loudest came from the room I wanted. I pounded hard on the thin door, trying to compete against the thumping bass and the shrieking vocals. The volume was turned down suddenly. I knocked again, a little softer this time.

"It's open," came a voice from within.

I walked in and saw two young guys, a skinny kid with a wispy mustache dressed only in shorts, and a hulking brute sitting on one of the beds, smoking a bong. Their eyes were badly bloodshot, and an acrid stink of pot greeted my nostrils. The big kid glowered at me from where he sat, but didn't stop his activity.

"Mike?" I said.

"Yeah?" The skinny guy swallowed hard. "You a cop?"

"No. My name's Zack Taylor. Can I talk to you a minute?"

"What about?"

"Ben Sterling."

"Ben?" He seemed puzzled.

"I was a friend of his."

The kid looked at the guy sitting on the bed and shrugged. "Sure, why not?" He went to the stereo and turned the sound down further so we could talk.

The room was a mess, decorated in basic young man. Clothes and empty beer cans lay scattered about. An advertising poster featured a busty, young, bikini-clad, blond woman holding out a bottle of beer. There wasn't a trace of Ben left here.

I didn't want to sit, but it would put them more at ease and seem less like an interrogation. Apart from the other bed, the only choice was a dilapidated chair that was draped with a black T-shirt sporting the logo of a rock band over two mostly-naked women holding a skull. I moved the shirt and took the chair.

"That's Jeff." Mike waved at the bruiser, who was sucking in his cheeks as he took a hit. I nodded.

Jeff exhaled and looked at me. "Ben, huh? Dude blew his brains out. Pretty fucked up, man."

I was about to respond, and not in a good way, when Mike spoke up. "This won't take too long, will it? I gotta get to work."

"Not long at all." I looked around. "You didn't talk to the police here, did you?" Instead of being embarrassed, Mike grinned.

"Nah, they talked to us all one by one up in the Zoo. I moved some stuff out before they came."

"You got some problem with us having a little fun?" Jeff said to me.

I looked at him. "No problem. Smoke your brains out. But that stuff's supposed to make you mellow. So lighten up."

"Don't fucking tell me what to do, man."

I rolled my eyes, turning to Mike. "What can you tell me about Ben?"

"Well, uh, he was a pretty cool guy, and we got along okay." Mike sniffed. "Not like that guy I roomed with last season. He was something else. Remember him?" Mike shook his head.

"Goddamned faggot," came the reply from Jeff.

"What did Ben do on his days off?" I asked.

"He'd go to Portland," Mike said. "He worked out at some karate studio there."

"Do you know which one?" I said.

"Nah. I wanted to go, but we had different days off."

"Was he seeing anybody?"

"You mean a girl?" Mike stroked his mustache. "Yeah, some chick in Portland. Uh, Sandy, I think it was. He never told me the rest. Cocktail waitress."

"Do you know where she worked?"

"Somewhere in the Old Port." Mike shrugged.

"Is that a bar?"

Jeff brayed a laugh. "A bar. No, it's a shitload of bars."

"Yeah," Mike said. "Other things, too, shops, restaurants, you know."

"Okay." I nodded. "Did he have any problems with anyone here?"

Mike shot a quick glance at Jeff and looked away. "Uh, no, I guess not."

"You sure about that?"

"Hey, man, he said *no*," Jeff spoke up. "Why don't you leave it alone?"

"Listen," I said, trying to control my temper. "You've been a great help and all, but could I speak to Mike alone?"

"What for? You're asking questions like a fucking cop, man."

"Yeah," said Mike. "Why do you want to know that, anyway?"

"Ben didn't commit suicide," I said, watching them. "He was murdered. Someone shot him."

"No fucking way," said Jeff from the bed. He put the bong down on the floor.

Mike's eyes grew wide. "You ain't shittin' me, are you?"

"Ben would never do it," I said. "He wasn't like that."

"Well, I thought it was pretty freakin' weird. Murdered, though, Jesus Christ." Mike shook his head.

"You asshole," said Jeff, standing up. He loomed over me in the chair. "You're looking for someone to be a suspect. Like on TV, set someone up for the cops."

I shifted ever so slightly in the chair, changing my balance in case I had to make a move. I looked up at the guy, who wanted to fight. "Take it easy. I don't think you did it."

"Fucking right, I didn't. So why don't you get lost?"

He reached down to grab my shirt, and I slapped his hand away and popped him a light little backfist to the family jewels. He stopped reaching, and his mouth hung open. I stood and pushed him back onto the bed.

"Mike, could you step out into the hall for a minute?"

I took Mike by the arm, and he moved with me, but he looked panicked.

"Easy, man, I just roomed with the guy!"

As we moved into the hall, we almost bumped into someone else, another guy wearing checked black-and-white pants and a white cook's jacket, with a floppy white chef's hat that looked like a fallen soufflé.

"Problem?" He looked us over.

"This guy was asking about Ben," Mike said. I let go of his arm.

From behind the door came a muffled cry.

"Mike, don't tell that asshole anything. I'm going to fucking kill him if he's still here when I get up."

The new guy cut in. "Mike, why don't you go and get ready for work." He looked at me like he was mad. "Let's you and me take a little walk."

I handed Mike one of the motel matchbooks, and followed the mad guy outside.

# CHAPTER 10

Once we were out of earshot of the building, the guy suddenly stopped. "You come by here again, I'm going to call security and have you arrested," he snarled.

"What for?"

"You know what for. You come by here, selling your shit to these guys. But I have to work with them, and if they're messed up, we have to deal with it. So leave now and don't come back."

"I think you have me confused with someone else," I said.

"I know you're selling dope to those guys, so don't—"

"Whoa," I said, holding up my hand to stop him. "Wrong. I don't know them, I don't sell dope, I don't know who is. My name is Zack Taylor, and I'm here asking about Ben. I was a friend of his."

The guy had stopped his angry mode and stared at me with his brow wrinkled. "Asking about what?"

"He didn't kill himself. He was murdered."

The guy stared at me some more, looking like he was rearranging his thinking. "I think I'd have preferred you to be the dope dealer," he said. "All right, we better go sit down and clear this up. I'm Brian, by the way." He suddenly stuck out his hand and we shook. "I'm the sous-chef here. Sorry about before."

"Forget it."

"Come to the Zoo with me." He walked toward the hotel. "So what was Jeff's problem?"

"Apart from the obvious?"

He smiled. "Yeah. Apart from that."

"He didn't seem to like me much," I said. "I asked them a few questions, if Ben had any problems with anyone here, and he got all paranoid."

"Ah. Maybe that's because Ben did have a problem with Jeff. Ben told him not to come by anymore to smoke dope in his room. Jeff got a little nasty, and took a swing at him. From what I hear, Jeff suddenly ran into a wall." Brian looked at me once again. "You a private detective or something?"

"No, just a friend who wants to find out what happened."

"The police already came by and asked us all a bunch of questions," he said.

"I know. But they still decided it was a suicide."

To get to the workers' entrance of the hotel, we had to walk past a monstrous green metal dumpster reeking of old garbage. In the August heat, the stench was overpowering.

"Isn't that special?" I said. "Is there some reason for putting that thing right where the help has to walk by it?"

"A deliberate reinforcement of the class structure. It reminds the peons of their true place."

"Oh." I smiled. "Sous-chef, huh? Not for long, I'll bet. You'll work up to chef yourself soon, right?"

"Not here. It's the same menu all the time. Tourist stuff, lobster and plain steak. I want my own place. Get to do the kind of food prep and presentation I like."

We went in through the screen door by the loading dock. Once inside, the hot, smothering air closed around us. We sat in a large room with painted animal murals on the walls (*ah, the Zoo*), and chairs set along long tables for eating.

"Hard to believe someone killed Ben," Brian said. "It's like on TV or something, you know?"

"Is there anyone else here he didn't get along with? Other than Mr. Personality back there?"

"Ben was a pretty good guy. Good worker. We'll miss him." He thought for a minute. "He did have some words with Chef, but ..."

"Tell me about that."

He looked around before speaking. "Chef, well, he's the boss. He likes things done his way. He went off on Ben one day over a delivery."

"Did Ben do something wrong?"

"Well, Chef told us he'd handle all the deliveries. He checks the stuff over, makes sure we're getting what we paid for. Some companies try to slip stuff by you, you know? One day Chef was in the can when a truck came by, so Ben went out to take care of it. Chef started hollering when he found out, got all bent out of shape."

"Was there something special about that delivery?"

He shrugged. "It's one of our regulars. We couldn't figure out what all the fuss was about. But Chef likes to lay down the law, and he goes off like that sometimes on all of us."

"Must be hard, working for someone like that."

"It's the business. Most of them are like that. You've got to pump out a couple hundred meals in 90 minutes. Then they have to deal with distributors, kitchen staff, the wait staff, customer complaints, food and bev managers. It's a lot of pressure. And you're always working over a steam table, oven, or grill, in the summer, no less."

"So why do you do it?"

He rubbed his face as if he was tired, then gave a little smile. "Hard to explain. When you're really good at it, it's like a form of art. At the top, you get to make the decisions. But to get there, ya gotta pay your dues."

"What do you know about Ben getting sick?" I asked.

"Late one afternoon, Ben talked about feeling crappy. He threw up a couple times. Drove himself to the hospital, though we offered to take him. That was the last we saw of him. Somebody's cousin works at Maine Medical, and we heard they pumped his stomach, and it was some kind of poisonous mushroom."

"Nobody else got sick, right?"

"No. Must have been a bad one in the batch we had, and Ben got it somehow. We sent the rest of what we had to be tested. They didn't find anything. Man, if a guest had got it, we'd be getting sued from here to Sunday."

"But Ben knew mushrooms. He wouldn't have made a dumb mistake like that."

He spread his hands. "What can I tell you?"

"So he went to the hospital and never made it back, right?"

"Yeah. How come you think someone killed him?"

"I knew the guy." I thought for a minute. "What about the drugs?" I said. "Has that been a real problem?"

He took off his hat to wipe his brow, then leaned his chair back without answering and studied me for a long moment. It looked as if there was something he didn't want to tell me.

"Look," I said. "I don't care what people do, and I'm not a cop. I'm just wondering if Ben saw something he shouldn't have, and somebody wanted to make sure he didn't tell anyone."

"Christ, you think he might have been killed in a drug deal? This isn't exactly New York, you know."

"It can happen anywhere." I looked at him.

He tipped his chair forward. "There's a rumor," he said, his voice dropping low. "There might be something harder going around, among some of the guests. There's some mighty rich people with nasty appetites."

"Do the police know about this?"

"Are you crazy? Nobody wants them sniffing around, looking for drugs. We'd lose half our staff and a lot of our guests. And you didn't hear it from me." He stood up. "I gotta get upstairs."

"Thanks. Here's my motel if you think of anything else. I suppose I should talk to this Chef ..."

"Grossman. Pardon me if I don't introduce you. He tends to shoot the messenger." He realized what he'd said, and made a face. "Sorry, man."

"It's okay. I'll find Grossman myself."

"He isn't going to like having you around like this, talking about murder and drugs."

"If he gets in the way, I can go around him or through him."

Brian gave a rueful smile. "He's a big guy, so either way is pretty tough. He could have you thrown out, or arrested for trespassing."

"I've been thrown out of places before."

"Okay," he said, as he walked toward the door. "Your funeral."

I watched him go, hoping he did not have the gift of prophecy.

Dale T. Phillips

# CHAPTER 11

The kitchen looked like an industrial Hell. Overhead lights glowed eerily through pockets of rising steam. Pots and utensils hung from metal hooks. The air, ineffectively churned by noisy ventilation fans, clung to me with greasy fingers. Workers called out over the clatter of metal trays, the banging of lids, doors, ovens, coolers. The aroma of cooking food blended with the scent of cleaning fluids.

The white-jacketed denizens of this world moved about their various tasks, but none looked big enough or old enough to be Grossman. Two people were behind a long, stainless-steel counter. It had built-in steam tables forming a barricade in front of a line of ovens and grills. One was the pockmarked kid I'd talked to, and the other was a young woman.

I finally found Grossman, chewing out some dark-skinned kid in an apron, by a sink piled high with pots and pans. There was no mistaking him. At six foot three, very round, and dressed in white as he was, he made me think of a giant snowball. On his head bobbed a brimless white paper stovepipe hat.

As I got closer, his puffy face looked as if it had been squashed together, with jowls that pushed in on the mouth.

69

Thick glasses magnified mean-looking eyes. Tobacco stains showed their tracks on his teeth and hands.

He finished his tirade with the kid and saw me. "What do you want?"

"I'd like to ask you about Ben Sterling."

"You're the one," he said. "I heard you was asking. I already talked to you people. What is it now?"

He must have assumed I was with the police. As long as I didn't say otherwise, well and good.

"We're beginning to think it wasn't a suicide," I said, trying to sound like a cop.

He looked at me a moment, brought up short. You could almost hear him thinking. He grunted and walked over to a small office which had been reclaimed from a storeroom. Sweat shone on the roll of fat at the back of his neck. He mopped it with a dirty handkerchief as I followed him in and shut the door behind us. He wedged himself behind a small desk and sat in a chair while I stood.

"How did you come to hire him?" I said.

"We were down in Florida, in Boca Raton, at the Commodore Club. We do winters down there and summers here. He dropped by one day, near the end of the season. Wanted to do the summer up here, and he had references, so I hired him."

I remembered when Ben had come to tell me about going to Maine. That was the last time I'd ever seen him. "You were happy with his work?"

"He knew what he was doing, but I had to get after him to do things. He was late a lot, and couldn't keep up the pace when we got busy. He drank some. I smelled it on his breath a couple of times. Mouthed off, too."

This wasn't like the Ben I knew. "Mouthed off?"

"You know, talking back when I told him to do something."

"And you don't like that."

70

"I got a kitchen to run. Then he disappears for a few days. I had to get other people to cover his shifts. So I canned him."

"You fired him because he was *sick*?"

"He was probably faking."

I felt my anger rising, the hot little spark glowing to life again. "He was throwing up before he left here. And it's tough to fake getting your stomach pumped."

"Whatever. But he ate here, you know, same as we all did. Nobody else got sick. We had to check everything out. Sent out every mushroom we had to be tested; they found nothing. Big pain in the ass. If he did get a bad mushroom, it wasn't from here, that's all I know."

"How do you know?"

"Because I check all the produce myself, when it comes in. I know what's what."

I studied him a moment. "Is that why you two had a run-in? Because he took a delivery order?"

He chewed the inside of his cheek for a minute, then shrugged. "Yeah, that's right. I want to check everything over, make sure they don't make any mistakes, make sure we get the best stuff. Fruits and vegetables, you gotta be careful. I told him, along with everyone else, to let me check the produce over, before the truck leaves."

"So he tried to help out because you weren't around, and you yelled at him."

"I yell at everybody when they fuck up. That was another reason I was getting rid of him."

"So did you call him at the hospital and fire him while he was sick, or were you going to wait until he got back?"

Grossman paused. "I called him. Told him he could come back and pack up his stuff, you know. But he never came back."

"No, he didn't. Because somebody put a bullet into him."

He stared at me. "Why do you say that?"

"Certain things don't add up."

"What things?"

"Why he'd do it, for one. He wasn't really the type, we know that."

"Who'd want to kill him?"

"That's what I want to find out. Do you know anybody else he was having problems with, besides yourself?"

"What do you mean, besides me?"

"Had it been suicide, you might have contributed to his death, yet you didn't seem much affected by it. Most people would feel something. That makes us want to ask more questions."

"What am I supposed to do?" He looked at me.

I thought of some anatomically inventive suggestions, but kept them to myself. "One of your workers was killed, and all you can do is badmouth him. I'd be interested in seeing how the other employees were affected."

He looked away. "I don't want you bothering my people, asking a lot of stupid questions."

"Why? What are you afraid of?"

"I got nothing to be afraid of. But you act like you don't believe me."

"Let's just say your version doesn't seem to fit any of the facts."

"You calling me a liar? I'm gonna file a complaint. Who's your boss? Lemme see your badge."

Damn. The jig was up. So I did my best Alfonso Bedoya imitation, from *The Treasure of the Sierra Madre*.

"*Badge*? I don't need no stinking badge. I was a friend of his."

"What?" His face flushed red. "You sonofabitch, get the hell out of here. Now." He cursed some more, and his face was turning purple. Maybe he'd work himself into a heart attack.

"I'll go," I said from the door. "But I know that Ben was murdered. And you're a goddamned liar. I'm going to find out why you're lying and who killed him."

"I'll throw you out myself," he said, 300 pounds of bulk rising from the chair.

"Go for it," I said. I was trembling with anger now, tense as a taut piano wire. If he'd touched me, I'd have hurt him. Big as he was, he saw what was in my eyes, and stopped. Instead, he picked up the phone and jabbed at the buttons with a sausage-shaped finger.

"Calling security. They'll throw you out."

"Always best to have someone else do the job when you can't handle it yourself." His face darkened even more. "But you may want to call your manager first and ask him about the liabilities on lawsuits."

As I'd hoped, he broke the connection and punched out a new number. I left the office, making a mental bet that I was going up the next level in the food chain.

Dale T. Phillips

# CHAPTER 12

The chef had made me angry, and outside in the cool air, I tried to calm down. It didn't help to see a man in a uniform coming toward me, with the cap and swagger of a cocky security guard.

Some guy in an expensive suit approached in a big hurry. His hair was moussed and carefully combed so that all the strands were perfectly aligned. He smiled broadly, displaying his well-capped teeth like a row of piano keys. He looked like a guy who would try to sell me an expensive used car.

The well-dressed man was moving quickly, and he reached me before the guard did. He stuck out a manicured hand for me to shake, complete with a gold ring and glittering, pricey watch. But after meeting Grossman, I didn't want to make nice. I looked at the hand like he was offering a turd. He withdrew it, his brows knitting into a brief frown I took for irritation.

"I'm Jackson Royce, Food and Beverage Manager." He nodded to indicate the guard standing a few feet away, thumbs hooked into his belt. "We going to be civil about this?"

I shrugged. "Why not?"

"Good, good," he said, smiling again. "Why don't we go up to my office?"

The three of us walked toward a set of small wooden buildings, nestled like sea birds over a roadway that had been cut down at an angle through the hard rock. We passed by a few parked cars, including a sleek, black Porsche. Royce slowed as we went past, his eyes scanning the surface. He reached over and flicked a small piece of debris from the hood before we moved on. I wanted to run my fingers all over the finish of the car, just to see if he'd have a fit.

At the top of the drive, we went up an outside stairway overlooking the drop. Obviously, Royce was not afraid of heights. The office was nothing out of the ordinary, except for the old-fashioned floor safe in the corner. Royce's name and title were splashed in several places, just to remind everyone of where the power was. Now I was in his territory, where he was comfortable and could play the game his way. The guard leaned against the wall by the door, arms crossed.

Royce indicated the chair in front of the desk. "Please, have a seat, Mister ... ah?"

"Zack Taylor."

"You've raised a very volatile subject, Mr. Taylor. We're still upset by it. May I ask, what is your official capacity?" He was showing me what a favor he was granting by talking to me when he didn't have to. A real buddy.

"I'm here on my own, to find out about Ben's death. He was a friend of mine."

"I see." Royce toyed with a gold pen from his desk. "We did cooperate fully with the police, and told them everything we knew. After that, I'm afraid it's not our policy to get involved in our employee's private lives."

"So you won't mind my asking around a bit."

"Actually, we would prefer to end this unfortunate affair. Publicity of this sort isn't good for business."

"And a murder is especially bad."

"Now, see, that's the problem," he said, shaking his head. "Statements like that serve to upset people. The police told us he took his own life, and we believe them."

"They may have some new information soon."

"Well, then, should they require anything else, we'll be happy to help in any way we can."

I was about to be sent packing with nothing to show for it. Might as well take a swing, see what came of it.

I watched his face carefully when I spoke. "Be sure to tell them that your chef is lying about Ben. They'll want to know why. Maybe then they'll look a little harder to find out who poisoned him before he got shot."

"Listen, you." The polite act was over. "I don't know what your game is, but you're going to be in a lot of trouble if you keep shooting your mouth off. You will not come here spreading wild rumors among the staff and guests. You are not welcome back, and if I find you here again, I'll have you arrested for trespassing. Do you understand?"

"Shall I escort him out, Mr. Royce?" The security guard was off the wall and ready for action. Here was where the toady could impress the boss.

I looked at the dumpy guard, who was a few inches taller and much wider than me. He looked like one of those fools who use their size to push people around. "I'm leaving now. Do not touch me."

The smirk was on his face as he reached for me. I grabbed his wrist and pulled, simultaneously sweeping his feet out from under him. I even turned him so that he landed on his butt, not his head. It took the wind out of his sails. I left quickly, without even a snappy exit line.

Dale T. Phillips

# CHAPTER 13

After my delightful reception at the resort, I returned to my room in Portland, where it was time to get ready for my match with Thibodeaux. I changed into workout clothes and started stretching, then jumping rope to get my heart rate up. When I was loose and sweating, I started my kata, the ritualized, formal routines of karate. The familiar patterns helped me focus. When my blows were crisp and I was moving well, I packed my gym bag with street clothes and sparring gear and called a cab, to avoid the parking hassle.

I entered Thibodeaux's studio a few minutes shy of six. Everyone turned to me to see tonight's designated victim, and the conversational buzz grew loud. About twenty people milled about the room, mostly younger people wearing the traditional white martial arts outfit called a *gi*. Two of the older crowd were in suits and ties, looking out of place. Thibodeaux had gathered quite an audience, as his type always does when they're sure of winning.

Thibodeaux, Mr. Show Biz himself, was smacking the heavy bag at the other end of the studio, doing flashy high kicks and spinning backfists. He wore a red, satin-like outfit plastered with tourney patches.

I found the locker room and changed for the fight. Most important was the heavy belt and cup apparatus to protect my groin. My own gi was traditional, basic white, the way it's supposed to be. Real martial arts is not about looking fashionable or flashy.

I rinsed out my mouthpiece, got my gym bag, and walked barefoot back out into the main room.

Thibodeaux was talking to the two suits and ushered them to chairs when he saw me come out. Everyone else sat on their knees at the edge of the broad flat mat. A big white circle in the mat's center showed the sparring area, familiar to many martial arts. This was just sparring, not a real kickboxing match, which required a regular boxing ring.

"Surprised you came." Thibodeaux grinned at me. I looked at him like he was a bug, and said nothing. His smile wavered and came back. He jerked his head toward a nervous-looking balding man in casual clothes. "This is Jim Kapinsky. He'll be ref."

I nodded by way of introduction. I did a couple of last-minute stretches to limber up, then put on my padded head protector and slipped my mouthpiece in. I donned the foot and hand pads as well. It all sounds like a lot, but when you've got two people kicking and punching each other with real force, it doesn't feel like much padding at all.

Thibodeaux was wearing gear similar to mine, but all in black. He probably thought it looked tougher. Kapinsky brought us both to the center and spoke.

"This is to be light contact, for points only. We don't want anyone getting hurt. Three rounds, rest between each unless somebody wants to stop before then. You okay on the rules?" He looked at me. I nodded. Thibodeaux and I bowed to each other and to Kapinsky, and went to opposite sides of the big mat. We didn't do the sportsmanlike touch of gloves, as you would in a friendly match.

I figured the sparring was a front, and Thibodeaux was going to kick my ass. It was just a question of how much damage I was going to take. He had the reach on me, pounds of muscle, a few years' speed, and a desire to hurt. All I had was a sense of regret that I hadn't had the control to keep myself out of trouble.

Alright, then, what would he do first? He'd likely rush me from the get-go and try to flatten me quick to impress his admirers and gain a big psychological edge.

As soon as Kapinsky signaled, Thibodeaux charged right in with hard front-kicks. I was prepared and dodged out of the way, but just barely, and he caught nothing but air. I danced backwards a little more. Since I retreated, he thought he had me intimidated, and kept coming, reaching a little farther with each kick, over-extending in his eagerness to nail me. Finally he was off-balance and open. As he recovered from a kick, I popped him one in the chest, pulling it at the last second to score, but not hurt.

There was a murmur from the crowd, and the smirk on Thibodeaux twisted into a snarl. He slowed down and got more cautious, stalking me like a cat, trying to cut off my escape. By the rules I had to stay on the mat, but he made me pay for it. There were fewer kicks, but he snapped them in hard. Mostly I blocked them with my arms and shoulders like I should, but he caught me a good one in the ribs, and didn't pull it like he was supposed to.

He had a power jab that kept hitting me before I knew it was coming, but at least I blocked and ducked enough to keep him from landing the follow-up combinations. I was so busy stopping his shots, I couldn't get off much of my own. After about a hundred years, Kapinsky ended the round.

My breath was already ragged, and my arms felt heavy from all the punishment they'd taken. I looked over at Thibodeaux and he was breathing even harder, but still looked like he had plenty in him. The next two rounds were going to suck, big time.

We went at it again. He closed with me to slug it out. So much for light contact. I did my turtle imitation, covering up while I waited for an opening. The flurry of punches eventually slowed, and I dug a right into his stomach, and followed with the left up top. It caught him by surprise, and he backpedaled to shake it off.

He recovered quickly and kept pounding me with those long, strong legs like twin battering rams, but the kicks had less snap now. That was good, since I was slowing down myself. His jab was also landing less often, and didn't have the sting in it any more. I used feints to good effect, stopping his attack and breaking up his rhythm.

He was also more cautious, staying out of my reach so I couldn't land anything. But that meant it was harder for him to get me as well.

Kapinsky called for another break, and Thibodeaux looked surprised. I guess he'd figured to have me down by now. Of course I didn't feel too peppy, but I had enough left to nail him if he got careless. It was still a fight. I sucked in as much air as I could. Thibodeaux looked pissed now, glancing furtively at the spectators. His show wasn't going as planned, and it got to him. This was his last chance to do something big.

When we started again, he came in like a freight train. He got a right through to my face that would have loosened some teeth if I hadn't had my mouth guard in. I tasted blood, and a little bit of anger.

Now I'd see if I could make him careless one more time. I deliberately slowed down, acting tired and hurt. After another high kick caught my shoulder, I even staggered a little. Sure enough, he got cocky and started dancing around, showing off for the crowd. I crouched like I was covering up, while I was ready to spring right down his throat.

When he front-kicked, I sidestepped and closed, driving a smashing right into his nose, with everything behind it. His feet went out from under him and he slammed down on his back, making a loud thump on the mat. Kapinsky jumped in, looking worried, but it was all over. I bowed and walked back to my side, breathing hard. A few of the older spectators applauded briefly.

Thibodeaux's pupils swarmed over him. No one came over to me. I spat out the mouthpiece and took off my headgear and pads, dropping them into the bag on the edge of the mat. I limped back to the locker room. My ribs and arms were sore and my mouth hurt where he'd nailed me. The mirror in the locker room showed a swelling upper lip with a small but bloody cut. A little cold water washed the blood away, but the lip had that sticky, cotton feeling. At least I wouldn't need stitches, and nothing was broken. I'd be sore as hell for a while, but I'd got off lucky. And maybe Thibodeaux would have a little less mouth and attitude. It was a good tradeoff. It had felt good, too good, to smash him in the face.

I took a quick shower to get the sweat off, discovering a few new hurt places. When I came back out in my street clothes, the suits had gone and Thibodeaux was still lying on the mat, a towel up to his face, and one bloody one on the floor next to him. Good thing he wore red pants, so the blood wouldn't show, as it was a bitch to wash out. Several of the kids shot poisonous looks at me. I didn't bother asking Thibodeaux about Ben just now, as I figured he wouldn't be too talkative.

Before I reached the door, the young guy I'd met before stepped in the way. His cheeks were flushed and his eyes blazed bright. He tried to look tough and mean, but he was too clean-cut, and you just wanted to pet him on the head like a puppy dog.

"You want to try that with me?" He couldn't even sound tough.

I shook my head. "Sorry, I've had enough."

"He had you beat until you cheated!"

"How'd you figure that?"

"You broke his nose."

"He'll live." I shrugged. "Though he won't be as pretty. If he's never had it broken before this, he's been lucky. See this?" I tapped my own crooked snout. "Four times, so far, three in the ring, one out. No big deal."

"But it was supposed to be light contact!"

"Anyone tell him that?" I touched my tongue to my swollen lip. "Since you hadn't noticed, he was trying to take my head off out there. Is that what he's teaching you?"

"He teaches us real good. If you weren't so chicken, you could find out."

"Sorry, kid. One lesson is enough for today." I stepped around him and got to the door.

"You better not come back here," he said to my back.

"Why on earth would I want to?" I murmured as I left.

# CHAPTER 14

Kapinsky the referee was outside, leaning against the building, waiting for me. He smiled and bounded over to shake my hand. He was a lot happier than I was.

"Great fight," he said. "Great fight. You did it. You really did it. Pow, right on his ass. One hell of a lesson."

"I got lucky. He had me beat."

"No way. You set him up, a couple of times. I saw it. And man, after you got him with that combination, wow. I've never seen him stay off of someone like that."

"That's what you call staying off? It feels like he took sledgehammers to my arms."

"You're still walking, aren't you? His other opponents end up on their back. He just pounds the shit out of them."

"Speaking of which, you have some different rules of 'light contact' up here. He was trying to take my head off."

Kapinsky shook his head. "I'm sorry about that, man, truly I am. Thibodeaux likes things run his way. I didn't want to do it, but he made me. I was there mostly for show. But I thought you knew the score."

"Yeah, I knew it, but it wasn't any fun to go through, just the same."

"But you did it. You took him out."

"He was cocky. If he'd taken his time and been careful, he wouldn't have had a problem."

"Yeah, but he can't do that. He's the big fish in the little pond, and thinks he's fucking invincible. But you popped him. Broke his fucking nose. *Damn*, that was sweet."

Kapinsky acted like a kid who'd just been given a pony for Christmas.

"There's a couple of thousand guys would do a lot worse to him than I did."

"But no one's done it in a long time. He's going to be pissed." Kapinsky grinned.

"He better get used to it, if he's going to have an attitude like that. Still, I shouldn't have lost control and hit him like that."

"Oh, no, that was great. Besides, what choice did you have, the way he was coming at you?"

I shrugged. "Maybe he doesn't have any control, but I'm supposed to know better."

"Hey, look, can I buy you some dinner? For taking that prick down a peg." He paused and nervously licked his lips. "And I could tell you about your friend."

There were warning bells going off in my head, but he had information.

"You knew Ben?"

"He came to my studio after he had an experience here similar to yours."

"Yeah, I'd like to hear about that. How did you know he was my friend?"

"When Thibodeaux called, he said you were a friend of the other guy he'd beat, and he'd give you the same treatment."

"Jesus," I shook my head. "He is a case, isn't he?"

Kapinsky took me to a Chinese restaurant and mentioned that this area was the Old Port. Somewhere around here was a cocktail waitress that had known Ben. I asked Kapinsky how many bars were around. At least a couple dozen, he said. Damn. It wasn't going to be easy.

Kapinsky ordered a drink and tried to get me to order one.

"No, thanks."

"C'mon, get a drink. You've earned it."

"I don't drink," I said abruptly.

"Oh." He looked embarrassed. "Hope you don't mind if I do."

I shrugged. The waiter left and Kapinsky went on.

"I run a studio out on Washington Street, but it's not like his." Kapinsky shook his head. "I don't train my people to go out picking fights to show how tough they are. His students are always in trouble. Two of them just got busted for assault."

"Great teacher."

"Yeah, he's a real pain in the ass. He's tried to fight everyone around. Calls himself 'The Champion of Portland,' all that crap. Doesn't know anything about the true spirit of martial arts.

"Anyway, he gives me a call a couple months ago. He's set up a match, asked me if I could ref. I said sure. I was hoping he'd get beat and learn to keep his mouth shut.

"The opponent was Ben. Jesus, he was good. Thibodeaux couldn't land a solid blow, and Ben scored whenever he wanted, nice and light. It was a pleasure to watch him."

"Yeah, Ben made it look elegant." I took a swig of my soda, and held an ice cube against my cut lip with my tongue. Kapinsky had another drink brought over and we ordered our food.

"So every time Thibodeaux kicks or punches he comes up empty, and he gets madder and madder. He goes in wild and hard, and finally landed one. Then he jumps back, with that sneer on his face, like a nasty little brat. Ben looks at him a minute, shakes his head in disgust, and took off his pads. He just walked off. Thibodeaux lost it. He was screaming at Ben to get back on the mat, but Ben had nothing to prove. Everyone knew he was better.

"So I asked Ben if he wanted to come to my studio. He was a real asset, let me tell you. Made me feel bad, he was so much better than me. Shocked us when we heard the news. Couldn't believe he'd killed himself."

"He didn't," I said. "He was murdered."

Kapinsky stared. "You're serious, aren't you? Jesus, the police didn't say anything about that."

"They didn't know then. They do now."

"Who'd kill him?"

"That's what I'm here to find out. What about Thibodeaux? You say he was pretty upset?"

"Yeah. Yeah, he could kill someone." Kapinsky looked like he was mulling over something unpleasant.

"What is it?"

"Oh, nothing. I was just thinking. Ben was shot, right?"

"Yes, why?"

"So it would be someone who couldn't take him in hand-to-hand and knew it."

"Maybe."

"Maybe indeed. You could get the cops to search his place. Maybe they'd turn up something."

"It's a start. What about his students? Their god was defeated, maybe someone couldn't take that."

"Pretty stupid reason for killing someone."

"Most killings are for stupid reasons. His sidekick challenged me tonight as I was trying to leave."

"Chip, the little puppy? I doubt he'd know how."

"You think of anyone else might have a reason? Any problems Ben might have had with someone?"

"Sorry, he kept the personal stuff to himself."

The food arrived, and I tried a forkful. It was good, but the spices fired up my lip. A mouthful of cold soda helped that, but what I really wanted was one of Kapinskys' drinks. The iced glass looked enticing. Kapinsky must have thought so too. He was on his third now. There was an edge under the excitement. I wanted to ask more questions.

"What about his being sick? What do you know about that?"

"Nothing. He only came in Wednesdays, his day off. He was supposed to be in that Wednesday, but that was the day he ... it happened."

We ate in silence for a while and Kapinsky finished the last of his drink. He immediately waved to the waiter and motioned for another. He looked at me, looked away, and bit his lip. He was about to sell me something.

The drink arrived, and he took a long gulp. He set the glass down carefully, his face flushed from the booze. He took a deep breath and looked at me.

"You ever think about opening your own dojo?"

"Not really."

"Oh." He frowned, thinking it through. "You going to be in the area long?"

"At least until I find out who killed Ben."

"Want a place to work out while you're here? Maybe teach a few classes? Same stuff Ben was doing."

"You offering me a job?"

"Why not? Actually I'm thinking of moving out to California, starting a place out there. Maybe you get to like it here, you might want to try your hand at running your own studio."

"Man, I left California as soon as I could. Why you want to go there?"

"I uh, need a change of scenery." He looked uncomfortable.

"I come out here, you want to go there. Everybody wants to be somewhere else."

The check came, and Kapinsky looked it over.

"Give you a lift?" he asked.

My head hurt and I was sore all over. I could have used a ride, but after the drinks he'd had, and the sales pitch, I didn't want to be around him anymore.

"No, thanks. I want to do a bit of looking around."

"Okay. So how about stopping by sometime, taking a look?"

"Yeah, why not? No guarantees, you know."

"Sure, sure. Stop by whenever. Here's the card, has the address right there."

"Okay, I will. Thanks for the dinner."

"No problem. Be seeing you."

I limped into the warm summer night air, feeling like I'd been hustled.

# CHAPTER 15

*Ben and my brother Tim were being attacked. I moved in to help, but the attackers turned into shadows and drifted away. Both Ben and Tim had open, horrible wounds. They looked at me with silent, reproachful faces covered in blood. Finally I got to them, but they told me they were dead. I looked for a place to bury them. Then we were on a boat, and I rolled their bodies overboard. They began to swim, and I called to them. They kept swimming away, and soon I couldn't see them anymore. Someone else was driving the boat, and I couldn't make the driver stop.*

It was dark in the room when I awoke, and the dream melted away, the edges retreating as consciousness returned. The feeling of loss and guilt remained, however. I lay shivering, trying to forget, and wanting a drink very badly. Every part of me hurt.

The clock said three-fifteen, and I noticed my hands were shaking. Not a good time to start drinking, but I wanted it like a junkie wants a fix. Only booze would take away the pain in my mind, take away the pain in my body. Simple. Christ, I was bad off.

Thank God you couldn't get a drink at this time of the morning. The only thing I had was a bottle of tomato juice. I tried to get up to get it, but I was like a board that wouldn't bend. The effort was too much, so I just lay there. The television was still on, showing an old episode of *Hawaii Five-O*, with the stalwart Jack Lord as Steve McGarrett. Good old McGarrett. He could uncover the killers and not have bad dreams while doing it. Too bad he wasn't on this case.

I tried to get back to sleep, but the more I pushed out the thought of the earlier dream, the more it came haunting. The trouble with being lonely is that you remember all the things you shouldn't. It was a while before sleep finally came, and by then McGarrett had chased the bad dreams away.

I woke up groggy some hours later. It was finally daylight. It hurt even to just lie there, and then I tried to move. My bruised, aching body reminded me of how dumb I had been. Every limb was stiff, my lip was still puffed out, I had contusions and abrasions I could have done without, and there was one really sharp pain down low on the left side under my ribs. But as I went over my catalog of hurts, I kept remembering Danny's face as my right hand made contact with it, and figured it had been worth it.

It took a while to hobble to the shower, but once there the hot spray felt wonderful, even though it stung. I soaked in the heat and stayed under until I could move a bit. Moving took a little of the stiffness away, and by the time I got out, I felt like someday I might be whole again. I toweled dry and dressed as slowly and carefully as an old man.

About all I was good for now was stakeout duty, so I decided to watch Thibodeaux's studio. There was a little breakfast restaurant within sight of the door to the studio. Perfect. Inside, I took a table by the window.

By the time I got to order, I was ravenous, and settled for a feed that would fill a lumberjack: a three-egg omelet stuffed with cheese and onions, served up with sausage, hash browns, toast, and coffee. It was pretty decent food as coffee-shop fare went, though I'd have eaten it even if it wasn't. I tried to make it last so I'd have an excuse to sit longer, but it was gone before I knew it. With a full stomach and a refill of coffee, I felt ready to claim human status again.

Seeing the waitress walk by got me thinking of Maureen. There was no physical resemblance, just a kind of shared weariness around the eyes. I hoped Maureen was all right, and decided to call her. It surprised me to realize that. A year or two before and I wouldn't have felt so charitable. It seemed I was taking more of an interest in people, in the whole world around me. Maybe I was getting soft, developing feelings and all.

A little later Chip went to the door of the studio, unlocked it, and went inside. Nothing else happened, so I sat there and played with the sugar packets. They had pictures of old-time sailing ships on them. You could still see sailing ships off the Maine coast. In Miami, it was all power boats.

One thing I should have known that when you're on stakeout, you shouldn't drink too much coffee. I'd had two refills, and was going to accept a third when my bladder told me I'd need to make some room. I did my business and came back to my table, but ten minutes later needed to go again. Great detective I was. If anything happened, it would no doubt take place while I was in the john.

So I vowed to stay at my post and refused the refill pot when it came by. Twenty minutes later I was rewarded by seeing Thibodeaux make a slow, stiff walk to the door of his studio. He wore sunglasses, and had some major bandage action over his nose. He went inside, and I was left with my sugar packets again.

I stretched it out for another twenty minutes, but realized that I seemed too much like a guy on stakeout. I paid up and left five dollars for the waitress as a tip to make up for monopolizing the table. She lit up with a big smile and thanked me like she meant it. At least I'd made someone's day.

The telephone book listed a Daniel Thibodeaux on Cumberland Street, very close to where I was. It might be helpful to see where he lived, find out a little more about him. And maybe I could even get inside. Carrying professional lockpicks was a crime, but I had my Swiss Army knife, which could open many a cheap lock. I'd learned some special skills while working for a former employer.

The address was one of those small sets of apartments jammed in between two buildings. The front door was old and solid, with an oval of glass etched with flowers. The wall by it showed four names, each with a buzzer. Thibodeaux was in apartment D.

I'd need a cover in case anyone got suspicious as to what I was doing there. Especially if someone was in the apartment when I tried to get in. Up the street were newspaper vending machines and some advertising and real-estate fliers. I took a handful of the fliers and came back. A young guy came out through the door just as I got out front, and he even held it for me as I thanked him and went in. I was surprised at that, because in security-conscious Miami, they would have slammed the door in my face before I could get inside, or demanded to see my key before letting me by.

The interior could have used a little sprucing up. I walked up the stairs and found "D". Before you try to break into a place, you should always check to see if someone is home. Saves embarrassing explanations. Lucky I did, for someone came to the door and opened it.

The someone was a young woman who didn't much care about her appearance. Her hair was a mess, her eyes were red and puffy, and a cigarette hung from the corner of a mean-looking mouth. She wore shorts and a red T-shirt with no bra. I tried to act embarrassed, and shifted my eyes to look past her into the room. The place was cluttered, with beer cans standing on a coffee table, and a pizza box that gaped at me with open jaws. Through the open door came the unmistakable sweetish odor of pot.

"What?" She crossed her arms in defiance, and stared me down as the smoke curled around her head. This place couldn't have had a working smoke detector, I thought. I held the rolled-up fliers with both hands, and acted befuddled.

"Is the uh, man of the house at home?"

"Are you for real? No, the fucking man of the fucking house is not home. He's at his fucking karate studio where he got his fucking nose broken last night. And I hope whoever did it comes back to finish the job."

"Would ... would you like a copy of the Watchtower?"

"The Wat ... Oh, Sweet Jesus. No, I don't want your goddamn Watchtower. Go fuck yourself. And don't ever come back here, or I'll call the cops. We have a buzzer downstairs to keep freaks like you out. Get out of here, now!"

I ran down the stairs as if she'd scared me off, but I was laughing to myself. I'd been like Bogie in *The Big Sleep*, where his detective character, Marlowe, acts as a goofy birdwatcher at one point to get into a bookstore without suspicion. Here I'd pulled it off, and the woman probably wouldn't even remember my face, just that it was some dumb religious huckster.

All I'd found out was that Thibodeaux's taste in women didn't run to the high-class or neat type, and that his home life was undoubtedly not the happiest. I'd come back some other time, when the lady of the house wasn't home.

Dale T. Phillips

# CHAPTER 16

I'd been thinking of how to get someone else interested in the circumstances of Ben's death. Although it was a long shot, I'd see if I could interest a reporter. After all, there weren't that many murders in Maine. Any spotlight could help put the pressure on the killer. And provide a link, in case I was killed.

My soreness made it a good day to take it easy. The public library wasn't far away, and the walk helped me loosen up. A helpful librarian pointed me toward back editions of *The Maine Times*, a regional paper that published investigative pieces. I scanned some issues and found what I wanted: a writer named J.C. Reed, who had a series of articles with the right kind of thought process. Just in case, I got two more names as backup.

Portland was great because everything was easily reachable on foot. The Maine Times office was just down the street. Once there, a few questions got me pointed in the right direction. I knocked on the door to Reed's office.

"Yeah," came a response from within.

Reed was a sturdy-looking older man. He was balding on top, so he compensated with a beard, all of which was white.

He briefly looked up as I came in, and returned his attention to the paper he was reading.

"Mr. Reed, I asked for the best investigative journalist and was sent to you."

"Then somebody lied to you. That'd be Bob Furness down the hall. Go see him."

I laughed in surprise, reevaluating him on the spot. He was a player. His voice was pure clam chowder, bred from generations of Mainers.

"Sorry," I said. "I guess ass-kissing doesn't work on you. How about outright bribery? Can I buy you lunch and tell you a story?"

He considered for a moment, then shrugged and put down his paper. "I always knew this job would pay off someday." He came around the desk to shake my hand, and we introduced ourselves formally.

We went to a restaurant called the Great Lost Bear, down on Forest Avenue. It was a funky joint, lots of stuff on the walls, hand-lettered signs abounding. Reed ordered some microbrewed beer and looked at me sideways when I didn't join him.

"Too early in the day for you?"

"It's not that. I had a real bad problem once. If I dip my toe now, I'll drown."

He nodded. "I've had my problems with it myself from time to time. Maybe it's the whole Hemingway thing." He struck a pose in profile. "What do you think? Am I ready for the lookalike contest in Key West?"

"Absolutely," I chuckled. Now that he pointed it out, he really did look a bit like Papa. "Put on the bill cap and you're a dead ringer."

"Then bring on the bulls and red wine, and let's go punch someone."

"With a name like J.C. you want to fight?"

"It stands for Joshua Chamberlain, the greatest soldier of the Civil War, the man who saved the Union at Gettysburg. So yes, I want to fight."

"Yeah, didn't he accept Lee's surrender?"

"That's right," Reed said, giving me an approving look. "You know your stuff. That wasn't in the movie, which is all most people know about him."

"That was something, ordering his men to fix bayonets and charge, when they didn't have a bullet between them."

"Yes, not bad for a professor of Rhetoric. So, you read a bit. And you have some problem that only J.C. can fix. So what did they tell you when you asked what I was like?"

"They said you were an ornery cuss who'd tear my head off."

"True enough," he said, sipping his beer. "Didn't scare you, huh? Your need must be great."

"Let me tell you a story," I said. "Of a man who lived his whole life to help others, who tried to make the world a better place." And I told him as he drank his beer, looking like a sage in his white whiskers, eyes half-closed as he absorbed my words. I didn't tell him everything, of course, but I did say Ben had saved my life and how he'd done it.

When I had finished, and J.C. had drained his second beer, he looked at me.

"So you want me to write the tale of mysterious murder. Don't you know that journalists today don't investigate? They do little more than print press releases. They want stories handed to them on a platter, not go mucking about, getting all dirty by actually going out in the field."

I looked at him, waiting.

"On the other hand, there is a certain noirish aspect that might yield something up. A little *Death in Venice* sort of thing. Yes, possibly. No promises, mind. Have to convince my editor. But we could see."

Good enough for a start.

Dale T. Phillips

# CHAPTER 17

With Reed agreeing to look into Ben's death, I was feeling good, so I decided to risk calling the lovely nurse to see what might develop.

The phone book listed an A. Chambers. I fed in some money and punched out the number, crossing my fingers. Someone picked up the receiver.

"Hello."

"Allison Chambers please."

"Speaking."

"Hello. This is Zack Taylor. The rude fellow with the dead friend and the bad attitude?"

"Like I could forget."

"Well, I was wondering if you'd, uh, like to have a cup of coffee."

There was a pause. I realized I was holding my breath.

"Coffee."

"Uh huh."

There was another pause.

"Well. All right." I started breathing again, and almost missed her next words. "There's a place called Green Mountain Roasters, down by Exchange Street. Do you know where it is?"

"I'll find it."

"Say, half an hour?"

"Half an hour it is. See you then."

I hung up the phone feeling like a giddy seventeen-year-old getting a date for the prom. I very much wanted to see her, even though it was pulling my thoughts away from the investigation. This was for selfish reasons only.

So to feel a little less selfish, I bought a souvenir T-shirt and a lobster keychain, and sent them with a note to Esteban down in Miami, care of Hernando. Esteban would probably wear the shirt until it was in tatters, like he had with the last one I'd given him.

The coffeehouse was busy, even this late in the day, with professional workers stopping for a quick brew to get them through the evening, and a few black-clad art students to give it the real coffeehouse flavor. I got some mocha concoction and waited at a table for about five minutes before Allison came in. She looked even better without the nurse outfit. I wondered why there wasn't a crowd of men following her.

"Hello again," I greeted her.

"Hey." She smiled, and that was a damn fine thing.

"Can I get you something?" I offered.

"An espresso, please."

I went up to the counter and brought back the tiny cup that looked as if it was from a child's tea set. We sat and sipped for a moment. It would be up to me to break the silence.

"I'd like to apologize for my bad start before."

"You're forgiven. It's understandable if you went through the hospital staff. How'd you like the troll at the desk on our floor?"

"You mean Nurse Ratched? She was the essence of courtesy and helpfulness."

"I'm sure." She smiled wryly and picked up the cup with a dainty motion of thumb and forefinger. I was full of feeling, but had no idea what to say to this woman.

Everything I could say was immediately censored internally as being trite and banal, when I wanted more than anything to be witty and fun and interesting.

"So are you finding anything out?"

"A little. I spoke with the man who'd been in Ben's room while he was sick. Didn't seem to be anything out of the ordinary."

But that reminded me of the old man and his wife.

"Something wrong?" she said.

"I went out to see the guy at his home outside of town. It's an older couple, and the home's getting run-down. They're being hounded for four hundred dollars that the insurance company won't pay, and they just don't have it. They were afraid I was the bill collector."

"That's terrible."

"Yeah, the poor woman cried when she found out I wasn't there to ask them for money." I shook my head.

"It's hard for a lot of people. They can't afford to get sick. I wish I had enough money to give to folks like that who need a little help."

"That why you got into nursing, because you like helping people?"

She smiled, but I thought I detected a ruefulness. "Nursing pays the bills. I started art school, but my dad died and my mom had a stroke. I had to work and take care of her while I got my RN. Maybe if things had been different ..." She shrugged, but didn't sound bitter.

"So your mom still lives around here?"

"Over in Westbrook, in a managed care facility. Not far from the paper mill."

"Paper mill?"

"Oh, you don't know about that? Up north, they chop down trees, crush them into pulpwood, and turn it into paper here. Stinks all the time from the chemical processes. People who live there get used to it, but it hits you when you go there. But Mom doesn't have much of a sense of smell anymore, and the facility is a good place. I keep up the house in town here. We've lived here all our lives. Old-time Maine Yankees."

Allison set down her cup. "Now your turn. Where do you come from?"

"You're going to laugh."

"No, I won't."

"Yes, you will."

"I won't. I promise."

"Okay. Fresno, California, turkey and raisin capital of the world."

"Turkeys?" She laughed. It was a nice sound that I wanted to hear again.

"Told you you'd laugh."

She kept giggling, covering her mouth. "You're pulling my leg."

"Swear to God. Big spreads with millions of the damn things. My family had one. You wouldn't believe the noise they could make. That's all you ever hear, even in your sleep. Hell of a racket. Wasn't exactly my calling to follow the family tradition, so I left. Still get jumpy around Thanksgiving, though."

Allison laughed again, and I reveled in it.

"Any brothers or sisters?" she asked.

"Two brothers, one sister." I hesitated, wondering what to say. "One brother died young."

She seemed to sense my discomfort and changed the subject. "So what did you do after you left?"

"Bounced around to this and that. Never settled down. Worked as a raft guide here in Maine one summer. Worked as a bodyguard for a while. No career path to speak of, no plan. Jobs to pay the rent and buy food, and save up for knockabout expeditions, that's all. Ben and I took some great trips."

"A life of adventure, huh?"

"More like avoiding responsibility and commitment."

"Thanks for the warning." She made a wry face. We laughed together.

"The summer I spent here in Maine was a good one," I said. "I was having a very bad time, and being out in the woods helped me find some peace."

"Maine is a good place for that. Maybe you can find what you're looking for here."

What she said suddenly reminded me of what I was here for, and the blunt, bitter words slipped out before I realized what I was saying.

"You mean a killer?"

She winced like I'd slapped her, and I knew just how badly I'd screwed up. I felt like a clod who'd just tracked mud across the clean carpet of very nice people.

"Sorry," I said, and meant it. "I do that sometimes."

"It's all right," she said. But there was a coolness behind her words. "You want to do the right thing for your friend."

The moment was gone, and we were strangers again. Damn me for an idiot.

She was game, though. "You were telling me about what you'd found out."

"I went out to the resort where Ben worked," I said.

"Which one? There's a lot around here."

"Pine Haven, just down the coast."

"Yes, I know it. We had lunch there one time."

"Well, Ben was a good worker," I said. "A great guy, but the chef was talking about having some problems with him. That makes me suspicious. And the manager there was very uncooperative and kicked me out."

"Why?"

"He says it's because I'll hurt the tourist trade if I bring up questions about a murder. I don't know if they're involved, but I don't like them. There's another guy, too, who was pretty disagreeable when I brought up Ben's name."

"Is that what happened to your lip?"

"You don't miss much, do you?"

"I've seen enough fight results in my line of work. You didn't have that last time I saw you."

"Well," I said, wondering how to downplay what happened. "Ben and I both did martial arts. This guy in town owns a studio that Ben went to. The guy thinks he's the best in the world and has to prove it to everyone. I got conned into a sparring match that turned out to be more. I was lucky to get out with only this."

"Do you fight a lot?" Some women liked this aspect, but I wasn't sure about this one.

"I don't go down the street looking for trouble, but I do kickboxing, and sparring in several styles."

"Mmmm."

"I must be boring you, talking about this stuff," I blurted out. "I'm not very good at this."

She looked at me, her expression hard to read. "It's okay," she said. "Most guys only want to talk about themselves, their jobs, or sports. You are different, I'll give you that." She smiled at me.

I thought I was trying too hard and was embarrassed. She spoke again.

"What was your friend like?"

"Ben? He was the best. Funny, kind, not afraid of anything. He liked adventure, challenging himself."

"When did you see him last?"

"Christmas. We talked about our next trip. We were going to hike the Andes, see Machu Picchu."

"After all that, won't you find Maine pretty dull?"

"'The wanderer's danger is to find comfort'," I quoted.

"Ah," she said. "I'd love to travel, but this is my home. My roots run pretty deep."

"It seems like a good place for staying put."

Our coffees were long gone, and there was a pause. We'd passed the stage of polite conversation, and it was time to go. I felt a desperate urge and reached deep within for some courage.

"So," I said. "Would you like to do this again? I know I'm a total jerk and all, but it's nice talking to you."

She studied me for a long moment. "Okay. Coffee's pretty safe."

"Yes," I agreed. "Maybe someday we can work up to a lunch."

She smiled. "Perhaps."

"Thank you for meeting me."

We made polite goodbyes, and I felt like seven kinds of fool after she'd left. I thought about how wonderful she was, how different from me. She spent her life trying to help people, and I spent mine trying to hide from them. But being around her made me want to be a better person.

Dale T. Phillips

# CHAPTER 18

Using the number I got from the matchbook I'd taken, I placed a call to the Rest E-Z Diner to see how Maureen was doing. I thought it would be safe to go through Shirley, so I got her on the line.

"Shirley, this is Zack Taylor. I was there a few days ago with Maureen."

"Yeah."

"I wanted to know how she was doing. She wasn't too well when I saw her."

"She's a whole lot worse off now, thanks to you. Bobby Lee heard about a stranger here, and he'd had a stranger at his door, so he figured something was up and beat her."

"Oh, God. Shirley, I'm sorry. Is she okay?"

"No, she's not okay. He put her in the hospital again. Busted her up real bad. I'm goin' over there later."

"Damn it, isn't there any law down there?"

"The law is whatever men say it is. And they say if someone wants the police, they have to file a complaint. You see Maureen doing that? He'd kill her. Good Lord, a dog gets beat, and they at least give 'em a fine."

"Is there anything I can do?"

"You could shoot that sonofabitch. I'd do it myself, and be proud to say I did, if I didn't have three others depending on me."

"Couldn't she go somewhere else for a while?"

"He'd find her. And he'd do worse."

I tried to think of something. This was my fault, and I wanted to do something to make it better. "Shirley, you still there?"

"Yeah, it's your nickel. There's nobody here right now, anyway."

"What if Maureen had a chance to go somewhere, start over, without him? What if someone offered to take her anywhere else, someplace where he couldn't find her?"

"Well, now, that'd be real sweet. I suppose she'd just up and go in her new Cadillac and new clothes, while Bobby Lee waved goodbye? You poor fool, how would she get by? She ain't had much schoolin', and about all she's ever done was waitressing. How's she gonna get by, pay the rent, buy the groceries? I work all the time and can barely get by."

I had no answer. The amount of money I had could see me through for a while, but I didn't have enough to give Maureen the kind of help she needed. For any long-term solution, she'd probably need therapy, too, to keep her from hooking up with another man like Bobby Lee.

"But would she leave him if there was a chance? Could she leave everything behind if she could get out safely, with some way to keep her afloat for a while? There are women's organizations that help out in cases like this."

"Honey, if a rock fell on him tomorrow, she'd walk away without a tear."

"Then could you tell her to hang in there, and prepare herself for getting out?"

"Men been making promises to her all her life, and all she's ever got out of it was more pain."

"There was one who didn't hurt her."

"The way I heard it, he got her hurt anyway, by buttin' in just like you. And now he's dead. You gonna replace him?

You gonna ride in here on your big white horse, sweep her away from Bobby Lee and marry her, and live happily ever after?"

I swallowed. She was right. I wasn't Ben. "I'd like to believe there's something that can be done."

"Well, you just go right on believing it. Along with believing in Santa Claus and the goddamn Easter Bunny, pardon my French. But unless you're ready to put it all on the line, and got some kind of magic powers, maybe you better keep your do-gooding bottom the hell away from here."

"I want to help."

She sighed. "I know, honey, so do I. I'm a Christian woman, and I know how it is. But some things you can't fix. So find something up there you can fix, and trust in the Lord for everything else." Her voice called to someone. "Someone's coming in, so I gotta go. It's been real nice talking with you now."

After I spoke with Shirley, I went back to my room and took a hard look at my finances. I couldn't give Maureen a fresh start, but Shirley had told me to find something I could fix.

I thought of the Deckers in their tiny house, old and tired and afraid to answer the door or the telephone, afraid to open the mail, all for the sake of a few hundred dollars they didn't have. Some medical insurance company had guys in suits making six-figure salaries by squeezing the pennies from people like the Deckers.

I drove to the hospital and for four hundred and three dollars and fourteen cents, the Decker's bill was settled. The hospital would call them and let them know the bill was paid in full. I knew Ben would have approved.

Dale T. Phillips

# CHAPTER 19

I hadn't been making much progress in finding Ben's killer, so I thought I'd go back to Pine Haven and see if I could annoy someone there.

It was late in the afternoon, getting on toward dinner, and there was a knot of people smoking by the back entrance to the hotel. The waiters wore black pants with white shirts, dark green uniform jackets, and bow ties to match. The waitresses wore dresses in the same shade of green, and a few of the kitchen help were decked out in their usual white jackets and checked pants.

Brian, the sous-chef, came out as I approached, and lit his own cigarette. The people around him looked at me, looked at each other, stubbed out their cigarettes, and pointedly went inside at once, leaving Brian and me standing alone. So much for winning the hearts and minds.

"Have I got something catching?" I asked.

"No, but we're catching it. We're having an all-hands meeting in ten minutes. Kitchen staff, Wait staff, Housekeeping, Security, everybody."

"Can I come?"

He smiled. "It's all about you. A lot of people know about it already and don't want to be seen talking to you."

"Except you."

"Fuck 'em. They already chewed me out for talking to you."

"Sorry," I said.

"S'alright. I'm a big boy, though I am getting tired of them busting my balls. This whole thing is whacked, you know?"

"Sure is," I agreed.

"Ben was a good guy. Things haven't been right here since he died."

"Were they before?"

"They weren't as tense. Now it seems everyone has a bug up their ass."

"You think somebody knows something?"

"Don't know. It's just a strange vibe."

"I'd really like to talk to more people."

"Don't think that's gonna happen. They want your head on a platter. And they're going to tell everyone to run from you like you were Freddy and Jason combined." Brian stubbed out his cigarette.

"What if I crashed the meeting anyway? Went out in a blaze of glory?"

"They'll have security."

"The doughboy rent-a-cop? Not much of a deterrent there."

"There's others."

"Well, I could at least let everybody know what the real story is before they haul me away."

He smiled. "You like causing trouble, don't you?"

"When I have to."

"You want to listen in first, hear what they say?"

I grinned. "That could be fun."

"There's a set of stairs up to the dining hall from the side banquet room on the lower level. They never lock it, so you could wait a few minutes until everyone's upstairs, and slip on up. 'Course you didn't hear it from me."

"You? Ya bastard, ya didn't tell me jack."

"I better get on up."

"Thanks, man."

"Yeah. Good luck finding out who killed him."

Brian left, and I hung out for a few minutes until I thought it was safe. Then I went searching for the banquet room. It was off the corridor, with white-cloth-covered round tables. In the dim light they looked like pristine mushrooms. I found the stairs leading up. There was the buzz of a restless crowd.

"Okay everybody, settle down," Royce's voice rose over the clatter. The noise quieted down. The show was about to begin.

Royce spoke again. "You all remember the unfortunate circumstances when we lost one of our own. It was a tragic thing, and we're all sorry for what happened. The police investigated the cause of death and determined it was suicide. A sad thing, but we consider the matter closed. We need to put it behind us and continue on with the season.

"Recently somebody came by posing as a police officer, asking a lot of questions about the incident. We told him we had fully cooperated with the police, and everyone was satisfied that things were settled. He got belligerent, started accusing us of all manner of things, and even assaulted Larry.

"We had no choice but to tell him he was no longer welcome here, and would be considered to be trespassing if he returned. He seems to be trying to stir up trouble for some reason. Now, nobody wants business to be affected, but if people thought something was wrong, that could mean fewer guests. Fewer guests equals less money, so that guy could be taking money out of the wallet of each and every one of you.

"So for everyone's sake, if you see this man, let us know. You are not to talk to him or approach him in any way. Just call security or me, and we'll handle it."

Another voice asked a question. "What's he look like?"

Royce described me to the crowd, and there was a low murmur. Royce called out. "What is it?"

"That was the guy outside just a few minutes ago."

"What?" The alarm in Royce's voice was good for me to hear. "Where?"

"Out by the loading dock."

"Joe, Ralph, check it out." Royce sounded tense. "Did he talk to anybody? What did he say?"

"Brian stayed out there," someone called out.

"Did he? Brian, what did he say to you?"

I felt bad for the poor guy. Ah, well. Time to make my entrance. I stepped out into the huge dining hall. There was a gasp. I saw the staff seated at a number of tables, with Royce standing opposite, along with two remaining security guards as flankers. The wave of bad feeling was tangible.

"Actually," I said, "he didn't tell me a damn thing, except that I shouldn't be here." I looked around. "Nobody will tell me anything. What are you people afraid of?"

The guard I'd tangled with previously lurched in my direction, but Royce stopped him, and spoke quietly in his ear.

"I'm not some con artist," I continued. "But Royce is. Larry here was the one who assaulted me. Ben was my friend, and he didn't commit suicide. Anything you can tell me might help catch his killers." I quickly mentioned the motel name where I could be reached. Maybe someone would call.

Now Larry the guard and another, older man, also in a brown uniform, moved toward me. My time was up. I repeated the name of the motel, told everyone I was leaving, and walked to the exit with my two new escorts.

They stayed with me all the way to my car. Larry whipped out a notebook and wrote down my license plate number. "We gotcha now, asshole," he tapped the notebook. "I see this car again, I'll have it towed. We see you again, we'll bust your ass to jail."

I was not in the mood to be needled. "So you think you're a real cop now, Larry?"

"This is my house, boy, and you don't get to come back."

"Wow, you're so forceful," I mocked him. He took a step forward. Apparently, he had a short memory.

"Larry," the other man warned. Larry stopped, saving himself more embarrassment.

I got in the car and put it in gear. The window was down, and Larry couldn't resist one last parting shot.

"Get lost, punk, and stay away if you know what's good for you."

But I sure as hell didn't know what was good for me, and I sure as hell would be back.

Dale T. Phillips

# CHAPTER 20

So far, my score as an investigator was lousy. I'd come up zeroes with the hospital, with the martial arts angle, and now was blocked from further information at the place where Ben had worked. That didn't leave much.

So maybe I could find the cocktail waitress that had talked to Ben in one of Portland's myriad watering holes. The Old Port area was a formerly seedy waterfront district that had been rejuvenated into upscale shops, restaurants, nightclubs, and bars. I discovered to my dismay just how many bars. With the help of a local nightlife paper, I made out a long list of names and started at the top.

The first place was a trendy fern bar, all brass and glass and hanging plants. The clientele was the junior-exec crowd, aggressive young men in tailored suits with spiked or wet-look hair, swigging Heinekens and Coronas. The women looked stately and crisp, and sipped colored drinks. Both the men and women studiously avoided looking available. The regulars loudly hailed each other with forced good cheer, sounding like they were trying hard to prove they were having a great time. It was too much like Miami.

I showed Ben's picture to one waitress who wasn't yet busy. She chewed gum and had too much hair piled up on one side of her head, making her look lopsided. She said she didn't recognize him, and she didn't offer to ask any of the other waitresses. Too busy being aloof, I guess.

The bartender came by and asked me if I wanted a drink. I settled for a club soda. When he brought the glass, I put down a couple of bucks and showed him the picture. He didn't recognize Ben either. I checked the other waitresses one by one, but no one claimed to have seen Ben. I abandoned what was left of my club soda on the bar, drew a line through the name of the place on my homemade list, and went to the next bar, not far away.

I checked out working-class bars, bars with lawyers, even a punk-rock bar. It was getting on in the evening, and I was getting discouraged and irritable from resisting the temptation to drink. Everybody else was drinking and having a good time, and I wanted to be like that, instead of constantly living with my pain.

On my way out of yet another dead-end set of questions, someone deliberately blocked my path. It was Chip, the faithful puppy from Thibodeaux's dojo. His face was flushed with booze. He had three friends behind him, arms crossed, unsmiling.

"Hey, asshole," he slurred. "I wanna to talk to you."

"I am trying to leave," I said, slowly and calmly. "I do not wish to fight, and you are blocking my path of retreat. If you threaten me, it is assault, if you strike me it is battery, and the police will put you in jail. Now please let me leave."

"What are you, a lawyer?" He did his best to sneer. "We get assault charges all the time. Doesn't scare us any, does it, Jason?"

The referred-to young man behind the kid looked distinctly uncomfortable. He hadn't been at the fight at the dojo and must have been one of the ones in trouble Kapinsky was telling me about. If so, another assault charge would be very bad news for him. He looked like he didn't want to play. The others didn't look too happy, either.

"C'mon, Chip, let's go," said one. "This guy's too chickenshit to fight, anyway. He's not worth it." He put a hand on Chip's shoulder, but the kid shook it off and glared at me.

"Think you're so damned tough, why don't you fight me, huh?"

"I told you, I don't want to fight, I want to leave. Are you going to let me go, or are the police going to get involved?"

"Let's go, Chip," someone else chimed in.

"I want to hear him ask me. Come on, tough guy. Ask me real nice and I'll let you leave."

The anger was coming, a rumbling red wave. This had to end quickly, before I really hurt him. As I stepped to go around, he reached for me with his right, and I grabbed the wrist. I pulled down and twisted, applying pressure with my other arm against the elbow joint. He gasped and pawed ineffectually at his trapped arm, but he was helpless. I glanced at his companions. If they tried to jump in, I could break the arm, so they backed off, giving me plenty of room.

I frog-marched Chip out to the sidewalk, and let him go with a shove. He fell hard, scrambled to his feet, and tried to lunge at me, but all three of his buddies grabbed him and held him back. It saved him a lot of pain and some expensive hospital bills.

He spat out profanities and threats as I walked away, shouting until I was gone.

I was shaking with rage now, angry at him and angry at myself. I'd come very close to doing some real damage. Way too close. Some people want to pass on their pain to others, and I was edging into that darkness. There was a sour taste in my mouth, and I stopped and spat. I leaned against a wall and realized how badly I wanted a drink. The thought of the pain going away, even for a little while, was tempting. The voice inside told me to forget tomorrow, just ease the hurt tonight.

The wall was rough brick, and I pounded my hands against it. When it hurt enough to bring me back to the rational world, my hands were cut and bloody. The greater pain was still there, but I looked upon it coldly, dispassionately, and pushed it to the back of my mind. Disgusted with myself, I straightened up, shook like a dog, and went back to my task.

At the next bar, I went into the men's room to wash my hands, the hot water stinging my wounds. I splashed water on my face, dried off, and was finally ready to face the world once more.

With the photograph in hand, I started the questions again. But no one recognized Ben, and I was soon back out on the street. The next place was only a few doors down. It was also a bust. At least these places weren't far apart from each other, so I was able to work through them.

With only eight more places left on my list, I was seriously doubting I'd come across anything, but I pushed myself to make the effort. The next bar was a comfy, quiet little joint, with a nice, unpretentious feel. It was a place Ben would have liked.

The first waitress looked at the picture and shook her head no, but the second was a hit.

"Oh, yeah, he was in here. I think Sandy knew him." She pointed at another waitress across the room. I thanked her and followed Sandy to the bar station where she gave her drink orders to the bartender. She gave me the professional smile. "Can I get you something?"

"Could I talk to you about Ben?" She started at the mention of his name. I showed her the picture of the two of us together.

"Two minutes," I said. She nodded.

"Hang on a sec."

She went to deliver the drinks and was right back. She looked me up and down. "You don't look like a cop."

"He was my friend." I showed her the picture again. "That's me."

"So it is," she said, and looked back up. "What do you want?"

"Can you tell me about him?"

"Not much to tell. He came here a few times, was polite, well-behaved. Not like some other guys. That's about it."

I gave her the look which told her I wasn't buying it. "There's more."

"Look, I don't want any trouble."

"From what?"

"I gotta go."

"Sandy," I said. "He didn't kill himself, somebody shot him."

I watched her very closely. She didn't know until I told her. But the news didn't explode her world. She looked sad, rather than shocked, as she digested the information. I guess she knew the night people well.

She ran her hand through her hair. "Who?"

"That's what I'm trying to find out."

"And so you found me."

I nodded.

She looked thoughtful. "Well, that explains things. He sure was about the last person I'd expect to kill himself. He really seemed to like living, you know? But then it was in the paper, and I was wondering how in hell I'd guessed so wrong."

"You didn't. So what's the problem?"

"Look, my ex was in here one night, and he sort of grabbed me. Ben stepped in."

"Did they fight?"

"They went outside. Ben came back a little later. Vince took off, and I didn't see him again."

"Vince is the ex?" I said.

"Yeah," she said. "I asked Ben what happened, and he just said to let him know if Vince came back."

"So then what?"

"So we talked a few times after that and he asked me out. We went to the movies. Some guys only want to get in your pants, but he acted nice, like he was out for company rather than a quick lay. You can tell. We had a nice time. I think

123

something might have happened. But then he didn't call, and I saw it in the paper."

"So you didn't know he was sick?"

"What do you mean?"

"He was in the hospital for three days with food poisoning. He was throwing up, and weak. He went back to work before he'd even recovered. Then someone killed him."

"Well, I wondered. Damn."

"Yeah. Sorry it didn't work out. I think you both missed something special."

She shrugged, as if bad news and missed opportunities were nothing new.

"So tell me about this Vince," I said.

She bit her lower lip. "Well, he's a biker, and he's got a temper. He's been in trouble a couple of times. Fights and stuff. But killing somebody ..."

"Does Vince have rough friends, maybe?"

"Yeah."

"Maybe I better talk to him. What's his last name?"

"Beaulier." She spelled it for me. "Jeez, I don't know. He won't want to talk to you."

"I know, but I have to check these things out."

She shrugged. "Your funeral." That saying again. It was beginning to spook me.

"Where can I find him?"

"Most likely at the Cave. It's a biker bar in Lewiston. Better watch yourself there, though. They'll kick your ass just for fun."

"How will I know him?"

"He's got long, dark hair and one of his eyes droops a little."

"How do I get there?"

She sketched a rough map on a cocktail napkin and handed it to me. "Hey, what about that karate guy Ben fought?"

"Yeah, I heard about the fight."

"And how the guy wanted a rematch, and he wouldn't leave Ben alone?"

"What's that?"

"Yeah, he went to the place where Ben worked out and challenged him again."

"When was this?"

"I guess about a week before Ben died."

"A week? You're sure about that?"

"Yeah, I remember. That was the last time we spoke."

I seized on that piece of information like a drowning man grabs for a rope.

Dale T. Phillips

# CHAPTER 21

Another night of bad dreams haunted me, for I still hadn't adjusted to this place, or the new hours. Still stiff and sore from the fight, I stood in the shower under the hot water to loosen up. Then I began stretching, slowly and carefully, until I had some movement. I put on workout clothes, took my wallet and room key, and went for a jog. I did a slow trot for half an hour, and considered that well done. I rewarded myself with a convenience store juice and a muffin.

I'd showered again, dressed, and was feeling better, when the knock came at the door of my motel room.

"Who is it?"

"Police. Would you open up, please?"

"Could I see some identification?" I called out. Through the peephole, I saw a leather wallet that held a genuine-looking badge. It was no guarantee, but good enough.

I opened the door to see two men in suits. One was tall, about six foot six, sun-browned and fit, looking more like a forest ranger than a cop. Knobby wrists stuck out past the cuffs of his suit. His age I guessed at early fifties.

The other cop looked a few years older, but was almost a foot shorter and wider. He was going bald, but did a comb-over with a few strands of black hair to kid himself and no one else that he still had something going on top. His suit fit badly, and had no natural fibers in it. The black penny loafers were cheap, and badly worn. His face had a droopy look to it, like he'd seen it all and was weary of what he'd seen.

The tall cop spoke. "I'm Detective McClaren, this is Sergeant Lagasse. Are you Zack Taylor?"

"Yes."

"Were you out at the Pine Haven Resort yesterday and the day before?"

"Yes."

"We'd like to talk to you. Would you come with us, please?"

This wasn't at the top of my list of things I wanted to do right now, but it didn't seem prudent to refuse. I sat in the back seat of their car as we drove away. All I could see of them was the back of each head.

They took me to a small interrogation room. McClaren sat behind a table, which held a tape recorder and a folder. Lagasse leaned against the wall, chewing on a toothpick. The ends of his fingers were brownish-yellow. Smoker, then, probably trying to quit. He looked me up and down in an arrogant way. I knew the type. He'd been a cop about four to five years too long. He'd be counting the days to retirement and pension, but wouldn't know what to do with himself once he was off the force.

Since I'd been in this kind of situation before, I guessed how they would play this out. Lagasse would play tough, McClaren would be the cooler. They'd whipsaw me around until I caught myself in a contradiction, and they'd zero in with accusations until even I believed I was guilty. But I had a few tricks up my sleeve.

McClaren cleared his throat and spoke the interview setup for the recorder, then asked me, "Do you wish to have an attorney present?"

"No."

They looked at each other, and McClaren shrugged slightly, and restated for the record the fact that I had declined an attorney. Then he addressed me. "Are you Zachary Taylor, formerly of Las Vegas, Nevada?"

"Yes," I replied.

"What kind of a name is that?" Lagasse piped up. They weren't wasting any time. And I'd have bet that Lagasse relished his role.

"Just like the President," I said. He looked puzzled. Obviously not a scholar. I smiled. "But someone named 'Gassy' shouldn't comment on others' names."

Lagasse colored red. "You're pretty mouthy for a guy in trouble. You assaulted a security guard who was trying to remove you from the property while you were trespassing."

"What I was doing was asking questions about my murdered friend who had worked there. When they didn't like the way it was going, they got the rent-a-cop to roust me. I started to leave, and admonished him against physical contact. It was he who assaulted me as I was leaving."

"You kicked him with a shod foot," McClaren interjected. "That's considered a deadly weapon."

"I didn't kick him. I did a foot sweep to take him off balance, and let him down easy. The only thing hurt was his pride."

"What about your face?" said Lagasse. "Looks like he got a few licks in."

"I spar in kickboxing."

"So you're some kind of chop-socky master?" Lagasse sneered.

"Ooh, the Bad Cop speaks again," I said, without even looking at Lagasse. "What, you didn't read the report?"

"We read it," said McClaren. "We didn't much like what we read."

"Like the part where I hit a cop and went to jail?"

"That part in particular. Someone sure got hurt that time," said McClaren. "What happened?"

"The Feds know how to drop the hammer."

"How did you get involved with the Feds?"

I took a deep breath. "They were questioning me because of my former job. I worked as personal security for Carlo Tortelli."

"'Carlo the Knife', former New York Mob boss." McClaren nodded. "So you were connected to organized crime."

"It wasn't like that," I said. "Years ago, one of his associates tried a hit on Carlo, put three bullets into him. Carlo went into early retirement out west.

"I was in a martial arts show in Vegas, where I did disarming techniques. Carlo came by after a show and wanted to see if I really could stop a good knife man. He showed me a four-inch blade. I was young and cocky, and offered to let him try.

"He was good, but lucky for me he didn't have the speed anymore. I managed to disarm him. He was spooked around guns, he said, and none of his regular guys had my specialty. He offered me a job at about eight times what I was making, so I took it. Most of the time I just stood around outside a hotel room while he diddled his mistress.

"Nobody talked family business around me. After a few months, I got bored and moved on. That ended my involvement."

McClaren spoke up. "And the Feds?"

"About a year after I'd left, they brought me in for questioning. I didn't know anything, but that didn't matter. After maybe six hours, they hadn't got anywhere. One guy kept busting my balls, pushing me around. When he shoved me one time too many, I hit him."

"There's a copy of a note says that he needed facial reconstruction for a fractured cheekbone," McClaren said.

"I only hit him once. I was out of control. And just for the record, he was a dirty cop who later went to federal prison. But on the advice of my attorney, I pleaded out and did four months."

"So did you like your time in the joint?" Lagasse all but sneered. "Whose bitch were you?"

I turned my head to look at him. "I would expect a comment like that from a foul-mouthed little troll like you."

Lagasse blanched and came up out of his slouch with his fists clenched. "Why you goddamned ..."

"Sergeant," McClaren's voice was like a whip crack. It stopped Lagasse from grabbing me and causing a real mess. History would have repeated itself.

Lagasse unclenched his fists and shrugged. That was probably his response to everything when he couldn't jeer. He slumped back against the wall and furiously chewed his toothpick. McClaren turned his attention back to me.

"So what brings you to Maine, Mr. Taylor?"

"Ben Sterling's death was murder, not a suicide."

"And how do you know Benjamin Sterling?"

"We grew up together out in Fresno."

"But you weren't at the funeral?"

"I drove up from Florida as soon as I heard."

"Long way to come for a mistake," said Lagasse.

"Why are you so sure it's a mistake?"

Lagasse grinned. "Twenty-two years on the force, a little research, and the M.E.'s report. I've seen this type before."

"Type? And what type would that be, Sergeant?" I asked.

"Loner, loser, failed marriage, dead-end job. Gets sick, goes into the hospital for a few days. Comes out without a job anymore, sees there isn't much of a future for him. Nothing going right, no one to talk to, he gets a gun, drives out to a deserted spot, boom. End of story."

I swallowed hard, anger boiling up in me. "He wouldn't do that. Not ever."

"People do funny things sometimes." He shrugged.

"And this is pretty funny to you, isn't it?" I snapped.

The look of amusement left his face as he came off the wall once more. "I'll tell you one thing. You're not funny," he said softly, but with an undertone of menace.

"Hey," McClaren said. "Dial it down."

"Listen," I said to Lagasse. "You know a few things about his life, but nothing about the man. So your hasty view that it was suicide is unprofessional."

That stung Lagasse, as I knew it would. An outsider, a civilian, had questioned his competence, the thing he thought he was good at, and now he'd bludgeon me with everything he had on the case.

"Oh yeah, smartass? Your buddy was found behind the wheel of his own car, one bullet through the temple, fired at close range. He had his wallet on him with sixty-seven dollars, and his watch. In the car with him was a .38 Special, Smith and Wesson. Numbers filed off."

"He wasn't still holding it?"

"You shoot yourself in the head, you don't hang onto the gun unless you've got it taped to your hand. His prints were all over it, and tests showed he'd fired it. Ballistics matched."

"Anybody hear it?"

"It was nighttime at an industrial park down by Marginal Way. Nobody around to hear a thing."

I chewed my lip, thinking. He waited, as if eager to shoot down everything I brought up.

"Could he have been moved there after he'd been shot somewhere else?"

"Not according to the M.E."

We sat for another minute, Lagasse grinning like he smelled victory.

"You said he was shot 'at close range', right?" I was grasping at anything.

"That's right. About six inches away. Angle and exit wounds are consistent."

"Wouldn't a suicide put the gun right up against his head?"

He looked annoyed. "Maybe, maybe not."

I had to take a shot. "He was shot from the right side, correct? But he was left-handed."

"Let me tell you, buster, we ran this through," he said. "We heard this guy is supposed to be some kind of karate or kung-fu expert, and you want me to believe someone sitting right next to him was able to blow his brains out while he sat there? There were no ligature marks, so he wasn't bound up in any way. Tox screen came back negative, he wasn't drugged.

"We got no one with reason to pop him, and no way of doing it. Jesus, excuse me if we didn't call in the FBI. But now we're supposed to go to the chief and say 'Sorry, sir, we screwed the pooch on this one. This needs to be reopened as a homicide.' And when he asks why, we'll say 'because a friend of his, who worked for the Mob, says he didn't do it.' And we look like fucking idiots."

The comment I really wanted to make was far too easy. "Listen, Sergeant, that Mob stuff was ten years ago. I was a kid. I was just around to give an old man a sense of security. That's all."

"You work with scum, you get dirty."

"You work with lawyers. What does that make you?"

Out of the corner of my eye, I saw McClaren suppress a smile.

"Real funny. You know what I think?" Lagasse was getting into it. "I think you guys were both dirty. You think somebody whacked him and you want us to do your bird-dogging. You Mob boys are supposed to take care of your own dirty laundry."

"Ben never had anything to do with that. And what kind of crook goes to the cops?"

"So maybe you're a lousy crook as well."

"Get your head out of your ass, Lagasse. You might see better."

Lagasse took a step toward me as McClaren slapped his hand on the table.

"Enough," he said. "Sergeant, why don't you go get a cup of coffee?"

"Good idea," Lagasse said. "Something in here stinks, anyway."

McClaren shut off the tape recorder and watched him go. He leaned back in his chair and rubbed the side of his nose.

"Okay, just you and me. Any ideas on who might have wanted him dead? Or why?"

"No. I just got here."

"So you have no motive for a killing, no suspects, no information, really, just a notion that he wouldn't have done it."

"He wouldn't have. He wasn't like that. When I find out something, I'll let you know."

"Let me give you a piece of advice." McClaren leaned forward. "I suggest you get back in your car and return to Florida and let us handle it."

"I'm not going anywhere, so stop blowing smoke up my ass," I said. "You're not going to do a damn thing unless the killer walks in here and confesses. As a suicide, it's a nice, neat package, the way you guys like it."

McClaren frowned. "You have issues with the police, that's one thing. But you're not on TV, so don't go poking around, trying to play private eye. You told us your story, and if he was killed, we have a problem on our hands. But we don't need you getting in the way. You know what the game is. We can nail you with obstruction and have you right back in here for a long time. So keep your nose clean and we won't have any problems. Why don't you think about it? I'll have a uniform drive you back."

I did think about it, all the way back to my room. To hell with them. Warning or no warning, I wasn't about to just sit back and do nothing.

# CHAPTER 22

After my little tête-à-tête with the police, I went to Thibodeaux's studio to find out about the second confrontation. The place was locked, but I figured someone would show up soon. I looked around and moved to a less obtrusive spot, where I could see the door without being seen.

Twenty minutes later, Chip slowly walked up to the door with his head down. Sunglasses covered his eyes. He took out a set of keys and dropped them. Cursing, he bent down to retrieve them, and when he straightened up, I was right behind him.

He never even knew I was there until he finally managed to get the door open, when I gave him a little nudge through it with my foot. He stumbled and lost his balance, and sprawled out on the floor. I felt for the wall switch and turned on the lights. He turned to see who had pushed him. His sunglasses had fallen off, and as he blinked, I saw his red, puffy eyes.

He staggered to his feet, hands so slow in coming up for the defense it was comical. Had I wanted to hit him, he couldn't have protected himself.

"Relax, kid, I just want to talk. Have a little too much to drink last night?"

"Hell d'you want?"

"Just some answers to a few questions."

"I got nothing to say to you."

"Last night you were pretty eager to talk. Oh, put down your hands. You look ridiculous."

He hesitated. Finally he dropped his defensive stance and settled for surly. "You better get out of here."

"Or what? You'll throw me out? We both know that's not going to happen."

He mumbled something I didn't catch.

"What's that?" I said.

"Call the cops."

"Great. We'll tell them about your assault on me last night, then we can move on to accessory to murder."

"What are you talking about?"

"Ben had another run-in with you clowns, just before he was killed."

"I don't know anything about that. Leave me alone."

He turned away. I was tired of his attitude. From my drunk period, I remembered what a skull-splitting hangover felt like. I drew in my breath and screamed a piercing *kiai*, the power yell of martial arts. He moaned and held his head like his brains were going to fall out.

"What the fuck, man?" He snarled like a junkyard dog. I grabbed him by the hair and shook him hard. He gurgled, and I let go and stepped back. He dropped to his knees and threw up on the floor of the dojo. When he was finished, all the fight and bluster were gone, and he was on the edge of tears.

"Want to tell me about it now?" I said, when he'd recovered.

"Danny, it was Danny," he sobbed. "He wanted to fight the guy, all-out, no holds barred. He went to that other school. Your friend was there."

"So what happened?"

"He said no."

"He said more than that."

"He said that Danny had no honor," Chip said, wiping his mouth. "I almost jumped him."

"Be glad you didn't. He'd have torn your lungs out."

"He shouldn't have said that."

"What, the truth? That Thibodeaux is an overgrown bully who can't take the medicine he dishes out?"

"That's not true!" Chip winced at the volume of his own voice.

"So why does he have you running around picking fights to defend his so-called honor?"

"He doesn't tell me to. I'm proud to do it."

"No doubt. Maybe if you live long enough, you'll understand what's wrong about all this."

He said nothing, and just held his head.

"So go on. What happened then?"

"Danny started saying how it's not much good to learn how to fight if you're too scared to fight. Your friend just laughed and turned his back on us, and told us he'd call the cops if we didn't leave."

"Let me guess. You birds ran home."

"He was too scared to fight, there was nothing else to do."

"And that was it?"

"Yeah."

Chip was a bad liar. There was more.

"Your Danny didn't by chance make some remarks as he left, did he?"

Chip's face got redder, but he said nothing.

"Let me guess. Loudmouth started shooting off how this wasn't the end of it, makes a few threats. And a few days later Ben turns up murdered."

"He didn't kill him!" Chip whined. "He wouldn't do that."

"Not even when Ben was showing him up for the fool he was? My guess is, he didn't like that."

137

"You bastard. You're just like him."

"What's the matter, you want me killed, too? This isn't the Wild West, kid, we don't have to see who's the better gun."

"He'll get you. You'll have to fight him again."

"If he killed Ben or had someone else do it, he'll fight me alright. Otherwise, no, he won't."

"We won't forget this."

"Go clean yourself up, kid. You look like hell."

I left the place with a sour taste in my mouth, although certainly not as bad as Chip had.

# CHAPTER 23

It was time to see what was up at the Pine Haven resort. I couldn't take my car there anymore, so I went to a rental place and got a good rate for the week on an old clunker, though newer than mine.

I couldn't risk contact, so I'd also have to hang out at a distance and spy on them with binoculars. The Yellow Pages listed several optical shops, and I drove over to Exchange Street and purchased a high-quality set.

Maine license plates call the state "Vacationland", and the drive to Pine Haven proved them right. The sun was good and warm in a crisp, blue sky. With the window down as I drove, I enjoyed the fresh air, thinking of the contrast between here and Miami. Here the heat didn't beat you down, and the air refreshed you, instead of sucking the energy from your lungs.

The guest parking lot at Pine Haven was crowded with cars, and I didn't see any patrolling security guards. I parked near the exit, facing out, so I could leave in a hurry if the need arose. On the other side of the parking lot were groomed paths and hiking trails leading in all directions around the resort grounds. Many people were out walking, smiling and nodding to each other as they passed, enjoying the day. I was not out of place with my binoculars, as there were plenty of nature lovers here.

There were good sight lines to the hotel from the trails, and I found a spot with unobstructed views of Royce's office door, the back door of the hotel where the help went in, and the front of the workers dormitories. It was a perfect place for a stakeout, cool and quiet, shaded by the tall trees. A light breeze ruffled the mix of leaves and evergreen branches around me, and a tangy scent reminded me that the ocean was nearby. Easy to see why Ben had liked it here.

I raised the binoculars and adjusted them for my visual inspection. There were people moving around, but I couldn't read their lips to see what they were saying. That's another thing that always looks easy in the movies.

So I sat there, listening to the birds sing and feeling the breeze in my hair. I thought of what I would do after finding Ben's killer. My life had had a deliberate aimlessness to it, but I'd shared some good times with Ben. He knew my past and forgave me, though I couldn't forgive myself. I felt pretty empty right about now. Revenge carries you to a certain point, but what about afterward?

I also thought about the nurse I'd met, and wondered if she'd want to have anything to do with me. Maybe she was used to guys that had so much going on in their lives that they didn't have time for someone else. I certainly had time for her, but what could I offer her? Some leftover ghosts and martial arts expertise. Not the most stellar of resumes.

An explosion of color caught my eye. It was Royce, wearing bright, godawful, multicolored running tights. With the maroon shirt and the neon running shoes, he looked like a mobile beer sign. He checked his watch and started off at a trot. I didn't follow, because there is no way to be unobtrusive when following a running man in the woods, and the way he was dressed, I doubted he'd be up to much in the way of criminal acts.

I stayed on through lunch, eating the sandwich I'd picked up at a sub shop on my way over. Every once in a while I'd get up and move around and stretch, and I was able to move well for the first time since the fight.

Hours passed, and nothing of note happened. I watched comings and goings. Royce didn't come back this way after his run, so he must have taken some other route back to his room. Or maybe I'd missed something.

Around two in the afternoon, Grossman came out of the hotel and went to the dormitory. A short while later he came out, dressed in street clothes. He went to a white Cadillac parked next to the dorms and got in. I figured I could catch up to him somewhere along the road. It beat sitting here waiting for somebody to hold up a sign saying they were guilty.

I took a few shortcuts through the trees and got to my rental car. I didn't quite peel out, but was going faster than was prudent. I pushed it down the winding road, punishing the car in my haste. Gunning it down the stretches, I barely slowed for the corners, holding tight to the steering wheel and fighting for control. A long stretch of road showed the caddy about a mile ahead, behind another car. I made up some time on that flat stretch, and took it a little easier until we got to the highway.

Grossman got on the highway and headed north, not shy about letting the caddy have some gas now. I had to use a heavy foot to keep up, and noticed the needle was over eighty.

He got off at the exit for the Maine Mall, and I followed him there through all the traffic lights. The huge shopping center lot was busy, and he drove around for ten minutes looking for a parking spot close to the entrance. I parked before he did, and walked over to watch the doors going in. He came rolling along, his size making him easy to tail, and I followed him in, concealing myself in the crowd.

I've never been much of a consumer, and shopping malls seem like the place where bored people come together to buy things to fill their empty lives. The stores have no soul, offering the same useless crap all over the country.

Grossman stopped in to a number of places, including an electronic gadget boutique, a men's clothing store, and a cigar store. He bought something in every one, and every time I could see the register, he paid in cash. I quickly scribbled the name of each place in my little notebook.

Then came something I couldn't believe. Grossman stopped in the food court area at a well-known burger chain and got in line. So much for the gourmet chef. Though he got his food for free at the resort, here he was buying junk food between lunch and dinner.

He wolfed down two burgers at one of the tables in the open area, stuffing french fries in at the same time. He shook the bag of fries, getting every last one, and left the trash on the table when he got up. When he got in line for an ice cream cone, I almost went over to sign him up for a Richard Simmons exercise class.

Grossman went into more stores. He must have spent several hundred dollars. And his Caddy looked new. I wondered where he got the money.

He went back to his car, and I managed to catch up to him a few miles down the road, breaking a few speed laws in the process.

Grossman got off at the exit for the resort and drove back to Pine Haven. I had been hoping for something more revealing, but at least I knew he had expensive habits. It was late afternoon, and I went back to my place in the bushes until Grossman came out of the dorms in his cook's outfit and went into the hotel for the dinner shift. I watched for a while longer before giving it up as a lost cause, and headed back to Portland.

# CHAPTER 24

While eating my supper at a pizza place on Forest Avenue, I thought about my next move. Sandy's biker ex needed to be checked out, though it was likely to be nothing but trouble.

Northeast of Portland are two towns on opposite banks of the Androscoggin River, forming a "Twin City" of "L-A", for Lewiston-Auburn. There was little resemblance between the two, or to the real L.A., for that matter. Auburn was more upscale, and had a regional shopping mall, while Lewiston was a blue-collar town from a manufacturing past. The mills were now silent, and little had arisen to replace them. The descendants of the French-Canadian immigrant millworkers now contended with chronic unemployment.

The gateway to Lewiston from the highway was a row of sandwich shops and burger, chicken, and pizza fast-food joints, with a Chinese restaurant or two thrown in for variety. Further in, I noticed the Department of Motor Vehicles was cheek-by-jowl with the unemployment office. No matter which side of the building you went to, you had to stand in line. Good training for life here. Get your license and spend the rest of your life waiting for something and driving around looking for work.

The downtown had undergone extensive renewal, evidenced by the broad sidewalks that butted into the street and the trees planted at regular intervals. The main drag was one-way, and I cruised past the pawn shops, stores, and private clubs. One look at the half-deserted boulevards and I wondered how the businesses here stayed solvent.

The Cave was a few streets away from the main drag. It was a classic dive bar, with a half-dozen motorcycles and three cars parked in the tiny lot. Out front was one of those wheeled-trailer advertising signs, propped up by cinder blocks. It told of a Tuesday night two-for-one special on beer.

People who ask a lot of questions are not welcome in biker bars. No matter how I played it, this was going to be bad. I was liable to get the snot kicked out of me unless I could put a lid on my penchant for smartass remarks.

The Cave was aptly named. In the dim, smoky interior that reeked of sweat and stale beer, it took my eyes a few seconds to adjust to the gloom. Two guys sat at the bar, and behind it was one tall, bald, mean-looking mother of a bartender. A skinny guy played pinball in the corner, and three others were by the pool table, drinking beer from longneck bottles. The jukebox pounded out a Rolling Stones tune that had been old thirty years ago.

Everyone looked at me except the kid playing pinball. Nobody spoke. It was eerily reminiscent of a Western movie, where I was the stranger coming through the saloon's batwing doors, looking for a gunfight.

One of the pool players had a dyed-blond buzz cut. The other two had long hair, one of them a short guy with a skimpy mustache. The bigger guy had one eye that drooped.

"Vince Beaulier?" I asked.

Nobody said anything. I tried again. "What's the matter, Vince, you shy?"

He turned to glare at me. "Who the fuck are you?"

Great. Tough guy with an attitude. Well, I hadn't expected to be greeted like a long-lost brother. I gave him my name. His eyes narrowed as he looked me over.

"You're not a cop." An affirmation, not a question.

"No, but I'd like to talk to you for a moment, if I could."

He and the big, blond guy exchanged glances. Buzz-cut had intense, blue-gray eyes that bored into you like twin ice picks. He took out a cigarette and lit it, and shrugged ever so slightly. Ah, the leader.

"So talk." Beaulier said.

I held out the photo. "Recognize him?"

Beaulier's gaze flicked to the picture and his face stiffened. The social chill in the room went down a few more degrees. Any colder and ice would form.

"Maybe."

A real blabbermouth. "When did you see him last?"

Beaulier gave me a hard look. "Why you wanna know?"

"He's dead. I wondered if you'd talked with him."

Shorty grinned, exposing teeth badly in need of cleaning and straightening. "Sure he ain't a cop, Vince? Sounds like a fuckin' cop to me."

"He ain't no cop. But I don't know what he is."

Buzz-cut smiled and croaked in a hoarse voice damaged by too many cancer sticks. "Private dick." He made it sound like a funny insult.

Shorty barked a quick laugh.

"That true?" Beaulier cracked a smile, but a mean one. "You a private dick?"

"I'm just trying to find out who talked to him before he died."

Beaulier leaned over to make another shot. He missed the three-ball off a side rail. Nobody was in a rush here to hand out information.

"How'd you find me?"

"Waitress in Portland."

"Stupid bitch talks too much."

"So how about it?"

Beaulier looked at me like I was dogshit stuck to his shoe. "Why the fuck should I tell you anything?"

I thought to myself '*because if you don't, I'm going to stuff your head up your ass,*' but decided on a different tactic.

"Twenty bucks." Hey, it always worked on TV.

Beaulier grinned. I was glad I was so entertaining. "Make it fifty," he said.

Shorty barked again. I was beginning to think he was a pet dog.

"I don't have fifty."

"Tough shit. I don't feel like talking to you." He defiantly took a swig of beer.

I ran through my options, none of them good. Time to kick things up a notch.

"Feel like talking to the police, then?"

"What?" Yeah, that got a reaction.

"This man was murdered. You had an argument with him just before he was killed."

"You threatening me? You fuckin' threatening me?" His voice rose in angry disbelief.

"Easy, Vince." Buzz-cut put out his hand.

"Easy my ass."

"Remember your parole."

"Fuck parole. I'm gonna bust his head."

A loud smack rang out over everything, as the bartender slammed a baseball bat on the bar. His point was made. Nobody moved. The jukebox had stopped, and the silence was magnified. But in my head, I heard the music to *The Good, the Bad, and the Ugly.*

"Outside." When the big bartender spoke, it was like the Word of God.

"You heard him, dirtbag. Outside." Vince had his snarl down quite well.

I went out the front, with the three of them in tow. At three-to-one odds, I'd have to think of something fast, unless I wanted to get hurt, or run off like a candy-assed baboon.

The wheeled sign gave me an idea. I walked over and hoisted one of the cinder blocks up on to the flat part of the hitch. They watched me, wondering what was up.

"Pop quiz, Vince," I said. "Which is harder, your head, or this concrete?"

I took several deep breaths and focused my energy. I raised my arm and chopped down with the edge of my hand against the block. I'd carefully aimed for the spot where it was thinnest, over the opening, and the block split in a very satisfactory way. An easy enough trick with the proper training, but always very impressive. My hand stung a bit, but I ignored it, and looked at the three. Yes, they were impressed. Vince looked thoughtful, which was probably something different for him.

Buzz-cut walked to one of the bikes and produced a heavy-looking wrench that was over a foot long. He went to the block I'd broken, raised the wrench, and smashed it down into the block, which broke again. He gave me a look as he tapped the wrench in his hand.

Trumped, I laughed. Buzz-cut stared at me in disbelief, then cracked a smile. Shorty and Vince broke up. The tension eased. Buzz-cut lit another cigarette. Once we'd stopped laughing, I figured I'd try again.

"So how about it, Vince? When did you see him last?"

Buzz-cut coughed, very gently.

Vince scuffed his feet, like a kid reluctantly confessing a playground infraction. "'Coupla weeks ago."

"You had some trouble, right?"

"It was all that bitch's fault. She was mouthin' off, giving me lip, so I was getting ready to smack her around a little. But this fucking guy tells me to lay off, like she was his old lady. We went outside and I was gonna kick his ass, but he starts talking cops. I was pissed, but hell, I don't wanna go back to Thomaston. No beer and no pussy."

I chose not to remind Vince that just a minute or two before he had been ready to engage in an activity that would most certainly have sent him back. The human brain is a marvelous thing.

"So what happened?"

"Aw, I was gettin' tired of her shit, anyway, so I split. Plenty of others."

"And you never saw him again?"

"No. Told him if I did, I'd stomp him good, teach him a lesson."

I tried so very hard not to, knowing what it would lead to, but a smile stole across my face.

"What's so fuckin' funny? You don't think I could?"

"He could have broken every bone in your body."

"That right? Think you're pretty fuckin' tough, huh? All that kung-fu shit? I'll fuckin' kill you, man."

"Let it go," Buzz-cut rasped. He gripped Beaulier's arm and held him there as I walked away. Beaulier spat out obscenities polished from long practice as I got in my car.

"This ain't over, motherfucker! I'll fix your ass!" He flipped me the bird as I drove away. Another fan.

He was angry and violent, had spent some time in jail. Could he have killed in cold blood? Maybe. Buzz-cut was a tough number. Maybe he liked to help his friends with revenge. I added them to the list of suspects, depressed that it was getting longer.

# CHAPTER 25

I was a failure. Instead of digging up information when I talked to people, I wound up making more enemies. And every enemy was another door slammed shut to further information. There weren't many doors left. About all I could do was follow and do surveillance on people who wouldn't talk to me, but it was a long list.

Kapinsky's dojo was in a run-down strip mall, a gathering of hopelessness. The sign for his school was small and stuck where you'd never see it, unless you already knew it was there. The dojo was wedged between a tanning salon and a closed store with the front windows soaped over. The only other businesses were a takeout sandwich place and a shabby laundromat. The parking lot had crater-like potholes and crumbling concrete around the light fixtures, with dead hedges around the borders, and litter everywhere.

The interior of the dojo gave off the same air of neglect and decline. Other studios I'd seen that had reached this stage didn't remain in business long. Many good karate instructors were poor businessmen. This was not an endeavor where you made big bucks, but did it for the love of the sport. All the same, I wondered why things were going

149

so badly to seed. A fresh coat of paint and a little work wouldn't hurt this place. It needed some life.

When I halloed loudly, Kapinsky poked his head through a doorway. He smiled and came out to greet me.

"Hey, hey. Great, you came. Let me show you around the place. Here's the office and part-time storeroom."

I looked in to be polite. "No computer?" I asked, eyebrow raised.

"Computer? What for?"

"Everything," I said. "How do you keep track of the students, how and when they pay, and the business bills?"

"Oh, I've got a ledger for all that. Cost me four bucks at LaVerdiere's. Why would I want a computer?"

"They do a lot more. You can write letters, create flyers and press releases, add some graphics, email them out. You know, make your own advertising."

"Huh, I never thought of that." He looked thoughtful.

"It sure helps the business."

"To tell the truth, business hasn't been all that good."

"The location doesn't seem to help." I nodded. "You need a good anchor store in this mall."

"Yeah, the economy's hurting everyone."

"Your sign could be bigger."

"I've been meaning to do something about that. Hey." He laughed. "You haven't even seen the whole place and you got ideas. Guess you are the right guy."

He took me into the locker room. One of the overhead lights was out, and the remaining light threw eerie shadows over the benches, peeling paint, and battered set of lockers. In back was a urinal and a toilet stall with no door. The sink had rust stains, and over it was a smudged and cracked metal mirror. From the tiny shower stall came the smell of mold.

"Women's room same as this?" I asked.

"We, uh, kind of share the facilities. The plumbing's not working on the other side. Anyway, we only have two girls in the class. They take turns with the guys."

I kept silent, nodding, though I was embarrassed. I'd only seen one or two studios worse than this, both in much worse neighborhoods, in much bigger cities. Kapinsky was smiling like a man trying to sell a car while hoping you wouldn't notice it didn't have an engine. I shrugged. It was his place, and if he wanted to let it fall apart, that was his decision.

We left the locker room, and went back out to the main hall, stopping before a huge wooden cabinet with a combination padlock on the front.

"Here's the weapons closet," Kapinsky said, spinning the dial to open the lock. He opened the doors to show an array of martial arts weapons used for training advanced students. I saw metal, wooden, and bamboo swords, sais, nunchakus, assorted shuriken, and a variety of wooden staffs. There were some nice pieces there.

"Some of these look new. Use these much?"

"Nah. Don't really like them." Kapinsky picked up one of the metal swords and idly swung it. "Bought them about two years ago when I wanted to start the studio." He put the sword back and ran his hands over some of the other equipment. He closed the cabinet after a long look. "Ben was pretty good with these. He was getting some interest going."

The mere mention of Ben cut me. I changed the subject. "Did you buy the place outright or do you have a lease?"

"Lease. Still got eight months left, unfortunately, otherwise I'd be out of here. Borrowed the money from my sister, so I can't default. And the guy that owns this mall is a bastard, said he'll tie me up in court if I don't pay. He went after the folks next door when they wanted out, sent them into bankruptcy."

He paused, and looked at me directly for the first time. "You could have it all for just taking over the lease. Weapons, mats, students, everything."

It looked like a bad deal, but then again, I had some ideas for what to do if I decided to try it. Considering the neglect of the exterior, I could probably work some kind of

151

reduction in the lease, or else convince the manager to spruce up the mall grounds.

It would need lots of interior work, too, but I could do most of that myself. I knew some ways to get a fresh crop of students, generate some income. It would never be a big moneymaker, but it would be a cheap way of starting my own school.

We wound up back in his office. I felt a twinge of pain when I tried to sit.

Kapinsky noticed and nodded sympathetically. "Little stiff, still?"

"Some," I admitted. "Came too close to getting my head taken off, though."

"I'd say you handled yourself pretty well."

"Danny doesn't seem to understand the concept of rules."

"That's the goddamn truth. Sure was good to see you clean his clock." He said it with some heat.

"Past history with you two?"

He blanched, as if I'd gut-punched him. "No, nothing like that. Just, you know, because he's an asshole and all."

"Uh-huh."

"Hey, I'd like you to meet my students," he abruptly changed the subject. "See what you think. Feeling up to it?"

Maybe somebody among his students could tell me something useful. "Sure."

He brightened up, like a puppy who'd just got tossed a bone. "Terrific. Hey, let's celebrate." He reached into a drawer and pulled out a bottle of Scotch. Blended, not even single malt.

"Before class?" I was appalled. If Kapinsky was drinking now, he had a problem. Was the place falling apart the cause of the problem, or a result of it?

"Never too early for a celebration. I feel your coming here is good luck. What say?" He poured a healthy slug into a paper cup, but I stopped him before he could fill a second one for me.

"No thanks. I don't drink, remember?"

He looked at me with an unreadable expression, then shrugged and put the bottle away.

"Here's to ya," he said, and took a generous swallow. "I know what you mean. I probably should cut it out. Ah, well, when I get to California and away from here, everything will be different."

I didn't disillusion him, but I knew people usually take their problems with them.

"Tell me about Ben," I said.

"Well, like I said, he had the match with Thibodeaux, and I talked with him for a while. He came on down, just like you are, and decided to stay on and help out."

Ben would have seen this place as a challenge, and he hated waste. Yes, I could see him lending a hand here.

"How often was he here?"

"Once a week, when he was off. He worked six days a week, you know. Some resort down the coast."

"Pine Haven."

"Yeah, that's it. He'd come in and work out with my top students."

"Any problems with anyone?"

"Not at all. They took a real shine to him."

"He take a special interest in any particular student?"

"No, but he was only here, what, five times, really." Kapinsky looked at his empty cup.

"You know where else he went on his days off?"

"I think he mentioned the Old Port one time, like he was going there when class got done. Can't tell you where, though."

"He didn't talk about seeing anyone?" I said. "Mention any names?"

He shook his head.

"How'd you hear about his death?" I said.

"It was on the radio first, but they didn't say who it was. You know, unidentified male. Later it was in the paper. We were all pretty shocked."

153

"Can you think of any reason for anyone to kill him?"

"Maybe Thibodeaux couldn't take being shown up."

"Could he do it?" I watched him carefully.

"That rat bastard could do just about anything," Kapinsky said. It was plain there was something deeper there.

Kapinsky looked at the drawer now, obviously wanting another. Neither of us spoke. I couldn't think of any more questions at the moment, and things were getting awkward.

"You wanna meet the gang? The class starts in a few minutes."

"Sure," I said. I wandered out to the main room and looked around some more, running things through in my head. Time passed, and Kapinsky was still in his office. He finally came out, and it was clear he'd had more to drink.

I decided to press it. "What happened the night Thibodeaux came to challenge Ben the second time?"

"What?" He looked up. "I uh, I was out that night."

I looked at him.

"You weren't here for the class?"

Kapinsky was the sensei, the teacher. There was a responsibility when someone signed up for classes.

"Ben was teaching. He had everything under control."

"Who closed up?"

"Ben. He left the key in the box outside."

"Did he open, too?"

"No, I took off when he got here. I gave him the keys and left."

"Your students didn't mind?"

"They liked Ben better," he said, and turned his head away.

"You don't want to teach anymore?"

Kapinsky sagged. "I just like a night off once in a while."

"You take off other nights?"

"Sometimes."

He was hiding something. "So the night you're gone, someone comes in to insult and challenge the person teaching your students. How do you feel about that?"

Kapinsky shrugged and wouldn't meet my eyes. I stepped closer.

"Hey," I said softly. "What's going on?"

Kapinsky didn't answer. I put my hand on his shoulder. He flinched and pulled away.

"Ben was murdered," I said. "Something happened, something which maybe has a connection, or maybe not. But I need to know."

Kapinsky was looking at the floor. He swallowed a couple of times, and finally spoke, his voice so low I could barely hear him.

"Thibodeaux came here right after I'd started the place. I was closing up. He wanted to fight, to prove he was better. I refused, and he slapped me, hard. It made me plenty mad, the way it was supposed to, so we went at it. I wanted to knock that stupid smirk off his face. I should have known better.

"Third degree black belt, years of training, and Thibodeaux smacked me around like a rag doll. Kicked me in the ribs so hard I thought they were broken. Used his elbows and knees. Knocked me down and pounded my kidneys so bad, I pissed blood the next day. Then he started choking me, until I thought he'd kill me. I couldn't breathe, and the lights were going out. Just then he let me go.

"He laughed and said he might be back some time, in case I ever forgot the lesson. And there wasn't anything I could do. A martial arts instructor getting beat up by one guy? The police would have laughed in my face, and I would have lost all my students.

"So I got afraid and started to let everything slide, hoping he'd leave me alone. A beating like that does something to you. I don't feel like teaching anymore, I just want to get out. There's a chance for me out in California. But this fucking lease has got me trapped.

155

"Then Ben appeared. When he was here, I felt less afraid. I let him take over the classes, and wished he'd taken them all.

"And Thibodeaux came back. Soon after, Ben was dead, and I was alone again. Until you came. He called and told me to come ref that night, and I didn't dare say no. I loved seeing you bust his nose like you did. I hate being his goddamned little yo-yo, letting him spin me around any time.

"You tell me Ben was murdered, and I get a chill down my spine that won't go away. I don't want to know any more. I just want to run, but I can't even do that. Pretty pathetic, huh?"

Before I could respond, the front door opened and a young man came in, waving a greeting. I turned to Kapinsky and kept my voice low. "Pull yourself together, introduce me, and you can get through it. I'll help."

Kapinsky looked at me and nodded, just keeping away tears of shame. He rubbed his face and tried a brave smile. He managed to introduce me to the newcomer, who then went to change. I kept an eye on Kapinsky. He was shaken, but was controlling it.

More people arrived, and I met them all. He began the class, though there were only four students. Two more came in later, but it was a poor showing. I couldn't much blame anyone for not being enthusiastic about coming here to work out. It was plain Kapinsky's heart wasn't in it, and the depressing surroundings only made it worse.

I managed to talk to each person one-on-one, asking them about Ben. They were a nice enough bunch. They had all liked Ben, and liked the change from Kapinsky's lackluster teaching. They confirmed that Thibodeaux had come in and challenged Ben, and that Ben had laughed at him and made him look foolish.

As soon as the class was over, Kapinsky went back to his office. The last of the students left. I ducked my head in and said goodbye. He waved a hand in response, staring at the bottle on his desk. I couldn't say much, having once taken that road myself.

Dale T. Phillips

# CHAPTER 26

I'd finally had a decent night's sleep, and most of the soreness was gone. So it was time to go see if anything was happening at Pine Haven. I bought a sub and a bottle of iced tea to see me through lunch, and headed down the coast.

There was a good crowd of people strolling the trails at Pine Haven, looking well-fed, pleasant, and unworried. Sure. They didn't have any murderers to catch. I hiked to my surveillance spot in the woods and adjusted the binoculars.

Not much happened for a long while. People went about their business as I watched away, feeling like the Jimmy Stewart character in *Rear Window*. Though he'd been hampered with a broken leg, he'd had the lovely Grace Kelly to help him out. I'd gladly trade a broken leg for that kind of help.

I stretched and flexed my limbs, feeling out all of the remaining sore spots. At least Thibodeaux's nose would still hurt. It wouldn't cure his cockiness, but now he'd have a reminder for the next time he tried to push someone around. I felt sorry for the kid who followed him, though, basking in the reflected glory of a two-bit tin idol.

When I was growing up, my heroes were people like Thomas Jefferson, Abraham Lincoln, Marie Curie, Martin

159

Luther King, Jr.; pioneers, inventors, explorers, scientists, men and women who made the world a better place. Ask a kid today who their heroes are, and you'd get a list of overpaid rock musicians, movie stars, and professional athletes, people who were entertainers and nothing else. Many of these would be losers who, despite their money and fame, repeatedly wound up getting arrested for stupid stuff, like drug and assault charges.

Sure, put me in charge and I'd make it a better world. I gave up the deep thoughts and ate my sandwich.

Then more watching.

There was a flash of excitement. Royce walked from the hotel to his office, carrying a satchel. I watched him unlock the door and go in. Maybe he kept secrets there. Maybe I should pay his office a late-night visit. But then maybe he had it wired with an alarm, and I'd get busted. Anyway, I'd seen that old secure steel box, and I was no safecracker.

More nothing happened. People came and went, but did nothing to arouse my suspicions. An hour and a half doesn't seem like much time, but it can drag on for years. Every so often I watched the birds and squirrels just for a change of pace. How did the police stand it on long stakeouts? People work hard at doing nothing most of the time, but if you force them to do nothing, they can't take it.

Because of my casual approach, I almost missed Royce when he came out, despite how he was dressed. He sported sunglasses attached to a loop around his neck, a pressed pair of shorts with huge square pockets on the front, a teal polo shirt with the collar stylishly turned up, and docksider-type shoes on his feet, with no socks. He looked like an ad for L.L. Bean. All he needed was a tanned, skinny, young wife dripping with jewelry to complete the picture of yuppie tourist.

Royce began taking a protective cover off his Porsche. I started for the parking lot. I got back to the car and tore off down the road, knowing I'd never keep up with the Porsche if he wanted to go fast. He was out before me, but I wasn't far behind.

Luckily there was other traffic on the winding road. Royce was behind slow-moving drivers, with no place to pass, and I caught up with the parade a few miles down the road. On the long stretch, I saw cars ahead of Royce, and there were three more between me and the Porsche. By the time we got to the highway, I was only two cars behind.

Royce headed north on 295, passed through Portland, and turned onto Route 1, towards Falmouth. I saw residential areas where the houses were big and luxurious. There wasn't any peeling paint or junked cars in these yards. It was all immaculately manicured lawns, stone gates, and high fences. This was a very different Maine from the Deckers' little home.

We ended down by the shore. Royce turned off into a high-fenced boatyard, and I drove on past. I parked on the street, and quickly walked back.

There was a building inside the fence, which people had to pass to get to the boats out by the docks. I spotted Royce on the dock, carrying the satchel past the moored pleasure craft. These were a lot of shiny toys that weren't being used.

Royce boarded a sleek power cruiser, but a houseboat blocked my view of him. If he went for a cruise, I was out of luck. Could I rent a boat and follow? It didn't seem likely, nice day though it was for a boat ride.

About ten minutes later, he came back out onto the dock. Interesting. What had he gone there for? He walked back out past the gatehouse, waved to the man inside, and went back to his car. I hoofed it back to my car so I could follow.

Royce retraced his path. I was able to stay just far enough behind, since he didn't turn off anywhere. He led me straight back to Pine Haven. Damn. I was hoping for more. He parked the car, carefully replaced the protective cover, and walked up the flight of stairs to his office.

I had the itch to take a closer look at that boat and get on it, if possible. I drove back, trying to think of a story to get past security at the boatyard, or yacht club, or whatever the hell they called it.

At a convenience store near the waterfront, I bought a cheap Styrofoam cooler, a bag of ice, and a six-pack of soda. Then I drove back to the boatyard, pulled into the parking lot, and watched.

There were people around, and a fair amount of activity. The boatyard guy was dressed in shorts and a T-shirt. He was talking to an older couple on a sailboat. I shouldered the cooler and sauntered on down the other dock. The area was well-kept and clean, with all the amenities. The cost for tying up here was probably more than most people in Maine made in a year.

I stepped onto Royce's boat from the dock. I opened a soda and made a casual inspection, like a guy on his friend's boat. By the cockpit was a waterproof cylinder. I opened it and pulled out the marine navigation charts, showing the depth of the offshore waters, the buoys and shoals. Before I saw any more, a voice hailed me from the dock.

"Excuse me, sir." It was the boatyard guy.

"Yes?"

"Can I help you?"

"Oh, no thanks."

"I'm sorry, sir, but who are you?" Polite, but firm.

"Tom Parker. I'm Royce's cousin."

"Actually, he's already been here and gone."

"Gone? Well, he probably went out for the beer. This stuff won't do." I showed him my soda.

"Um, sir? Mr. Royce did not tell me you were coming. His instructions have always been that no one should be let on board."

I grinned and spread my arms. "Well I'm already aboard."

"Yes, sir, but I'm going to have to ask you to please step off."

"What, you mean I can't even sit down and have a drink while I wait for him?"

"Afraid not, sir. Mr. Royce's orders. I could try to call him for you."

"He's supposed to be here already. That means he's on the way. What am I supposed to do?"

"You're welcome to wait in the boathouse, sir."

If this had been Miami, fifty dollars might have persuaded the guy to let me stay. But it wouldn't play here. He knew how to deal with characters like me, and wouldn't be bluffed. I'd have to pull out of this situation, but there was no graceful way to do it. Anger would allow me a logical exit.

"Great, just great. I'll go wait in the car then."

I stormed off and sat in the car for a few minutes for show, drumming my fingers on the wheel, looking like a man who had lost all patience. Finally I started the engine and drove off.

Damnit. Schemes like this always worked for the hero on television. Maybe I wasn't superspy Napoleon Solo, but I had persistence. If a boldfaced walk-on wouldn't work, maybe stealth would.

I was a fairly good swimmer, so I drove back to Portland and checked the Yellow Pages for a shop that rented diving equipment.

In a place down on Marginal Way, I rented a mask, a wetsuit, and a pair of fins, declining the scuba tanks. I had a plan, but it needed darkness to work. The moon was full and bright in the sky these nights, so I'd have to wait for clouds.

Dale T. Phillips

# CHAPTER 27

Lady Luck had given me the cold shoulder the day before, so I was hoping for much better today. After fruitlessly laying in the bushes all day at Pine Haven, I'd then spent even more fruitless hours in a car staking out the Cave, hoping for some sort of break. Vince and his buddies hadn't even shown up by closing time.

To top it off, I'd finally reached Allison on the phone in the afternoon to ask her to dinner, but she couldn't make it.

I called her again in the morning, and found my luck had turned. She offered a picnic, since the weather was nice. The sun was out, the sky was blue, and it was looking good. But I was feeling guilty, because Ben's killer had seen another sunrise unpunished. Feeling bad about letting a lovely woman divert me from my goal, I thought I'd try to make some progress.

Since I couldn't watch my entire little band of suspects, I picked the closest, deciding to go for Thibodeaux's apartment. I drove in and found a parking spot. There was even half an hour left on the meter. It really was my lucky day. Maybe I should buy a lottery ticket.

With a cup of coffee and a newspaper, I began my stakeout. The coffee was a small this time, as I'd learned my lesson about liquids on surveillance duty. I found a comfortable place to sit, with the warm morning sun on my back. There were a few others doing as little as I was, so I attracted no attention. It was socially acceptable here to just kick back on a summer weekday morning and watch the world go by.

Twice over the next hour and a half the door to Thibodeaux's apartment building opened as people came out. The coffee had long gone cold, and I was reading some articles for the third time. My butt was getting tired, and it was only nine-thirty in the morning.

And then I hit the jackpot. Both Thibodeaux and the foul-mouthed young woman from his apartment came out onto the sidewalk. They talked for a minute and split up, he with his gym bag, she with her purse. They didn't kiss when they parted.

Breaking and entering was a very bad idea, but I had no better plan. But how to get inside? I needed an excuse to be there. I looked around and spotted a nearby drugstore, and got an idea. I went in and bought a clipboard, some paper, and a pen. Now all I needed was my story. By the time I'd paid for everything, I'd put my ruse together.

I opened the pad of paper and tore some off the front, inserting the remainder in the clipboard, so the pad would look used. From the apartment listings, I wrote the residents' names on the top sheet of paper. I rang the buzzer by one of the names. No answer. I tried another, and an answering buzz told me the door was unlocked. I took a deep breath and went in.

A man in T-shirt and baggy pants looked down the staircase at me as I walked up.

"Yeah? What is it?"

"Health Inspector," I said as I made it to the top of the stairs. The man was thin, and looked to be in his late fifties. His hair was slicked back, and he looked at me with tired eyes.

"Health Inspector?"

"That's right, Mr. ..?"

"Cloney."

"Right." I looked down at my sheet and tapped the name with my pen. "Here you are. 4B."

"What's this about?"

"Well, Mr. Cloney, someone in this building called us and reported seeing a rat."

"A rat?" His eyes went wide.

"That was the report."

"Better not be any friggin' rats in here," he muttered.

"Any open garbage containers, or food left out, anything like that?"

"Better not be." A man of limited vocabulary.

"Would you mind if I took a quick look into your place? So I can say I checked?"

"I don't got no friggin' rats," he said, but led me back to his door. I took a perfunctory pass through the place, and cheerfully told him he was checked off. Much to my relief, he stayed in his apartment when I left, probably looking around for traces of vermin.

The hallway was now empty. I took out my Swiss Army knife and opened one of the small blades as I approached the door to Thibodeaux's apartment. I knocked loudly and listened carefully at the door. There was no sound within. I set down the clipboard and set about jimmying the lock. It was a cheap one, and I had it sprung in under a minute. I picked up the clipboard and stepped inside, closing the door behind me, being careful to lock it.

"Hello," I said loudly, still being cautious. "Anybody home?" I wanted to be sure I had the place to myself before I poked around. A quick check of all the rooms confirmed that I was alone. I set down the clipboard and got to work. No need for gloves in a place like this; fingerprints wouldn't matter.

I was looking for anything which might point toward some kind of crime big enough to kill for. Any little thing could point to something else. Documents, pictures, large stashes of cash, a gun maybe. So I had to be thorough, but I also didn't want any traces of what I'd been doing. The same boys in Vegas that had given me tips on picking a lock had given me pointers about tossing a room, and I remembered them well.

The apartment was a mess. The kitchen held numerous places which could hide small things: boxes, cans, packages of all sorts. Everything went back more or less in the same spot. Due to the lack of housekeeping on the occupant's part, I felt whatever I shifted wouldn't be noticed.

Check the stuff in the freezer, even the ice cube trays. Unless they'd stuffed things inside the ice cream or the hamburger packages, there was nothing. Check the undersides and backs of all drawers and cabinets. Again, nothing. Now the appliances and the spaces between appliances. Look for traces of things having been moved recently. Nada. Just grease and dust.

Living room next, although people seldom keep things there that they want to hide. Pull the cushions, lift the furniture, roll the rugs, check lamps, check inside picture frames. Zip.

Bedroom next. A few karate trophies. How nice. Dressers and closets. Cigarettes and a dirty ashtray on the nightstand by the bed. A box of condoms was the only incriminating thing in the nightstand drawer. Pillows, remove the cases, check for repair jobs where someone might have put something in and resewed. Pull the sheets off and check the mattress, same way. Flip it and check the bottom. Then the box spring. Bupkis. Putting the bed back together was the hard part, trying to make an artificial mess.

I had got things back into a reasonable semblance of sloppy when I heard someone turn a key in the apartment door. Panicked, I dove into the closet. Slats in the closet door allowed me to see out.

It was the girlfriend. She came into the bedroom, went to the nightstand, and picked up the pack of cigarettes. I hoped she'd leave, but she lit one of the cigarettes and picked up the phone to make a call. Here I was, hiding in a smelly closet, crouched in fear, while she chatted with someone. She didn't even talk about anything incriminating. She finally hung up, after what seemed like a year, and just as I was thinking I was home free, I remembered I'd left the clipboard in the living room, right out in the open. Damn me for an idiot.

If there is a Hell, it certainly involves a lot of waiting. Everything was hanging on whether or not she'd discover something which obviously hadn't been there a few minutes before. I realized I was holding my breath, and quietly let it out. Bad housekeeping won out, and after an eternity, I heard the apartment door open and close, and the lock turn. I spent a minute getting my heart rate back to normal, and continued my search.

On to the bathroom, which could have used a good cleaning. Under the sink, same routine as in the kitchen. Check the mirror, sometimes things were tucked behind. Tap the shower curtain rod, just in case. Lift the lid on the tank, and bingo. People often hide things there, where every pro would check. I pulled out a waterproof bag with white powder inside. It was a fairly small stash, probably cocaine, but not enough for any heavy dealing. This was the recreational hoard. I carefully replaced everything as it was, and continued looking.

There was a stack of papers in a basket by the phone, which I went through quickly. Bills and letters, nothing of note. I'd done the whole apartment in just over an hour, and there was nothing to connect Thibodeaux to Ben's death. I took a last pass through to make sure everything was as it should be, and let myself out, taking my clipboard and locking the door behind me.

As I left, I felt as if I was being watched. I looked all around and saw nothing suspicious, but the feeling stayed with me.

Dale T. Phillips

# CHAPTER 28

I rang the bell of the big house, and Allison came to the door. She was the epitome of summertime, with khaki shorts and a navy-blue, short-sleeved cotton blouse, showing golden-brown arms and legs. She had a light scent of perfume that reminded me of strawberries. I stood gawking like a schoolboy.

"You found it." She smiled like sunshine itself.

"These are some beautiful old Victorian houses," I looked out, and the sweeping panorama of Casco Bay gave you the impression that you were master of all you surveyed. "Reminds me of San Francisco."

"My grandfather bought this house way back when," she said. "Houses built back then looked outward to the world. Lots of windows out front, and porches, so they could see what was happening. Now it seems people huddle in their backyards, and don't know their neighbors."

"It's a big place. You live here by yourself?"

"I rent out to two nursing students. Couldn't afford to keep it otherwise. Here, take this." She handed me a large, wicker picnic basket.

"Oof. What did you pack? A couple of turkeys?"

"Always with the turkeys," she said, and grinned. "Well, you looked like you have a healthy appetite. Ooo, nice car."

I laughed. "Thought you'd be impressed."

My car was a big, ugly, green monstrosity that got me where I needed to go. It was so old-fashioned, it still had a bench seat in front that could hold three people, without a gear box or storage container between the driver and passenger. I wanted her to see the real me.

She smiled when I opened the car door for her and closed it after she got in. I stowed the basket in back and we got going. She gave directions while we made small talk. We drove over a bridge into South Portland, and followed the shore down to Cape Elizabeth.

We arrived at an expanse of hilly greenery, nestled against the ocean, with a lovely lighthouse standing sentinel over the whole place. Fort Williams Park was a big place of people flying kites, throwing Frisbees, and clustering in laughing groups at picnic tables. I felt like a visitor from another planet. This sunny daytime world was different from the dark places I'd known all these years. I envied them their happiness.

We spread out a blanket on an available patch of grass with a view of the ocean. The blue-green waves were the color of peacock's feathers. I drank in the caressing breeze, and wondered why I'd missed out on so much life.

"Like it?" Allison smiled at me.

"It's beautiful."

"See that lighthouse? It was the first one completed after the founding of the United States. It's the oldest one in continuous use, and it's the most photographed and painted. Edward Hopper did some beautiful paintings of it."

"The same guy who did *Nighthawks.*"

"That's right."

"That's one of my favorites. But how could he capture all this daylight beauty," I spread my arms, "and then paint things so bleak they capture the quintessence of night?"

"Quintessence of night?" She laughed. "Who talks like that?"

"Article by an art critic," I said. "I remember that phrase. He was talking about the stark loneliness and alienation of the city. How the darkness of night mirrors the darkness of the soul, and how even bright lights can't drive it away."

"So you know about art," she said. "Or did you go to the bookstore and read up on it, just to impress me?"

I laughed. "Not a bad idea. If I'd thought of it, I would have."

She smiled. "Well, if you prefer a darker vision, we could come here on a rainy day, when it's deserted, gray, and scary. I did that once, late in the fall. There wasn't a soul around."

"Why?"

"We'd lost a patient, a seven-year-old girl. I needed to get away. The weather was so nasty no one else was around."

"I think even I would prefer it this way."

"Even if it doesn't fit with your experience?"

"I might try new experiences."

We started pulling various items from the basket. She brought out a bottle of white wine.

"What's the matter? We'll be discreet, no one will hassle us."

"I, uh, don't drink. One of the dark things from my past."

"Oh," she said, frowning. "Want me to put it away?"

"Go ahead, I just won't have any."

"We've got lemonade, too."

"Perfect."

I poured a cup of lemonade from the jug, while she opened her bottle with a corkscrew. I passed her a cup and she filled it. We touched our cups together in a toast.

"To beautiful days," she said.

I resisted the urge to add anything cutesy or force a compliment. She handed me a paper plate and I helped myself to a cold breast of chicken seasoned with rosemary,

173

some homemade potato salad, tabbouleh, and dark Greek olives from a deli container.

We ate slowly, taking our time and enjoying the food. I liked that she could just sit and be good company, without feeling the need to fill every space with conversation. I didn't like being around people who talked all the time.

Fat, lazy clouds drifted slowly through the sky. She poured more wine, her third cup. We set our plates aside and lay on our backs, looking up and telling each other what shapes we saw. She rolled onto her stomach and looked at me.

"So how's your mission going?" she asked.

I pulled up a long blade of grass and toyed with it.

"Not sure. Some progress, I guess. I am making people mad at me."

"And that's good?"

"If things get stirred up enough, something will happen, and somebody will make a mistake."

"That's dangerous though, right?"

I pondered for a minute how to answer. "Did you ever see lion tamers, and wonder how they do it? It's knowing how the animals behave. Keeping a certain distance, keeping your eyes on the cat at all times. Distract it with a chair."

"I always wondered why they use a chair."

"The four legs pointed at the cat confuses it. As long as everything goes right, the tamer comes out with a whole skin and everybody's happy."

"So how do you know what these animals are like?"

"I've been around their type."

"Were you a policeman?"

"No, but I worked as a bodyguard for a guy in Las Vegas. I didn't do anything illegal, just hung around to make sure nobody hurt him. I did get to know the criminal mind. After that, I had a few other security jobs. You learn to read people, evaluate them as a potential threat, and how to stop them. But I don't usually go looking for trouble."

"Except this time."

"This time it's different."

"And after?"

"We'll have to wait and see."

She rolled onto her back and looked up at the sky.

"So what about you," I said. "You still do your art, right? What do you work in?"

"Oils, mostly."

"Sold any?"

"A few. Not even enough to pay for my supplies. It's an expensive hobby."

"So why do you paint?"

"It's like making something come alive, just by applying dabs of color to a piece of canvas. You start with an idea and work towards making it happen. I guess it's my way of affirming life."

"That's a nice way of putting it," I said.

"How about you? What do you do to affirm life?"

"Let me think about that. Want to walk a bit?"

"Okay."

We got up and stretched, our stomachs still full. I marveled at the lighthouse, and we kept going until we came to some stone remains overlooking the ocean.

"This part of the fort," Allison said, "was built a long time ago, to keep somebody or other from invading. They kept manning it in the wars, but it never really saw any action. Now it's just something for people to climb on."

I looked at the crumbling walls, at the tunnels and passageways cut deep into the rock. There had been guns here, primed and loaded, men ready to fight and die, all for an enemy that never came. Now it was musty, dark, and useless. I kicked at some loose rubble.

It made me think of the walls I'd put up around myself to keep people out after Tim had died. Nobody had ever come close to breaching those defenses. I'd kept apart from life, a detached bystander, huddled in my little fort of pain. Ben had known me, but he'd been there while I put up the walls, and understood why they were built. He'd always been a part of life, unlike me. His relationships, even the failed marriage, were more than I'd ever had. Now even he was gone, and I was left with my own ruined walls. And here was a woman exploring those ruins, seeing if there was anything of value in the dusty stone.

"I don't know that I affirm life," I said. "I think for a long while I've been denying life. No, that's not quite right. Maybe more like avoiding it."

We stared out at the sea. Remembering Tim's death felt like rolling in broken glass. But it seemed right to finally speak about it now. I cleared my throat, and she looked at me as I spoke.

"When I was sixteen, I wanted a pistol. Just a twenty-two, to go out target shooting, plinking around. I thought I was old enough and responsible enough, and my parents got it for me. I was so happy, and I loved to shoot.

"Sometimes I'd take my younger brother Tim. He was such a great kid.

"Then one day, he was holding it and the gun went off and killed him. It was just one of those stupid, senseless accidents. One minute he was standing there, full of life, and the next he was dead.

"You think life is good, the sun is shining and all is right with the world. Then with one sharp crack, someone you love is dead. You hold them and see their expression, you feel them stop being. Everything gets black and twisted.

"So I had a lot I couldn't deal with. I took up karate, which helped to channel some of my anger. Ben was my friend, and took lessons with me. He tried his best to help me.

"Things got worse and worse, and I began drinking as soon as I was eighteen, to forget, and also to punish myself. There was some trouble then, too. When you're young and willing to fight, and filled with anger, there are a lot of people in the world willing to take you on.

"But the bottle was the one that was winning, and Ben shanghaied me and saved my life, kept me going. But not to any great purpose. I just kind of drifted. That's how I wound up working with crooks, and working as a bouncer."

I motioned with my arm.

"The daytime is for nice, happy people, like all these folks. They think there's a cure for every pain, a solution for every problem. The night is for people like me, people who deal with pain."

"Do you deal with it, or just avoid it as much as possible?"

I had no reply.

Allison spoke quietly. "My father was a policeman. Fourteen years. He'd seen the worst that human beings can do to each other. It affected him. A couple of times I came downstairs in the middle of the night and found him drinking at the kitchen table, crying."

"He knew."

"Yes, he did. He knew more than that, though. He knew that love is what matters, that shared pain is diminished, while shared joy is increased. He taught me to love, not to hate, to always go on. That was important later.

"He was killed on duty. Somebody shot him, murdered this wonderful man who was so full of love."

"I'm sorry."

"It was very hard. My mom and I always worried about him, and then the worst came true."

"What did you do?"

"We went on with life after a while." She shrugged.

I didn't say anything.

"I had my mother," she said. "She and I shared our memories of him. You had Ben." She looked at me, head cocked. "He kind of took the place of your brother, didn't he? That's why you two were so close."

I blinked. "I never thought of it that way."

"But now he's gone. I guess you're feeling pretty alone. What will you do now?"

"I don't know," I said honestly.

177

Allison drew a deep breath. "You could think about having a future. Neither of them would have wanted you to stop living, would they?"

I looked at her and smiled. "You're good at healing, aren't you?"

She shrugged. "I'm a nurse."

We looked out to sea some more. She turned and studied me. "You haven't talked about this much, have you?"

"No."

"I appreciate your telling me. You know, I like you, but I don't know if I can handle more violence. I'm going to worry about whether you'll get killed. I just don't know if I can live through that again."

"I understand."

"You shouldn't feel guilty for being alive, you know. You don't have to get yourself killed on this quest."

I was silent, turning over her words in my mind. It sounded like she knew some of what I'd been going through.

"You're something, you know that?" I smiled at her. She leaned over and kissed my cheek.

"So are you. Otherwise I wouldn't be here."

"Thank you," I whispered.

"Shall we go back?"

"Sure."

Something had passed between us, something I'd never felt before. It was strange, and I was curious about it. When I dropped her off at the house, she looked at me seriously.

"Think about what I said," she said. "The future could be very nice."

"Very much so." I nodded agreement. She leaned over and kissed me again, not a peck this time, but a real kiss. It sent a thrill right through me. It woke me up.

"Watch those lions. Call me," she said, and went up the walk, basket swinging in her hand. I sat there stunned, and more alive than I'd felt in a very long time. Her kiss was like going down the rapids, a lot of fun, but spinning out of control.

# CHAPTER 29

Nice as my afternoon with Allison had been, it was time to get back to work. My score was lousy so far, and I was getting frustrated. I'd followed two of the jerks from the resort, and all I'd found was that they liked money. Then I'd committed a breaking-and-entering felony, and my major discovery was that Thibodeaux had a crummy home life and used recreational drugs.

So I'd try for the biker. I took the rental car to Lewiston. There were way too many listings in the Lewiston directory for the last name of Beaulier, but no Vince. Calling all the names probably wouldn't get much information. Given Beaulier's history, anyone who knew him would be wary of telling a stranger his whereabouts. So that left staking out his favorite bar again.

The Cave was busy. No way was I going back in. The last time, I'd been lucky to get out intact. Movie heroes go into bars, fight all comers, and never get their asses kicked. The reality is that no matter how much karate you know, a small enclosed space filled with hostile antagonists is not the place to demonstrate it. Someone I know had done that once. I visited him in the hospital afterward. The doctors said he might walk again, but only with plastic knee replacements.

I parked in what I hoped was an inconspicuous spot and settled down to wait once more. It was at times like these that I almost wished I smoked, just to have something to do. Over in the lot, the concrete block I'd broken was still there. Maybe they'd left it as a monument to my impressive skill, or maybe they just didn't care. My money was on the latter.

Another biker pulled into the lot, his engine farting so loud it hurt. The noise bothered me so much I felt like going over and tearing the bike apart. And maybe an arm or leg of his while I was at it. I was getting cranky.

The only thing that happened in the next half hour was the departure of three Cave patrons. A few minutes later, two more came out. A closer scan through the binoculars confirmed that one was Beaulier. I started my car, and they took off in different directions. I followed Beaulier through a series of turns, trying not to get too close. I just managed to stay with him.

Another thing they make look easy in the movies is tailing people. It's not. It's almost impossible to stay close enough to not lose them without getting too close to tip them off.

Beaulier slowly cruised past a small park. A pair of teenagers, a boy and a girl, waved him down, and he pulled to the curb. I parked with the engine still running, and got out the binoculars. The two kids looked around and quickly walked over to where he sat on the bike. The boy looked a little like my brother Tim. He reached into his jeans and came out with money. He counted some out, keeping it low so only they could see it. Beaulier reached into his jacket and passed the kid something which instantly disappeared. The girl looked around anxiously during the transaction.

I ground my teeth. This demanded a reckoning. And if Beaulier was selling drugs to kids out in broad daylight, maybe he was capable of murder.

A police car appeared at the far end of the park. Beaulier saw it and roared away on his bike. I followed him across the bridge into Auburn, up a hill, and into the parking lot of a

Denny's restaurant. He got off the bike and hitched up his pants as he walked in.

I walked around the place, looking through the windows. Beaulier was sitting alone at a table, in a place where he wouldn't see me come in. I walked in and peered around like I was looking for someone, watching Beaulier's back. He was handing the menu back to the waitress. He stood up, and I ducked back around the corner. Where was he going? Bathroom. All that beer he'd probably sucked down at the Cave needed an outlet. I was closer, and got to the men's room first. No one else was there as I hid in a stall.

The door opened, and Beaulier came in. I waited until I heard the telltale splashing sounds at the urinal, then came out behind him. He half-turned to look when he realized someone was there, while keeping his lower half pointed in the right direction. For a moment. He did a doubletake and spun to face me.

"What do you want?" He all but spat at me.

"I want you to stop selling drugs to kids, for one. As of now you're out of business. You've got one chance to get your sick, sorry ass on that bike and keep on going to where I never see you again."

In one quick move, he had a knife out and made a lunge at me. I sidestepped the attack and grabbed his extended wrist, twisting it back and in until he dropped the knife. He swung at me with his other arm, a murderous haymaker with all his weight behind it. I got my chin out of the way just in time, and drilled a short punch just under his ribs. He sucked in some air, but still kept coming with a kick to my groin. I grabbed his leg, and swept his other leg out from under him. He fell hard, cracking his head against the bottom edge of the urinal. He slumped to the floor, out cold.

In his jacket were half a dozen plastic tubes with something that looked like the rock candy we used to get when I was a kid. I took all the vials out, as well as the cash he had tucked in his hip pocket, payment from the kid in the park. I went into a stall and emptied the contents of the vials into the toilet, ripped up the money, and threw it in as well, flushing everything down.

The empty tubes I stuffed into his mouth. I picked up his knife, put the blade flat under my foot, and snapped it off. As I did, the door opened, and someone else came in. A very surprised man with a Red Sox cap and thick glasses looked down at Beaulier lying on the floor, then at me. He backed out through the door without saying a word. I followed him out, and was gone before the police came by.

As I drove away, I realized I was shaking. Maybe Beaulier had been mixed up in Ben's death, or maybe I just wanted to hurt someone so bad I found an excuse to do so.

# CHAPTER 30

On my drive back to Portland, I wondered where thousands of years of evolution had gone. Mankind was little further along than the monkeys, and we killed for stupid things. We mouthed words of civilization and bashed each other's brains in. I needed to wash everything away in a river of alcohol, and wake up to find the ones I loved still alive, and me with no need or desire to hurt someone.

As I put the key in the lock, a shape emerged from the shadows of the stairwell. I turned, ready for trouble. The shape came into the light and I saw it was the cop, Lagasse.

"Scare ya?" he said.

"Surprised me."

"That's how easy it would be for someone to take you out if they wanted." He had a very satisfied smile, which looked creepy in the pale light.

"Thanks for the lesson, but I'm just not in the mood right now."

"Tough day, gumshoe?"

"You might say that."

He chuckled. I stood in the doorway and he nodded toward the room. "Mind if I come in?"

"Yes."

I went inside and flicked on the light. Lagasse came in anyway, glanced around the room, and sat in the chair. He put his feet up on the bed. It irritated me, like it was supposed to.

"So how's the revenge business?" He played with the toothpick in his mouth.

"Sucks. And the pay's lousy."

"No doubt. So you're still poking around?"

"I was told not to, remember?" I looked around for something to do, but decided to just endure.

"Don't hand me that happy horseshit," Lagasse said. "You're a cowboy, you don't take good advice."

"Not when my friend's lying dead and his killer is still walking the streets."

He was quiet for a minute. He rolled the toothpick from one side of his mouth to the other. "Why are you so sure?"

"Long story. About eighteen years' worth."

"His marriage didn't work out too well, did it?" Lagasse was talking as if he actually cared.

"Wrong people to put together." I shrugged.

"Happens sometimes."

"Yup," I agreed.

"Makes some people change."

"Nice try, but it doesn't fly."

Neither of us said anything. Most people are so uncomfortable being around cops that when there's silence, they'll blab anything. Police learn a lot with this technique. It doesn't work on me, though.

After a time he spoke again. "What was he like, after the marriage broke up?"

"Sad for a while. Couldn't understand what had gone wrong. It wasn't like he didn't treat her right. Maybe too well, I don't know. Anyway, I went to stay with him for a time, but he was back on his feet soon enough. He just loved life too much to mope around for long."

"You know if there's been anyone since?"

I thought of Sandy, and of how I'd just assaulted her ex-boyfriend. I'd save that card until after I saw Lagasse's hand.

"He hadn't mentioned anyone." There was truth to that, at least.

"So he's been by himself a long time."

"Not as long as some."

"Uh-huh," Lagasse nodded. "This resort work is seasonal, right, so where would he have gone after the season ended?"

"Any number of places."

"But if he'd been fired? Wouldn't it have been tough to find another place?"

"Not in the least. I see you've been talking to Grossman."

"He wasn't a big fan of your friend." Lagasse watched me closely.

"Chefs at resorts have advanced degrees in giving people grief. If you don't kiss their ass, they don't want you around." This discussion was beginning to piss me off.

"Had some experience with that?"

"Yeah," I said.

"According to him, your friend was about to be canned," Lagasse said.

"Because he had food poisoning and was in the hospital, for Christ's sake. The bastard called him there and told him to come back or else. Ben checked out of the hospital while he was still sick. He'd have been back to work the next morning."

"Sounds like he needed the job pretty bad."

"It's not the job," I said, shaking my head in exasperation. "Ben could've got a job any other place, I told you. But it's a matter of pride. Showing the jerk that no matter what he throws at you, it's not enough to stop you. We had a saying. 'Non carborundum illegitimatis'."

"What's that?"

"'Don't let the bastards grind you down'. And this guy is a Class A lying bastard."

"Not that you have an opinion." Lagasse smirked.

"Talk to some of the other help. I think you'll find his story doesn't hold water. And talk to that doper Jeff. He had a run-in with Ben, too."

Lagasse raised his eyebrows. "Well, thank you for telling me once more how to do my job. My, my, my, talk to the other help. Now why didn't I think of that? I come to talk and get a free job training seminar instead. My goodness, I sure do learn a lot from you."

"You could learn where the door is."

"I thought you were interested in helping out," Lagasse said.

"Oh, have you changed your mind?"

"Not a bit. I know you're running some kind of scam, I just don't know what it is yet."

I was tired of his needling. "Still believe it's a drug deal gone sour, huh? You've been in the sticks too long."

That one got him. His face clouded with red. I cut off his response. "Yeah, Sergeant, go ahead and get mad. Keep on concentrating on me while the killer walks away. Goddammit, why are you so convinced it's something to do with me?"

"Because you don't fit."

"What? Don't fit what?"

"You don't fit the equation. You've been dirty in the past. What else am I supposed to think?"

"Don't call it thinking, if that's the way you feel."

Lagasse stood up and came over to me. I held his gaze without flinching.

"You lied to me, you goddamned punk. That guy was right-handed. You knew it."

I shrugged. "You were going to just let it alone, case closed. I had to say something to get you off your ass."

"You don't lie to me!" Lagasse shouted. "You got that?"

"My friend was murdered. You want to play Barney Fife and do nothing, well, I'll do whatever it takes to get you to do your job."

"*If* he was killed, we'll get whoever did it. The legal way, the hard way." Lagasse was building steam. "Guys want to be vigilantes. But when they try, innocent people end up getting hurt. You cross the line, I'll nail you."

"You've already threatened me."

"This isn't a threat. It's a promise."

"Great line. I'll have to remember that one."

"Sonofabitch." Lagasse turned and went for the door. I had a flash of insight.

"Hey," I called. He looked back at me.

"You didn't come here just to tell me off. You found something, didn't you? You found something out! What is it?"

"None of your goddamned business," he slammed the door behind him.

Dale T. Phillips

# CHAPTER 31

After Lagasse left, I wanted a drink so bad I was shaking. To distract myself, I started exercising, doing the most difficult kata routines. I sweated through it for a while, trying to focus on the physical aspects of what I was doing. My mind was still racing, so I showered and changed and decided to go by Kapinsky's dojo.

It was warm, and there were plenty of other people out walking. The strip mall was dismal, and the studio was unlit. I rapped loudly on the door, in case he was sitting there in the dark, but there was no response. While I stood there wondering what to do next, the back of my neck tingled. I resisted the urge to look around, but prepared myself to duck whatever might come my way.

If I was being followed, I'd be better able to handle whoever it was if they were on foot. So instead of going back to my car, I started walking, hoping my tail might follow.

Some of the women out by themselves looked as if they might be working girls. Up ahead of me, a tough-looking, bleached-blond woman in a short skirt leaned against a doorway, with a cigarette hanging from her mouth.

I smiled at her as I came up. Eyes as cold as icy metal looked back at me. "Hi there," I said. "I have an entirely legal proposition for you."

She looked me up and down, and almost cracked a smile. "That'd be something different."

"Somebody's following me, and he or they will come by here. Ten bucks if you can describe him to me when I come back."

The cold eyes flickered. "Twenty."

"What do I look, rich?"

"I got bills to pay." She coughed, a hard, wet, smoker's hack. She couldn't have been over twenty-five, but looked forty, even though she probably wouldn't make it to that age.

I softened, and nodded. "Okay, twenty. I'll just keep going down the street, and come back in about ten minutes."

She shrugged. "If I get lucky, I won't be here."

"Business that good?"

"A girl can dream."

"Okay, I'll be back in five."

"Whatever." She waved me away and coughed again, her shoulders racked with the spasm. I walked on. A few blocks later, I ducked down an alley to the next street over and doubled back. The hooker was still leaning against the doorway, lighting another cigarette. At her feet was a pile of discarded butts. Apparently business wasn't that good.

"Hey there," I said. "So, was I right?"

She held out her hand. I went into my wallet and found two tens, placing them in her palm. She glanced at the money before tucking the bills down the front of her low-cut blouse.

"Young guy, maybe twenty-two, twenty-three. Ugly little runt, looked like a mick. Shorter than you, but stockier, wrestler's build. Red Sox cap over sandy hair, cut short, like a college boy. Short-sleeved green shirt and jeans, sneakers."

"Anything else?" I asked.

She shrugged, and held out her hand with a sly look. I crossed her palm with another ten-spot.

She told me the rest. "Innocent face, real intent on what he was doing. Moved well, but didn't look like he'd done this before. Real nervous, you know, like a kid playing a grown-up game and afraid he'd get caught. About shit himself when he saw me looking at him."

Chip, Thibodeaux's sidekick. Had to be.

"Did he say anything?"

"Nah, he was too busy blushing. Went up the street after you." She stopped to cough again.

"Anything else?"

She straightened up, looked at me with her hard eyes, and ran a hand through her hair. "You tell me."

"Uh, no thanks. I've got something going on."

"Whatever." She shrugged again. I nodded by way of goodbye, but her stare was already off in the distance. I was no longer potential income, so I didn't exist anymore.

I got back to my car and looked around. His vehicle had to be nearby. All I needed to do was lay back and wait, and jump him when he returned. The streetlights threw off a lot of light, but there were plenty of dark places to duck into.

Ten minutes later, Chip came jogging into view, dressed just as the hooker had described. He stopped at an ugly brown SUV, and as he dug for his keys, I came up behind him. I grabbed his ear and twisted, heard him shriek, and the struggle was over. It's amazing how sensitive the ears are.

"You, young man, are beginning to piss me off."

"OW! OW! Leggo! Leggo!"

"Chip, my boy, you are what we call a slow learner. I do not like being insulted. I do not like being threatened. And I most certainly do not like being followed. You have done all three."

"Let me go, let me go, Jesus CHRIST!"

"Now, now, profanity won't help. I think it's time we had another talk. It's kind of like a game show. You provide the correct answers, and you get your ear back. Otherwise, I keep it for a souvenir."

"All right, all right, just take it easy."

"Okay, Chip, for our first question, what were you doing following me?"

"What do you think I was doing?" His snarl turned into another cry of pain as I gave an admonitory twist.

"Like I said, slow learner. Let's try again. Why are you following me?"

"You're stirring up trouble, getting the police to come by. They asked us about the fight. I want to make sure you don't pin something on our school."

"You're kidding me. You think that because I don't like your little tin idol I'm going to prove that Thibodeaux killed Ben, is that it?"

"You better not!"

I sighed deeply. It was unreal. "Look, kid. I want to find Ben's killer, that's all. This will shock you thoroughly, but I don't give a rat's ass about your hero or your school. I don't lay awake at night dreaming up revenge schemes. Get it? If it wasn't Thibodeaux, well and good. If you're so convinced about his innocence, you have nothing to fear."

"He didn't do it!"

"Fine. But lay off, because the police will start wondering if there is something to hide. Following people is a suspicious thing. They'll start to ask more questions, dig deeper. Maybe even take Thibodeaux and you in to the station for questioning. Something tells me that wouldn't sit too well with him."

"He doesn't know anything."

"How true." I grinned.

He blushed an angry red. "I mean he doesn't know that I followed you."

"Well, if you don't want him to know, you better go home and stay there. No more picking fights in bars when you're drunk, no more sojourns into the night or early morn. You keep your nose clean from now on. You got it?"

He mumbled something.

"I didn't quite catch that."

"I said okay."

"Good. And one more thing." I leaned in close, to speak right into the ear that wasn't being twisted. "You've been beating your chest whenever you see me, figuring you could take me. I am heartily sick of it, and sick of you. The next time I see you so much as look cross-eyed at me, I am going to smash your pearly-white teeth in and use them for a necklace. Now get out of here."

I released his ear, and he rubbed it, wincing.

"It's going to hurt like hell for a day or two, but there's no damage. If you go home and put some ice on it, it'll help a lot."

I wasn't surprised that he didn't thank me for my advice. He started the engine and peeled away in a cloud of smoking, screeching rubber, not even looking for other traffic. I watched him go, shaking my head. That boy was an accident waiting to happen.

Dale T. Phillips

# CHAPTER 32

Though I was getting sidetracked, I couldn't stop thinking about Allison. I kept remembering how she looked, how she smelled, how she laughed. So I called her. She had the day off and agreed to go to the movies that night.

After I hung up, it was time to go back and watch Pine Haven once more. With the binoculars, a sandwich, and a bottle of water, I was ready to stay all day.

Since I hadn't bothered any more employees, Royce and Grossman must have thought I'd gone away. As long as I didn't attract attention, I could skulk around and watch to my heart's content. Not that it was helping a great deal. But at least I was in my head, sorting things out, and not on the streets, beating someone up.

Lots of nothing happened. People went in and out of various buildings. Royce emerged from his office and went into the hotel. Jeff the goon walked to the hotel. Once in a while I'd turn the binoculars towards the ocean, just for something different. Several boats were on the waves, having fun in the sun. Me, I sat on the forest floor and watched people walk in and out of buildings.

At about two, Grossman came out from the hotel and walked back to his dormitory. Half an hour later, he came out dressed in street clothes, and went to his white Cadillac.

I sprinted back along the trails to the parking lot, got to the car, and followed. He drove to the highway and headed north. He exited a few miles later, and we were soon on Route 302.

We drove until there weren't any more buildings, before the Caddy pulled off onto a side road. I let him get ahead before following. We passed through acres of forest. A sign warned of a dangerous curve up ahead, so I slowed. Good thing I did, for when I came around the corner, I saw another long flat stretch of road, where the caddy was pulled over to the side, about half a mile up. I braked and backed up, hoping he hadn't seen me. I parked and dashed out, binoculars in hand.

The Caddy sat behind a big truck with logs stacked on back, long ones that stuck far out past the truck's bed. Grossman was standing by the side of the road, speaking to someone in the truck. I couldn't read lips, but I could read the New Brunswick license plate on the truck. I wrote down the number in my notebook.

The driver got out, a big guy wearing a T-shirt and jeans, with long hair under his cap. He hoisted himself up onto the logs and walked back along their length. He came back with an oversized toolbox. He handed down the box to Grossman and climbed down off the truck. Grossman walked back to the Caddy, not looking back. He put the toolbox in the trunk, closed it, and got back in the car.

I didn't want him spotting me, and odds were he'd return this way. I was back in the car in record time, did a U-turn, and roared off down the road, grateful for the twists and turns that would hide me from him until I could get some distance ahead.

My car rattled in protest as I pushed it hard. The buildings came back, so I pulled over into the lot of an auto body shop. Grossman purred on by, and I fell in behind once more, with another car between us.

Grossman made no more stops, and went back the way he had come, all the way to Pine Haven. By the time I got to my spot in the woods and raised the binoculars, he was huffing up the steps to Royce's office. He had the toolbox with him. When he came out, after about three minutes, he didn't have it anymore.

Royce came out twenty minutes later, carrying his briefcase. He set the case down and began taking the protective cover off his Porsche, and I started running for the parking lot. Here we go again. My poor car and legs were suffering from this caper.

We headed north, and once again we wound up at the Falmouth boatyard. Royce took the briefcase out to his boat, stayed for ten minutes, and came back. He made his way back to Pine Haven.

Both Royce and Grossman had made long drives for some reason. There was no way I could crack the safe in Royce's office. But one way or another, I was going to get on that boat and search it.

The clouds were rolling in, and the weather report had said it would be overcast tonight. No moon, lots of darkness. A perfect night for breaking the law.

Dale T. Phillips

# CHAPTER 33

The movie date was a complete disaster. When I'd picked Allison up, we went to an art house place on Exchange Street. All I was thinking about was how to get on Royce's boat without getting caught. When you're with a woman and your mind is elsewhere, she knows it.

We talked about it, and I told her I was going to do something later that was risky, but that might prove important. Like a dope, I insisted we stay and watch the movie, but I was so preoccupied I couldn't enjoy it. Allison got pissed at me, and the conversation got real quiet. I took her straight home afterward on a very tense ride, and knew I'd blown it big time.

But for now I had to ignore it, and get down to business. Back at my room, I took out a duffel bag and packed in the gear: binoculars, mask, wetsuit, fins. I added a towel, my Swiss Army knife, some plastic bags, and a small penlight. Then I changed into my bathing suit, and stretched for a few minutes to loosen up and clear my mind a little. I finished dressing and set out.

At the boatyard, I parked by the side of the road around the corner. The place wasn't empty at night, like I'd hoped. Through the binoculars, I saw a guy in the boathouse watching his television. He looked out from time to time at the lines of boats bobbing at their tethers. I didn't know if he made rounds along the docks, so I'd have to be extra careful and watch out for him.

The trouble was getting to the dock area. There was a high fence around the boatyard that extended out into the ocean. Off to one side of the boatyard, outside the fence, was a breakwater of rocks. If I was careful, I could walk out to the end and swim from there, saving myself some distance.

Back at the car, I took off my shoes, pants, and shirt, and pulled on the wetsuit. The penlight and the knife went into a plastic bag inside the suit where they would stay dry. I left the car unlocked with the keys under the seat. Fins and mask in hand, I walked out to the end of the breakwater and climbed down to the water. Sitting on the slippery rocks, I wedged my feet into the rubber fins. To keep the mask from fogging, I spit onto the faceplate, swished it around with a bit of water, and poured it out. I braced myself and flopped into the cold ocean water. The icy chill hit me with a shock.

I dove down, and the waves immediately pulled me seaward with an insistent tug. It was an effort to move against the current without too much splashing around. I came up for air near the end of the fence and hung onto it, panting and resting.

Some of the boats had lights on, and there were also dock lights to stay away from. To get to Royce's, I had to get around the big houseboat moored at the next slip, which loomed like an iceberg over Royce's smaller power cruiser.

The stern of Royce's boat had a low transom, the kind favored by divers and fishermen. Still in the water, I pulled off the mask and fins, and quietly deposited them over the transom. Trying to be as quiet as possible, I pulled myself up and on board. I waited, listening. No hue and cry, no alarm.

The big houseboat now hid me from the boathouse and blocked most of the light, but I still didn't want to stand up and risk being seen. I checked the passenger seats and cushions near the stern. They yielded nothing. The back deck lockers had a few life vests, but nothing else. I went to the wheel and looked around. The only moveable thing was the waterproof cylindrical case for maps and nautical charts that I'd seen before. It might be a good spot for hiding something, so I tucked that under my arm.

The door leading down to the cabins was locked. Using one of the blades from my Swiss Army knife, I slid it into the lock and felt for the pins. It took about five minutes of concentrated work, but finally it clicked open.

Just as I was about to go below, I heard low voices from the outside deck of the houseboat. I froze, hardly daring to breathe. Two forms, a man and a woman, were silhouetted against the dockyard lights. Since the eye reacts to movement, I kept absolutely still. The two figures murmured in low tones, embraced, and went back inside. I let out my breath.

After several minutes, I felt safe enough to move. The couple had better things to do than hang out and look for prowlers. I made my way down the steps, letting my eyes adjust to the gloom. I flicked on the penlight, being careful not to shine it out through the porthole window.

The son-of-a-bitch had another safe, a small one, set into the wall. This guy had more security than Fort Knox. He must be hiding something. If he had anything incriminating, he'd have tucked it in the safe, but I had to check anyway.

There was a ship-to-shore radio and a tiny refrigerator. I thought about unscrewing the back of the radio, but the screwdriver blade on the knife was the wrong size, so I left it alone. The fridge had three beers, a bottle of white wine, and some mineral water. I checked everything for false bottoms and sneaky hiding places.

A small room, almost a closet, held a chemical potty. I gritted my teeth and examined it. Luckily it was clean. I shone the light inside, and tipped it from side to side to make sure there was nothing hidden in waterproof bags. I washed my hands afterward with some of the opened mineral water.

There was nothing I could find, no payoff book, no guns, no big poster detailing any criminal plans. Checking under the bunks, I came up with nothing but a capped plastic vial and a beer bottle cap. They went into a bag, just so I wouldn't go away empty handed.

Maybe the map tube held a clue. I popped the end piece off and took everything out. Nautical charts, covered with little numbers showing shorelines, water depths, and buoys. A penciled-in line started from here and ended a few miles up the coast. I noted the location for later. Just to make sure the case didn't have a hidden compartment, I flashed the light inside and thumped along the length.

I looked around one last time, pissed that there was nothing that would incriminate Royce, and that I wasn't a safecracker. The penlight and knife went back in the bag inside my suit, the maps back in their case. Up the stairs, then slowly and quietly easing the door open just enough to slip out.

When I'd replaced the map case, I went back over the transom into the chilly water, trying to splash as little as possible. With the mask over my face and the fins back on, I swam back to the fence and rested against it once more. The cold of the water was making me numb, and I was pretty beat from fighting the current.

Coming to the breakwater, I stopped when I heard a male voice followed by a female giggle. What was this, the night for smooching couples? They sat up on the stones at the end of the breakwater, right where I'd come in. It put me in a bad spot. I couldn't swim underwater all the way around, but one wrong splash and they'd discover me.

There was about twenty yards of shore between the breakwater and the boatyard fence. Going there had risks. The couple might turn around and see me, plus I'd be visible from the boathouse. I treaded water silently, getting colder and more tired by the minute.

This side it would have to be. I swam up and crouched against the rocks, and pulled off my fins and mask. The rocks were slippery, and I hurt myself some as I scrambled over them on my hands and feet. The couple stayed involved with each other, and no one raised an alarm.

After what seemed like hours, I made it back to the car. I peeled off the wetsuit and rubbed myself dry with the towel. Once dressed and in the car, I felt better. Dog-tired and with chattering teeth, but better.

Back at my room I took a hot shower, trying to scald away the chill of the ocean. It helped, but what I really wanted was a drink. There was a lot tumbling around in my head, and I was too tired to deal with it all.

With the bathroom light on, I went to bed. Sleep brought me bloody dreams. There was my brother, his life pouring out of him in a red river that I tried to swim through. His face was replaced by Ben's, who looked at me and pointed to the hole in his head in mute reproach.

Dale T. Phillips

# CHAPTER 34

The next morning I placed a call to the reporter Reed, who had nothing to report. He hadn't made any progress, but I couldn't blame him much, as I hadn't either. I called Miami, and was able to speak to Esteban, which made him happy.

Soon after, I was back at the cemetery, in the hushed lanes of the dead. But even here in this place of rest there was no peace for me. A police car sat watch at the gate, and the uniformed cop inside spoke into his radio when he saw me.

While I waited for them to come get me, I told Ben all the things that had happened, and asked for a little help, if he had any influence. I wasn't getting very far at all. The secrets were locked up, and I couldn't punch them loose. Even my attempt at contact with a nice woman had ended in disaster. I had failed Tim long ago, failed Ben in the present, failed at everything.

In the quiet morning air you could hear every sound. Another car pulled up, and the engine shut off. Out stepped Lieutenant McClaren. I waited for the news of my fate.

Apparently he had some respect for the dead and the feelings of the living. He stood by the car, waiting, as if he had all the time in the world. I sighed and said goodbye to Ben, and walked over to meet my fate.

"Nice day." I nodded to him.

He nodded back. "Ayuh."

"What brings you out here?"

"Had a witness who found an unconscious guy in the bathroom at the Denny's in Lewiston. He saw the guy who did it, and got the license plate number on your rental. So?"

"Lewiston's out of your jurisdiction, isn't it?"

"Let me worry about that. Why'd you mess up Beaulier? You think he had something to do with your friend's death?"

"So you think I assaulted this Mister ... Beaulier, was it? Is he pressing charges?"

McClaren made a face. "Vince Beaulier has some experience with the police. Let's say he's not eager to increase his familiarity."

"So Mister Beaulier does indeed have a record. And if there's no charges, no crime has been committed."

"Don't play cute. Why'd you do it?"

"Did the police happen to find any plastic containers around Beaulier?" I asked.

"Maybe."

"Uh-huh. And if you were to make a guess as to the contents of said containers, would you perhaps surmise that Mister Beaulier had been in possession of certain illegal substances?"

"All right, they were crack vials."

"Suppose Mr. Beaulier had, previous to his unfortunate encounter, been peddling the aforementioned substances in an area frequented by minors. And suppose Mister Beaulier's idea of capitalism is to push said poison on kids."

"He was selling to kids?"

"Right out in the public park. So maybe some public-spirited citizen decided it was time to make Mister Beaulier see the error of his ways and issue a stern warning."

"Some warning. The guy's in Central Maine Medical."

I spread my arms. "An occupational hazard of his profession."

"So now you beat up drug dealers. That it?"

"Not me, Lieutenant, I've been warned against taking action against criminals."

"Damn it!" He exploded. "This is what I'm talking about. You go playing vigilante, someone's going to get killed. You see someone committing a crime, you call us. We're the law, we'll handle it."

"How many arrests were on his rap sheet, again?"

"You saying we can't do our job?"

"Punks like him have a million ways to get around the law. And he'd be right back selling to those kids. Right now, at least, I'll wager he's not doing any selling."

"So you going to start shooting them next? Or how about anyone you think had something to do with your friend's death? You gonna blow them away, too?"

"I know, I'm just in the way and all. You're welcome."

"What do you want? A medal?" McClaren looked plenty mad.

"No, just you off my back."

"You don't get it, do you? We're on opposite sides."

"Only because you want it that way."

"That's the way it is. Maybe Lagasse's right about you, maybe you were just getting rid of the competition."

"You think any self-respecting drug dealer would drive a car like mine?"

"Don't be flip. Maybe some time in a cell would change your attitude."

"And what, pray tell, would be the reason for that?"

"Suspicion. You were at the scene of a crime."

"Great. You'd file all that paperwork trumping up a charge, and I'd be out before you were done. Both of us have better things to do with our time."

"Got it all figured out, don't you?"

"No." I sighed. "No, I don't have anything figured out. Least of all who killed my friend. But I do know you are starting to piss me off."

"Oh good." McClaren's face actually hinted at a smile. "I was beginning to think I was losing my touch."

"Will that be all?" I turned to go.

"Wait." There was something in his tone of voice that made me stop. I looked at him. He looked at the sky, at the ground, everyplace but at me. "I don't know if you're aware of it, but even a scumbag like Beaulier has friends."

"Yeah, I met a couple of them already. Some squeaky little rat who wouldn't be any trouble, but the other one looked like bad news." I described him.

McClaren nodded. "Ollie Southern. Bad news is right. He leads Beaulier's gang. They're centered in Lewiston, but they get around. Besides the other stuff, Southern's personally been involved in a half-dozen assaults and at least three murders that we know of. One of them, he poured gasoline all over the guy and lit it, while the guy was still alive. We had to use dental records to identify the poor bastard.

"They won't take too kindly to your stomping Beaulier. They will feel obliged to do the same, or worse, to you."

"And I should look out."

"There's now going to be three dozen or more hardasses out hunting you down, ready to put a serious hurting on you."

"Ollie Baba and the forty thieves?"

McClaren shook his head. "Doesn't any of this get through to you? You might know karate, but you won't have a chance against these guys. They don't fight fair, and if they can't get you any other way, they'll just shoot you. We've got some pictures of some people they took shotguns to, if you want to come by and see them."

"You really paint a rosy picture."

"I'm telling it like it is. The smartest thing for you would be to get out of town for a while. A long while."

"And here I was thinking you actually cared."

"Sure, it would make my life simpler. I got a feeling that if you stick around much longer, we're going to be fishing your body out of Casco Bay."

"Or maybe one shot in the head, in a parked car, like Ben?"

McClaren looked at me. "I don't make that as their style," he said. "When they do somebody they like everyone to know it, so no one messes with them. Killing someone and making it look like suicide, that's not how they operate."

"Murder makes a lot of heat. They might have wanted a free ride."

"What are you going to do?"

"What I've been doing." I shrugged. "Hang around and make a nuisance of myself until someone gets tired of me and makes a play."

"You're determined to get yourself killed, aren't you?"

"Only if you'll catch them afterward."

McClaren shrugged and walked away.

"Lieutenant?"

He turned around.

"Thanks."

He looked as if he might say something, but he'd used up all his snappy lines and made a vague wave, like he was brushing away a fly.

Dale T. Phillips

# CHAPTER 35

So I wasn't going to be arrested. At least not just yet. And now McClaren might even do some more checking around. Maybe I wasn't a complete failure. Failure, after all, is when you stop trying, and I was going to keep hammering away until they killed me, locked me up, or something broke loose.

Visiting Ben at the cemetery had given me time to think, and a small measure of peace. Using it, I stopped by a florist and ordered some flowers to be delivered to Allison. On the card, I wrote a note apologizing for my behavior.

Then I drove back up to Pine Haven, resigning myself to more boring stakeout time. My old spot in the woods hadn't changed, so I nestled in for a wait. I turned the precision German lenses to the compound below, to watch all the little bugs scurrying about their business.

The afternoon wore on and turned cooler, the shadows stretching and deepening. A lone sailboat remained out on the water, silhouetted against the impressive sunset, with just the right amount of rosy pink clouds. No wonder Wyeth and Winslow Homer loved to paint here in Maine.

With the sun gone, it grew cold. I hadn't brought a jacket, and was getting chilled. Exercising helped a bit, but I was definitely uncomfortable.

The help drifted back out when their dinner shift ended. Grossman went to the dorms and didn't come out again. Royce walked up to his office. The light came on for a brief time and went off, and he came back down the stairs carrying his briefcase. He headed for his car, so I ran for mine, glad for the chance to get warm.

I concentrated on keeping a safe distance behind Royce, and he was keeping a reasonable pace. We drove some until I saw the sign for "Scarborough Downs," which I'd read was a racetrack. Maybe Royce was a big gambler. Maybe he'd embezzled to support his habit. Something to look into.

When we got to the gates, there were two cars between us. I parked and tried to keep an eye on Royce, and watched his back as he went into the grandstand. I took the binoculars, since they'd fit right in at a racetrack.

At the ocean I'd been cold, but here the August heat was more in effect. The grandstand area was air-conditioned, but it still couldn't hide the smells of popcorn, bad hot dogs, sweaty horses, and sweaty people. Discarded tickets lay scattered on the ground, all the false hopes and broken, small-time dreams. This world was far too familiar to me, for in the course of my bodyguard career, I'd chaperoned high-rollers at too many tracks and bookie joints, wasting my own life along with my clients'.

I looked around and saw those I knew to be regulars, who came here night after night, and were mostly sallow-complexioned, skinny little men in cheap suits and slicked-back hair, or fat, bald men who gnawed like beavers on soggy, foul-smelling cigars. These weren't the cheery, quirky characters out of Damon Runyon, but the tortured, lost gamblers of Dostoevsky. Their eyes were as dead as their dusty dreams of winning.

The people just out for a good time were buying two-dollar tickets to bet on which horse would win, but they acted as if their house was on the line. Some prayed, squeezing their eyes shut in fervent devotion, some cursed, some yelled encouragement. I shook my head. I'd seen more wagered on the turn of a single card than was wagered by everyone here combined in an entire night of betting. Of course, I'd also seen the body of a man who'd been killed over a five-dollar wager.

The horses had whimsical, colorful names, like Sukey's Rainbow and Attagal Sal. But here the horses pulled a two-wheeled rig with a seated driver, instead of carrying a jockey on their back. They were called trotters or pacers, and weren't allowed to break into a full run, some even wearing leg hobbles to control their gait. Other than that, it was pretty much the same idea. Get around the track before the others. Entertainment for some, money for others.

There was no sign of Royce. He wasn't at the ticket windows. I checked the men's restroom on the main floor, but he wasn't there. I went outside and searched with the binoculars. If he was out there, I couldn't see him. Upstairs was the Clubhouse, where they served sit-down food. I walked through and didn't spot him. Where the hell had he gone?

I kept making the rounds, circling the entire place every few minutes. Then I spotted Royce emerging from a corridor on the main floor. With him walked a big, soft-looking guy, a type I'd seen too much of. He looked like the typical small-time operator who wanted to be a big shot. A little wave in the front of his hair gave him a kind of bumpy crest. Royce said something to him and he laughed. Royce left, still carrying his briefcase. To hell with Royce. I wanted to check out the new player in the game.

Dale T. Phillips

# CHAPTER 36

One thing stood between me and Royce's buddy: a large
security guard, looming by the front of the corridor to keep
out the general public. I watched him, sizing him up. He was
a young kid with short, spiky brown hair. His thick neck
stuck out of the rent-a-cop's outfit like a stump, and the
beefy build would have qualified him for a linebacker
position on any college football team. He had the type of
frame that would turn to fat quickly when the workouts
stopped and the beer and pasta began to pile up.

He wore no gun, as his size alone would intimidate most
potential troublemakers, and his presence would keep the
rabble away from the offices of the mighty. He looked
bored, though, and didn't scan the room properly.

His interest picked up, however, whenever some girls
went by. His eyes got a hungry look. He puffed up and
preened a little until they went past, then his gaze shifted to
watch the round little bottoms walk away.

This could be my way in. I was thinking of bribing some
girl to distract him, when two soda-sipping teenagers did that
all on their own. They eyed him and giggled as they went
past, then stopped about ten feet away and started talking.
He was the essence of casual supercool as he sidled over and

joined the conversation. I moved by unnoticed and went down the corridor.

The office I'd seen Royce's buddy go into had no name on it. I went in without knocking. The guy was standing behind the desk, and looked up. He was about three inches taller than me. His sallow face resembled a lump of dough, and his slack gut drooped over the front of his pants. He wore an ugly sport coat that made him look like a second-rate insurance salesman.

I couldn't tell which smell was worse, his pervasive aftershave or the cigar in the ashtray that stank like a burning outhouse. The brass nameplate on his desk proclaimed "Ray St. Cyr, Assistant Manager." He wasn't smiling. I wasn't going to get the same reception as Royce had.

"How did you get in here?" he asked.

"I'm looking for Royce's business partner," I snapped.

Score on the first hit. He didn't want to admit anything right up front, but wasn't a good enough actor to hide it. I'd have loved to play poker with him.

I'd met his type before. I decided to play the mysterious man from the shadowy syndicate, higher up than his buddies. The fixer from the central office. I knew the jargon and the routine. Push him around first, get him on the defensive, drop some dark hints, dangle a little bait.

"What's this in relation to?" He coughed a nervous little hack.

"Do you know him, Ray? Is he your good buddy?"

Annoyance on the pasty features. Good. I pushed some folders aside, and parked a butt cheek on the corner of his desk.

"That depends," Ray answered. "Who's asking?" Pure imitation tough guy.

"The names wouldn't mean anything to you. To your bosses, they'd mean a lot."

"You mean you're not working alone."

"Bright boy. Now what's your business with Royce?"

"Why would you want to know a thing like that?"

"You're being awfully cagey, Ray, and I'm not a patient man. I don't work for patient men, either. Let's just say Mr. Royce has come to the attention of certain people. They are not happy with the way things have been run. Mistakes have been made, and some changes are necessary. So we'd like to know where you stand."

Ray had a worried look on his face. "I, uh, haven't heard anything about that. I'll have to make some calls."

"Can't do anything without orders, huh, Ray? I got it. If you're out of the loop, maybe I should be talking to your boss. How about it? Where does he stand?"

Ray was sweating now, though the air conditioner had a good chill going in the room. He pulled out a handkerchief and wiped his brow. "I'm sure you'll find him amenable to whatever you propose."

"Amenable? That's a big word, Ray. It shows you're a bright boy. But your buddies haven't been bright at all. In fact, they were pretty stupid."

"What do you mean? There haven't been any problems."

"No? What about that killing? I'd call that a pretty big problem."

"I don't know nothing about that."

"Sure, sure, Ray, I know the drill. But somebody screwed the pooch big time. Now the cops are involved."

"I was told things were fine."

"Well things aren't fine. The cops know it was murder now, and they're looking a lot deeper. They're watching Royce and even questioned him again. I don't suppose he bothered to mention that, did he?"

"No."

"I'm not surprised. Royce always has his own games and always lands on his feet. But someone else always takes the fall. Someone not really vital." I picked up his nameplate, breathed on it, and polished the surface.

Ray's pale face got three shades lighter, and panic flashed in his eyes. "Look," he stammered. "I haveta stay clean, on account of the Racing Commission and this job, you know.

Shit happens, well, that's business, but I don't know nothing about it. There's no way to connect me."

"That really doesn't matter, Ray. The cops are going to shake the tree hard, and they'll take what falls. No one else is going to want to go down for this one, so you're a prime candidate. They'll hand you over in gift-wrap. But not in any shape to talk. Maybe it'll be a car accident. Or maybe another suicide, one bullet through the bean, just like the other guy. Nice and neat, so everyone can go back to business as usual. But one guy won't be around to split that pie, leaving a little more for everyone else."

"They wouldn't do that."

"Why's that, Ray? You family? Hey, this is business. Tell me right now someone else they'd rather give up."

Ray chewed on that for a minute. "Why are you telling me all this?"

"You didn't make the mistake. Someone was too quick to start blowing away civilians. It's bad for business, and not the way we work nowadays. We want the guy who gave the order. And the trigger, too. We want to take them aside for some, shall we say, special counseling. You can set up a meeting for us, it can be all nice and quiet. Help yourself at the same time. Get yourself out of a jam and maybe grab a bigger slice of that pie."

"I told you, I don't get involved in that end of it."

"Like to keep your hands nice and clean, don't you, Ray? Sit back and collect your money and pretend there's no blood on you. Well, guess what? You play with this crowd, you roll in it, and you're covered with it just like everyone else. Now's the time to save your own ass and come out ahead. Question of survival. You or them. Which is it gonna be?"

"I need some time to think."

"Time's up, Ray. Just like on TV, 'This offer will not be repeated'."

"I just don't know." Something in his eyes changed. The deal wasn't closing. His wind was up, and I was losing him. "What's your name again?" He seemed suddenly determined.

"Taylor."

"Where'd you say you were out of? Boston?"

"Miami. A special job requires a specialist."

"Christ, you're not even carrying a gun."

"Attracts too much attention, Ray. I told you, that's not the way we work nowadays."

"I don't even know who the fuck you are. Something about this smells fishy."

"Almost as bad as your cologne."

Ray's face flushed a dangerous red. "You fuck, you're lying, you're not connected. Shit, Royce told me there was some guy snooping around, asking questions. That's you, isn't it? Jesus H. Christ."

"Two points for you, Ray. But what I said was true. Someone's going down for that killing, and these guys toss everyone else over first. You'll be the first to go. You're expendable."

"Shut the fuck up."

"You go to the DA now, you can cut a deal, come out with your skin. But you wait around, you'll be yesterday's garbage."

"No way. I'm clean, I can't be touched."

"You think so now, but ..."

"I told you to shut up. You are in deep fucking trouble."

"It's you who's in trouble. You'll have to talk to me sooner or later, Ray."

"How you figure that?"

"Because I'll follow you everywhere you go, and watch everything you do. You go out to eat, I'll be at the next table. You go to see some woman, I'll be there, taking it all down. I'll be all over you like a gator on a chicken."

Ray apparently decided his height over me and his bad-boy connections gave him the advantage. He came out from behind his desk, pointing a finger at me as he came closer.

"Let me tell you something. You don't come in here and talk that crap to me. Do you know who I am?"

I picked up the nameplate again and waved it at him. "Ray St. Cyr, Assistant Manager."

"Fuckin' right. And I can have your ass busted, boy. You got that?" He poked me in the chest with his finger.

"Don't do that," I said.

He blinked. "What?"

"Don't do that."

"Don't you fucking tell me what to do. I know some very big people."

"Are they doctors?"

"What?"

"They better be doctors, because you're going to be in a cast if you do that again."

"Tough guy, huh? You won't be so tough when ..." he poked me once more.

My left hand shot out, grabbing his wrist. My right grabbed his offending digit and wrenched it back until it snapped. Ray looked at it in disbelief for a second, jaw open in astonishment, before he began to howl.

"I see you're busy, Ray, so I'll come back. See you around."

He answered me with a string of curses. Ray was not very inventive in his invective. The security guard stood a few paces up the hall, looking at me like he was wondering where I'd come from and how I'd got past him.

"Ray caught his finger in the drawer," I said. "I'm going for some ice. You may want to give him a hand."

He glanced past me, and curiosity got the better of him. He went through the door to see what all the noise was about, and I hotfooted it out before Ray sicced the dogs on me.

# CHAPTER 37

The next morning found me once again back in the bushes at Pine Haven, watching to see if Royce or Grossman would stir from their lair. I'd turned over the rock, and I wanted to see where the bugs would run. They'd have to call in the troops to deal with me. The muscle would be around soon, and I'd better be ready.

By late in the afternoon, I was completely bored with lying around in the leaves. I drove back to my room, ready for a shower and a good meal, and maybe a call to Allison.

At the door I stopped, sensing trouble. Something was definitely wrong. Sniffing the air, there was a faint whiff of cologne. The last time I'd smelled it, it had been all over Ray. Squatting to inspect the door lock, I saw several shiny scratches from where they'd picked it to get in. Probably there now, waiting for me. I walked away from the door and looked around the motel parking lot, to make sure they didn't have any more backup. Around the corner was a big black Lincoln Continental, a car favored by bad boys who travel in bunches. Had to be theirs.

Part of me wanted to just call the cops and have the whole bunch arrested for breaking and entering. It would be fun to watch them squirm, though I wouldn't find out as much that way. But I wanted to confront them, to see if I could handle them, since someone in that room might be the one who had killed Ben. I took a deep breath and walked back to the room. I opened the door, turned on the light, and stepped in.

Three of them. One sitting on my bed, one back in the corner to my left, and one over by the bathroom against the far wall.

The man on my bed looked to be in his early thirties, and wore an expensive suit. He brought up a gun, pointing it at me. His black hair was carefully coiffed, in one of the mod styles you see on television. He'd be the boss of the muscle outfit. The black eyes sized me up, taking in the fact I wasn't armed and wasn't crapping my pants in fear at finding someone in my room holding a gun on me. I dubbed him "Slick." He grinned with one side of a nasty-looking slash of a mouth.

I looked around the room, the telltale mess advertising that it had been searched. The huge guy back in the corner to my left could barely fit between the floor and the ceiling. His hands were as big as dinner plates, and he looked like he could crush a bowling ball as easily as I could crush a beer can. With a jagged scar over one eyebrow and a fierce scowl, I'm sure he turned peoples' knees to jelly when he stared at them. This being Maine, I silently named him "Moose." He also had a gun under a suit that surprisingly fit quite well, with a turtleneck jersey instead of a dress shirt. This was at least a well-dressed bunch.

The guy next to the bathroom was about my size. He was a dangerous one, gray eyes, alert, and very fast-looking. He was well-balanced on the balls of his feet, ready for action. He wore dark leather gloves and tapped a blackjack against his leg. I tagged him "Speed."

Slick motioned me forward with his finger, and the big guy moved between me and the door. Speed moved up to my left, behind me. I noted each location, feeling the hairs on the back of my neck prickle.

"Come on in. We been waiting for you," Slick said.

And then Ray poked his head from around the corner inside the bathroom, glaring at me. He sported a well-taped splint on the finger I'd broken.

"That's him, that's the guy," Ray said, jabbing his bandaged digit at me.

"How's the finger, Ray?" I grinned at him.

"You son-of-a-bitch. It's your turn now. You're gonna—"

"Shut the fuck up," Slick cut Ray off. Ray clammed up fast, with a look on his face like a dog who had just been kicked. Slick rose slowly, holstered his gun inside his jacket, and adjusted his suit, drawing out the drama. He looked like he planned on having a good time.

They had me tightly boxed in, but I was doing mental calculations, choreographing my moves.

"So," said Slick. "You busted up Ray and come around looking for trouble. You found it. Who are you and what the fuck do you want?"

"I was a friend of Ben Sterling's."

"Who?"

"He was a cook from the Pine Haven Resort. Someone murdered him."

This created a moment of quiet while Slick digested this. "So what's that got to do with Ray?"

"There's some sort of connection between Jackson Royce from the resort and Ray here. When I tried to talk to Ray, he got rude and I broke his finger."

Slick looked disgusted. "Well, Ray doesn't know shit about any murdered cook. Do you, Ray?"

"No," Ray mumbled, eyes down.

"Well, I guess there's no problem, then," I said.

"Oh, there's a problem," Slick stepped closer to me. "You don't come around here talking like this. You're bad for business, so we're going to teach you a lesson. When you're able to move again, get the hell out and don't come back."

So, they were going to work me over, but Slick wanted to make a speech first. I decided he'd talked enough. I smashed him up under the nose with the heel of my right hand, snapping his head back and knocking him back onto the bed. Speed was already moving, blackjack raised. I checked his rush with a hard side kick cracked into his kneecap. He yelped as I dropped and spun to the left. The big hands of Moose closed on empty air where I had been, and I drove a right into his groin. Breath whuffed out of him as I straightened up.

Moose was now quite pliant as I hooked my foot behind his and thrust him into Speed, who couldn't get out of the way in time. They danced awkwardly for a moment until the back of Speed's legs hit the arm of a chair. Speed fell on his back across the arms of the chair, with Moose landing on top of him. The chair collapsed under their weight, and they were out of the fight.

Ray was groping in his pocket, hampered by his splinted finger and his terror. I took long steps and kicked for the family jewels like a field-goal champ. Ray let out a high squeak and collapsed, his eyes bulging.

Slick tried to get up, one hand holding the bloody shattered mess of his nose, the other clawing madly at his holster. I stepped in close and let him pull the gun, straightening the arm and twisting it before snapping it against my raised knee. He groaned and dropped the gun, and I hit him with another palm strike by the chin to put him out.

All the tough guys were down, and it was time to pull their teeth. I removed holsters and weapons, starting with Slick, who carried an expensive Glock. Speed had a pearl-handled .38, and the blackjack, which nobody used anymore. It was so old school I almost felt nostalgic. Moose was a surprise, carrying a .32. I would have figured him for a big-ass .45 or something comparable. They'd even given Ray a gun of sorts, a dainty .25 that was hardly bigger than a cigarette lighter, and what he'd been reaching for in his pocket when I kicked him.

I patted down each man carefully, in case there was more. I collected wallets as well. Slick had a condom in his, and Moose had a picture of a woman holding a baby. I removed each driver's license. Three of them had permits to carry concealed weapons, and I removed those as well, before tossing the wallets in a pile by the door.

They would get patched up and run back to their boss for instructions. They'd have a tough time explaining their failure, and it would take them time and resources to replace their guns and licenses.

I left them in the room and drove down to the water. The blackjack, guns, and holsters went far out into the tide. Then I drove over to the hospital, where they'd have to show. I parked where I could watch the emergency entrance without being seen.

A short time later, they pulled up in the big black Lincoln. They moved toward the hospital entrance, a slow, crippled group. When they were inside, I went for some dinner, knowing it would be a while before they got out. But I'd be back when they did.

Dale T. Phillips

# CHAPTER 38

They took a long time to come out of the hospital. Moose walked with a stiff, slow gait, and Slick sported a big arm cast and a bandaged face. I figured the other two would be staying awhile. Moose helped Slick into the big black Lincoln, even opening the door for him. Touching. They drove towards Falmouth without breaking any speed laws.

The neighborhood got more expensive and more private, and they pulled into a gated drive between big stone walls. Moose punched some numbers on a keypad, and the fancy iron gates swung open. The big car purred through and the gates closed, shutting out me and the rest of the world.

The stone walls completely surrounded the property, so I tried to keep them in sight as I went down a few side streets, looking for a way in. I parked in a nearby driveway, where the house lights were off. It was getting dark, which I hoped would make it hard to spot me. I cut through someone's tree-lined back yard, while a dog barked at me.

The wall was high, but I reached the top with a good jump. Luckily they didn't have spikes or broken glass on top, and I was able to hoist myself over. I dropped to the ground on the other side, listening for any alarms.

Using the trees for cover, I made my way to the house, skirting a fancy pool. In back of the house was a flagstone patio with huge stone urns at each corner. I sprinted across a short patch of open space and ducked behind an urn. A flash of light blinded me, and I thought I was caught.

The patio door opened and a big bruiser stepped out. He was only twice my size, not nearly as huge as Moose. He walked past me, inches away, as he looked around the back yard. He stepped off the patio and started around the perimeter. I dashed to the door and slipped through.

There was shouting in another part of the house. It sounded like someone was getting chewed out. I moved cautiously, hearing the voices through a closed door on the first floor. There was music from upstairs. I declined to use the staircase, as there was too much chance of getting caught out in the open.

The living room was expensively furnished, but offered no good hiding place. The kitchen was big, and had a pantry with a door. I crept in and closed it behind me. There wasn't much room and I tried not to move, afraid that I'd knock something over. The light was bad, but the acoustics were good, as I heard the boys getting their asses chewed. Footsteps thudded through the kitchen.

The ass-chewing went on for about another ten minutes before the boys were dismissed. I heard the front door open and close. The ass-chewer shouted for a drink, and someone hurried to the study. There was a brief murmured exchange before footsteps sounded in the kitchen. I thought for a minute. I hadn't heard or seen anyone else on this floor. I'd take out the bruiser and introduce myself to the boss.

I eased the pantry door open, just a crack. The big guy had his back to me, filling a silver bucket with ice cubes, and making a goodly amount of noise.

I came up behind him and used a neat little judo hold on his thick neck, squeezing his carotid artery until he lost consciousness. Leave that hold on a few seconds longer and you kill the person, but I released as soon as he was out, and half-dropped him to the floor. Removing his gun, I made sure the safety was on and tucked it in my pants. I picked up the bucket and walked toward the study. Before I got there, the voice yelled.

"Where the hell's that ice?"

"Right here," I said, entering the room. He stared at me as I took in the decor of Olde Worlde-Alastair Cooke wannabe. The bookcases had tasteful, hand-tooled, leather books, gilt-edged, and probably unread. A large wooden globe squatted beside the massive oak desk. The huge leather wingback chair was positioned just so in front of the fire. The laird himself was a beefy guy, late-fifties, balding and fleshy. He wore a maroon smoking jacket, and I wondered where the dog and pipe were to complete the picture.

"Where do you get your decorating ideas?" I shook my head. "Esquire meets Masterpiece Theater?"

"Who the hell are you? Where's Al?"

"Al is taking a nap. And you should know me. I just sent your boys back to you in pieces."

Light dawned in his eyes. He nodded. "Led you right to me, didn't they?" He sounded disgusted.

"Pigeons always fly home to roost."

"So what do you want?" He tried to sound casual as he reached in the desk. He was actually stupid enough to try it. "Money? I've got some here—"

The ice bucket caught him in the face, and I was at the desk in three strides. I rolled over it, sending things flying, and kicked him hard and full in the gut. He fell backwards, the jacket falling open. He cursed me with a bleeding mouth from the tumbled heap of ice cubes, pens, and twin desk lamps. I yanked open the drawers and removed the gun he'd been trying for.

"Not only do you have lousy taste in decorating and help, you are one slow learner." I shook my head. "I kicked the shit out of four of your boys, dumbass, five if you count Sleeping Beauty out in the kitchen. Now maybe you'll answer a few questions. Like first, who are you?"

"You ain't from here or you'd know that." He tried to sound menacing and important. He dabbed at his cut mouth with a silk handkerchief. I knew he'd have a hard time getting the blood out of that silk.

"You might impress the locals, but I've seen bigger and better. You are definitely small potatoes."

"I got connections ..."

"You got shit, and you know it. You call your bosses up and tell them you have a problem with some guy, they'll wonder why you can't handle it. They might even send a wreath along with the guy they send to replace you."

I nudged him with my shoe. "So why are you bringing in amateurs? What are you running? Some gambling scam?"

"I ain't telling you nothing."

"You're a tough guy, right, can take a little working over? Two days in the hospital, you figure, and you're back on solid foods? Let me tell you the facts of life. There's a vertebrae in your neck that I can snap so you won't be feeling anything from there on down ever again.

"You'll go from all this to a couple of square feet of hospital ceiling. Someone will feed you with a spoon while everyone around you clucks with pity. Your nose will itch, and you'll beg someone to scratch it. Each second that ticks by will seem like forever. You'll get pretty crazy the first year, but then it gets worse. You'll be pleading with your former associates to put a bullet into you."

He had been sitting up, but now he slumped. I prodded him again with my foot. "What's your name?"

"Tony Castle."

"Yeah, and I'll bet you were born with that name. What kind of operation are you running?"

"Gambling. Like you said."

I kicked him in the face, starting the bleeding anew. "Try again. What are you running?"

"Drugs, you crazy sonofabitch. This thing is all set up. Who sent you?" He almost spat as he glowered at me.

"Never mind. What's that got to do with Pine Haven?"

He shrugged. "You'll be dead soon anyway. The manager there, he did some dealings with a mutual acquaintance. He's a money guy, always looking for an angle. He meets a lot of rich people, and we wanted to expand our market."

These parasites always discussed dispensing human misery like it was part of American Free Enterprise. They thought of themselves as businessmen, and the way the world was going, it was getting harder to tell them apart. At least this explained how Royce could make payments on a Porsche and a high-class powerboat.

"So what about Ben Sterling?"

"Who?"

"When you have a man killed, you ought to at least know his name. He was the cook from the resort who was murdered."

Before I could ask him anything else, a girl's voice called out. "Dad? Dad, where are you?"

"Who's that?" I said to Castle.

"My daughter," he said, looking at me. I silently cursed. I didn't want a non-combatant mixed up with this. I could slap Tony around all night, but I didn't want to get tough with his kid, or even scare her. Time to go, then.

"Your lucky day, Tony. Don't get up, I'll let myself out. But don't worry, we'll talk again. Your money, guns, and goons, none of it matters. I got past everything, and I can get to you and stand next to your bed while you sleep. Anytime. You remember that. And I can hurt you in ways you haven't even thought of."

I sprinted across the lawn and made it back over the wall. The anger boiled inside me and I wanted some revenge. I had been so close to knowing it all. On the way back to my room, I stopped and threw the other two guns into the water. Any more, and the sea level would rise.

Back at the room, I looked at the wreckage from the earlier fight. I was shaking with rage, all control gone. In my mind, I saw my hands on Royce's throat, and the fat chef, too. Screw it. I needed a confrontation.

231

I went outside and got in my car, eager to drive to the resort. I wasn't sure what I would do when I got there.

Too late, my inner alarm went off. I'd been so intent on my anger, I hadn't checked around. I moved before I even knew what was coming, lunging across the seat to jack open the passenger side door. From the corner of my eye, I saw a vehicle rushing at the driver's side of my car, out of the darkness. I heard the impact, then I was flying through the open door, and then there was nothing but black silence.

# CHAPTER 39

Everything was dark. Muffled voices came from far away. I swam in a black sea of pain, and I was drowning in it. Pushing my way through the pain, I struggled to find a way up from the blackness.

There was some glorious light, so brilliant it hurt. I closed my eyes against it and went back to the darkness. The next time I came up, the light didn't hurt as bad.

Eyes fully open, finally, seeing sunlight, coming through a window. Remembering the line from Emily Dickinson, "There's a certain slant of light ...". I couldn't remember any more, so I mentally chanted the line over and over.

So. A window. A ceiling, too. A room of some sort. But where? Sheets so crisp they were stiff. A hospital, then. Damn. Hate hospitals. People go there to die. Like Ben. He'd gone to a hospital, and then escaped. But he died right after. See? One way or another they get you.

Someone nice, someone who worked in a hospital. Allison. Yes. Her face came into focus in my mind. Good. I was in a hospital. To see Allison? No. Too much pain. Something happened. Car? Yes, I'd been in a car. But after the car there was nothing. *A certain slant of light.* Light in my eyes, hurting. Nothing else. Remember it later. Sleep now.

I awoke in a hospital room, hurting. What happened? Why was I here, why was I here? I tried to move, and fresh pain shot through me. There was a voice as I went under again.

The next time I came up I was immediately aware of where I was and that something had happened. Thinking the pain couldn't get any worse, I did a severely limited visual inspection and flexed various parts to find out what was working and what had been smashed up. The hurting ratcheted up a few more notches. I hissed through clenched teeth and stopped. There were bandages, but not the feeling of any stitches or casts. A good sign. My head had contacted something even harder than itself, and moving it too fast made my vision swim. I tried a mental technique of gathering the pain together and focusing it somewhere else, but there was just so damn much of it.

The door to the room opened, but I couldn't turn to see who it was. Someone came to the side of the bed and squeezed my hand. She leaned over and I saw her. Allison.

"Hey, there," I said. She smiled, and I felt better.

"Hello again."

"We've got to stop meeting like this." I tried to grin, but even that hurt.

"I agree. The flowers were very nice, by the way. Were you afraid I wouldn't want to see you again? There are easier ways than this, you know."

"I can believe that. Ow," I said, trying to shift to see her better.

"Hurt much?"

"Nothing a thousand cc's of Percocet couldn't help."

She reached for my chart at the foot of the bed. "Says you're not due for another hour."

"Ha. That'd be fine, if I was still unconscious. I have a pretty high tolerance, you know, but this sets the teeth on edge. I promise I won't get addicted if you can stop the torture a few minutes early."

"I'll see what I can do." She replaced the chart.

"Thanks."

"You were lucky. Just banged up a bit. Mild concussion."

"What happened?"

"You don't know?" She frowned.

"I remember the car. Something coming toward me, then pain. And here."

"Someone rammed a truck into your car."

"Ah. That explains the bandages."

"This wasn't just a hit-and-run. Someone was really trying to kill you."

"Guess so."

"You knew this would happen, didn't you?"

"I figured something would. But this caught me by surprise. I wasn't as prepared as I thought."

"They almost succeeded."

"Yeah, but I think I know who did it. Are they still here? It might be a little inconvenient if I ran into them in the hallway. Four guys came into emergency yesterday, two stayed? One had been kicked in the groin and the other had a hurt back. And two others were treated and discharged."

"You did that? They were hurt pretty bad."

"They were trying to hurt me. And they had guns."

"So you beat them up." She was frowning. "But it didn't stop them, did it?"

"They're persistent."

"Well you don't have to worry about them being here. That was three days ago. One was released with a neck and back brace, and the other was let go when his voice resumed normal octaves. Besides," she said, looking into my eyes. "You're dead."

I raised my eyebrows, about all I could do. It still hurt. "Come again?"

"There was a policeman here, a Lieutenant McClaren. He had you listed as expiring in the night. He said it was in case whoever did this found out you were alive and tried again. Only a few of us know differently. You're in here under another name as a traffic accident victim."

235

"Bless his pea-picking heart. I didn't know he cared."

"Oh, he cares, all right. He's furious. Said he wanted you to recover, so he could arrest you himself. We're supposed to call him as soon as you wake up."

"My, my. Seems like I've stirred the pot some."

"So you can let him handle things now?"

"Well, he still needs to link Ben's death to these people. I doubt he can do it unless something else breaks or I get some proof."

"But if they find out you're alive, they'll come after you again."

"Yeah, but I've done so well up to now."

"I'm worried about you." She looked very serious.

"I like you too."

"Why don't you get some rest? I'll see about the meds."

"What about the Lieutenant?"

"He can wait awhile. You need to rest."

# CHAPTER 40

I was just finishing my first meal since the crash, when McClaren walked in. I groaned, but tried to put on a cheerful face.

"What, no flowers?" I said.

"You're dead, dumbass."

"Nice to see you, too. Yeah, I heard you pulled some strings. Thanks."

"Don't thank me. It was almost for real. I told you not to go poking around." He looked me over, noting the damage, and nodded. "Heard you must've popped out of that car like a champagne cork."

"So you just came to gloat?" I said.

"A little, maybe." There was a silence. "You going to tell me about it?"

"And you'll move heaven and earth to find out who did it?" I said. "For little ole me?"

"The law works for everyone."

"Even when someone's on your turf?"

He darkened as the color rose from the collar up. He was in better control of his anger than I was of mine, however, and the only other sign was a muscle that twitched along his jaw. I felt bad about baiting him, even if he was patting himself on the back for having told me how dangerous it all was.

"Sorry," I said. "I'm a bit touchy right now. The medication's wearing off again, and on top of it, I got careless, so I'm a might ticked."

"I hate to say 'I told you so', but I did mention you were out of your league."

"I'm still having a hard time believing it." I started to shake my head, but the sudden pain told me it was a bad idea. "I clobbered them pretty hard."

"Not hard enough, apparently. I just want to keep them from coming back to finish the job."

"Soon as I'm back on my feet, I'd actually like them to try." I moved a little, and hurt a lot. It could wait.

"So you saw who it was?"

"No, but I've got a pretty good idea."

"So give me some names." He leaned closer.

"You can't prove anything."

"Let me worry about that."

"You question them, they'll know I told you, so I must be still alive. By not doing anything, they'll think it worked."

"Damn near did, from the looks of things. What kind of vehicle was it?"

"I didn't see a thing. It was dark and I was trying to get out of the way."

"Who was driving?" McClaren asked.

"I already told you, I don't know."

"You know plenty. You better tell me. I have enough to hold you."

"For what? Getting hit by a truck?"

"How about this for starters?" McClaren held up a clear bag with a little plastic tube inside. "Where'd you get this?" He didn't sound friendly.

"Off a boat."

McClaren looked at me. "You know what this is?"

"More drug paraphernalia, I'd wager."

"It's another crack vial."

"Doesn't look like the ones Beaulier had."

"A confession at last." McClaren smiled in triumph. "No, this is different. And I want to know where it came from."

I considered for a minute. I almost shrugged, before I remembered how much it would hurt. "I was making an uninvited night visit aboard a private boat. That and a bottle cap are all I found."

McClaren turned the bag over in his hands. "Lot of this particular stuff has been turning up here. Heroin, too. Can you believe that shit is making a comeback? We would very much like to track it to its source." He looked up. "So why were you on the boat, and who owns it?"

"Belongs to Jackson Royce, the food and beverage manager at Pine Haven," I said. McClaren pulled out a notebook, and wrote the name down.

"Tell me about him," he said.

"He's a smarmy jerk, and he gave me the bum's rush when I asked questions. He drives a very expensive car. I followed him, and found he also owns a very expensive boat. Pretty good living for resort work. I dropped by his boat to see if I could find anything that would tie him to Ben's killing."

"I told you to let us handle it."

"You couldn't even get a search warrant for the boat without some probable cause."

"And this is all you found?"

"Yeah. I also found out he's tied in with some heavy people. You got much on Tony Castle?"

McClaren nodded. "Antonio Castellano, alias Tony Castle. We had three likely candidates we figured were responsible, and he's number two on the list. Haven't been able to get anything on him or his people, though. A couple of possession busts on some small fish. How did you get the connection? Another uninvited visit?"

"Matter of fact, yes. I followed Royce out to Scarborough Downs, saw him meet with an assistant manager there, a Ray St. Cyr. We had a discussion in which Ray came off the worse. Before I knew it, Ray and three other boys were waiting for me in my hotel room, after giving it a good tossing. They were going to persuade me to leave town after a sound thumping, but I convinced them otherwise. I followed them to the hospital and then to Castle's castle. Tony and I had a little talk, and he told me he and Royce were into some drug scam. We were interrupted before I could get any more details. I got back to my room, and that's when they hit me."

McClaren sat back in his chair, studying me. "Those the ones that came here recently?"

"You heard about that."

"You messed them up pretty good."

"Thought I had. They must have brought up some reserves," I said.

"They have plenty."

"So you probably went to my motel room. Is my stuff still there under lock and key?"

"Since you're deceased, your belongings were removed from your room, as well as what's left of your car. We have your stuff at the station as evidence. I'll keep it until I figure out what to do with you."

"Just what is it about me you find so hard to comprehend?"

"I do not like the fact you've worked with people like Castle. Why should I believe this isn't an organizational matter?"

"What, that I'm some kind of fixer for the big boys?"

"Something like that."

"Jesus, Lieutenant, remember the car I was driving?"

It actually made him smile. He shook his head. "You're right, you're too much of a smartass for them to have you around."

"Thanks for the vote of confidence."

"What should I do about you?" He looked at me.

"You could check auto body shops. Smashing my car must have at least scratched the paint on their truck."

"Thanks for telling me how to do my job. They'll have ditched the truck by now, which was probably stolen anyway. Hasn't turned up yet."

"So what do we do now?"

"We don't do anything." He pointed at me. "You sit on your ass and heal, or you can sit in a cell in the Cumberland County jail. Don't make me tell you again."

"After all the help I gave you?"

"Look, dumbass, you messed with the pros and almost got whacked. You won't be so lucky next time. And I don't want another homicide to deal with."

I was starting to get angry again. The pain was making me irritable. "Just for your information, I was overconfident because they didn't act like pros. By following the resort manager and chef, who both lied about Ben, I found the link to St. Cyr, and scared him so bad they sent some goons to rough me up. All four came here as a result. Then they led me straight back to their boss, and I took out his guard dog and slapped around the big guy himself until he gave me some answers. So, yeah, it seemed easy and I got careless. I won't underestimate them again. But I found out more in a couple of days than you have. That's really why you're pissed."

"Just hold it right there, cowboy. It's real easy to break into places for information when you don't have to worry about the law, or proof, or the goddamn lawyers waiting to sue you. Do you have any idea of the shitstorm we go through every time we lay a hand on someone? We got people complaining to the mayor if we use bad language, for Christ's sake."

"I didn't mean—"

"And then you come in, Mr. White Knight, because you don't think we can do anything. Your friend's dead, and you want to kick some ass. So you go looking for trouble, and find it, and I've almost got another corpse on my hands."

"How about if we get on the same side?" I said. "Stop riding me long enough, maybe we can work together. I can

241

take chances and act as bait to draw them out into the open where you can nail them. That's all I want."

McClaren sat back and sighed. He rubbed his head like he was tired. "I'll try one more time. I can't go around nursemaiding you. We have a job to do, and you're not part of it. In the movies and TV, cops want your help. But this is real, and you have no part in the investigation. We have to play by the rules and they don't. You don't carry a gun, and they do. That means you'll wind up just as dead as your friend. This ends your involvement, as of now."

"So what if you can't get them by the rules?"

"We will. Sooner or later." He was so sincere I almost believed it.

"Well, I guess there's not much I can do from this bed, anyway."

"Just remember, obstruction of justice is one charge I can make stick. And I can come up with others."

I turned my head away and winced as a bolt of pain jolted through my neck. "Could we continue this discussion some other time?"

"If we do, it'll be through bars."

"Yeah, yeah, I get the point."

"Look, I'm not doing it this way because I like it."

"Just business, right? Just doing your job? Funny thing, Lieutenant, Castle said the same thing."

McClaren looked at me and I saw the same type of anger I was all too familiar with. Then he shook his head and looked kind of sad. Though I respected him, we were still on opposite sides.

"Doctor tells me you'll be here for four or five more days," he said as he went out.

"Don't count on it," I said quietly to the closing door. I planned to be out of here a lot sooner than everyone thought.

# CHAPTER 41

Later on, after they gave me some painkillers that took the edge off, I figured it was a good time to start getting things back together. I began very slowly, alternately flexing and relaxing each muscle group, starting with my feet and working upward. It hurt, all right, but my vision didn't blur like before. I soon got tired, and relaxed on the clean sheets. An hour later, I tried again. It still hurt, and wore me out, but a little less than before.

I had a lot of time to think, and became convinced that Castle's boys had not been the ones to ram my car. They would have finished me off with a gun. That was definitely amateur night. So that left who? Southern? Thibodeaux? I didn't know that, but now I knew that there was a Pine Haven connection to a well-organized gang, with drugs and probably a lot of money involved. And that was likely the reason Ben was killed. Pine Haven was the weak link, so I'd concentrate my efforts there.

The doctor dropped by while I was resting, looked me over, mumbled something, and left. I had another little exercise session after he'd gone. Later, Allison came in, dressed in everyday clothes instead of her nurses' outfit.

"Hey," she said.

"Hey yourself. Not on duty, I take it."

"I'm on later. Thought I'd see how you were doing."

"Not too bad." I shrugged. "Just about to go to my tennis match."

"Funny."

"Just seeing if things still work," I said.

"You're in good shape, and all the damage is temporary. How's the pain?"

"Down to about a five on a scale of one to ten."

"What did the doctor say?" she asked.

"Not sure, since he didn't seem to be speaking to me. I felt a little bit like a piece of meat."

Allison grimaced.

"What's the matter?" I asked her.

"Some doctors won't connect with their patients," she replied. "It's almost like they shun human contact."

"Maybe they should have become lawyers instead," I said.

She laughed and reached over to brush my hair back off my forehead. I took her hand and kissed it. It didn't even hurt that much.

She smiled, making it worthwhile. "I brought you some books."

"Oh, thank God. Infomercials are now on during the daytime hours, and the scary part is, they're the most watchable thing on. Whatcha got?"

"A Tony Hillerman mystery, *The Right Stuff* by Tom Wolfe, and a book on sailing ships off the Maine coast." She looked at me. "How did I do?"

"Top marks. Thank you."

"Need anything else?"

"Where are my clothes?"

"The ones you were wearing when they brought you in were all torn and bloody. They took them for evidence. But you're not going anywhere for a few days."

"Do you think you could bring me something I could wear? I'd feel better, knowing they were there."

"Okay. I have to get going now."

"How about letting me show my gratitude?"

"You wish," she said, playfully smacking my hand. She walked to the door, me watching her all the way. How had the fool men in this town let her go?

Picking up the Hillerman book, I began reading about a mysterious killing in the desert. Maybe I could pick up some tips on how to solve a murder. Supper came and went, a very unexciting meal. The red Jell-o was tougher than the meat. If the bad guys hadn't killed me, maybe the food here would.

Hours later, I finished the Hillerman book. Bad guys had been caught, justice triumphed, and the Navajo policemen knew a little more about the world. No inside info for me on catching murderers, though, unless I became a Navajo shaman.

The book on ships had some beautiful color pictures, but my eyes were getting grainy. I was thinking of turning out the light and going to sleep, when Allison came in, now in her uniform. She put something in the little closet space, then came over and held my hand while she sat on the edge of the bed. She smelled of powder and perfume, and her skin was warm, with a creamy smoothness. My head spun, and not from the physical abuse I'd received. We talked for a while, then she was gone. I lay there, wondering if it had been real. It had seemed very much like a dream, but the scent and feel of her lingered. I drifted off to sleep, and had an uncommonly peaceful night, with no ghostly visits.

In the morning, I was able to move around at last, with only occasional jolts of real pain, and a lot of stiffness. Good enough. I had to get out of here. Hobbling to the bathroom, I got a look at myself in the mirror. I wouldn't win any beauty contests for a while. The area around my left eye was still badly bruised, my face was swollen in parts, and a handful of cuts made an interesting topographical map of red lines. In addition to badly needing a shave, I was having a very bad hair day.

I used the john, grateful to be free of bedpans, and washed up as well as I could. The cops probably wouldn't arrest me on sight, but I wouldn't be hired for any job involving meeting the public. I might scare the children.

I found the clothes Allison had left, and put them on. Miracle of miracles, my wallet was in the cupboard. I found some paper and a pen and wrote out a note telling the hospital to contact Lieutenant McClaren about the bill, and left the note on my pillow. Out in the hall, I just walked out like I was another visitor, a little slow, but okay for walking. People looked at me, but no one stopped me. They called a cab for me downstairs. I gave Allison's address and wondered how I'd be received.

It was no surprise that she was surprised to see me.

"What are you doing here? You should be in bed!"

"Is that a proposition?"

She blushed.

"Sorry," I said. "Can I come in?"

"Of course. But you really shouldn't be moving around."

"I'm not getting anything done just lying there. Read all the books you brought me, though."

"You did not."

"Okay, only two of them. Can you help me?"

She looked skeptical. "Help you what?"

"I need to find a new place to stay. And I need to get my stuff."

"What are you going to do?"

"Nothing dangerous. Tomorrow I'm going back to Pine Haven. The police can't hang around all day at that resort, but I can. That's all I'm going to do. Just watch."

"I don't think that's a good idea."

"It's not dangerous," I protested. "All I'm going to do is lie quietly in the bushes and do surveillance."

"Still on this mission."

"It's not much, but it's something."

"Even after they almost killed you." She was quiet for about a minute. I waited, watching her. She sighed and shook her head.

"My momma told me never to do this, but you can stay here if you want."

"You comfortable with that?" I looked closely at her.

"At least I'll know you're safe."

"Okay, but it's your home. When you want me out, just say so."

"All right. It's going to cost you, though." She came over to me. She kissed me long and slow, taking her time. I held her, feeling giddy. I felt uncomfortable because I couldn't yet tell her that I loved her, not while there was unfinished business with Ben's killers. It could get pretty ugly still, and if anything happened, well, she could go on a lot easier if she could tell herself it had been casual.

I was probably just being a fool, but this was something new for me, and I didn't know what else to do. Love would have to wait for vengeance.

Dale T. Phillips

# CHAPTER 42

Two days later, I had a rental car, a bottle of prescription painkillers, and was still on stakeout. Man of action, if your idea of action is lying around in the bushes wincing. I was once again watching the scene at Pine Haven, through the one remaining binocular lens. The other had cracked when my car got hit, so I had to close my left eye to use them. While I watched, I kept stretching every few minutes.

The question of who had tried to punch my ticket kept gnawing at me. Ramming a car was the sloppy move of an amateur. It didn't fit the profile for Castle's organization. The biker had been in the hospital, but one of his buddies could have lent a hand. Possible. I had the unpleasant feeling I was missing something important.

The day wore on, and there was no criminal action. I left the scene, feeling disappointed and useless. Back in Portland, I saw Allison for about ten minutes before she left for work. Left to myself for the night, I took a long bath to ease my aching body, and went to bed soon after.

The next morning I was hurting much less, and was up and out early to Pine Haven. A light patter of rain spit down from a dull gray sky. I got to my lookout spot in the wet bushes, and made myself as comfortable as possible in my

249

rain poncho, fighting off the mosquitoes that went for my face and hands.

A delivery truck with a Portland address on the side pulled up to the loading dock. Grossman came out to check the delivery. I watched carefully through the binoculars, but nothing seemed amiss. The truck left, and I relaxed and waited some more.

Around eleven o'clock, another truck pulled up, this one a produce truck, with a Boston address painted under the logo. There were two men in the cab of the truck. The driver got out, a big, mean-looking guy, with a huge beer belly. He went in through the loading dock door, returning with Grossman. The other guy stayed in the truck while the driver unloaded several boxes of produce. Grossman made marks on a clipboard. When they were done, the driver said something to Grossman, who shook his head in the negative.

The driver seemed to get angry, and started gesturing while he talked. He pointed a finger and they argued some. Grossman went inside. The guy in the truck looked all around, as if he expected trouble. The driver crossed his arms and looked defiant. I didn't think it was because they hadn't paid the bill for the lettuce.

A minute later, Royce came scrambling out of his office. He carried the toolbox I'd seen Grossman pick up, and he looked nervous, and mad, and in a hell of a hurry. He got to the dock and thrust the toolbox at the driver.

My bet was that I'd just seen a transfer of some of those drugs that McClaren was so hot to get his hands on. If I could intercept that box, it would stir up some major trouble. I got back to the car, knowing I could catch the truck, but wondering how I could overcome the two guys in it. I still wasn't a hundred percent, but I'd tail them and see what happened. Maybe I could get them apart and scoop up their delivery.

The rain was coming down harder now, and the truck took it slow over the slick roads. I caught up with it after a few miles, just as they got on the turnpike heading south. They must have arranged Pine Haven to be the last dropoff of the morning.

They pulled into the big rest stop in Kennebunk and parked with the semi trucks, tucked out of sight behind some other rigs. I parked in the car lot, and hustled over in time to see the driver come out from behind a couple of trailer trucks and head toward the food building.

I had to work fast. I pulled my poncho hood up and cinched it tight to frame my face. The car mirror showed that I looked like a complete dork.

I walked around to where the other guy in the truck could see me, waved at him frantically, and pointed to the back of the truck. He looked me over, glanced around, and rolled the window down a crack.

"Hey, mister," I said, in a high voice that made me sound like Jerry Lewis on acid. "You gotta leak in the back here. Might be gas. I smell gas. You better take a look."

I turned around and walked away, for he might be dumb enough to get out, but only if he thought I was gone. Once out of sight, I sprinted back, close to the rear of the delivery truck. I heard the sound of a door opening. He was careful, and I'd have to be even more so. As quiet as could be, adrenaline pumping, I slipped around the end and moved toward him.

But he was too alert, and spun to meet me. As he pulled out a knife, I kicked him in the midsection. He bounced off the truck, but still held the knife. I kicked him again, low to the knee, and heard him grunt in pain. One more kick to the knee, keeping my leg away from the blade, then I snapped a punch to his head. He staggered, and I kicked once more, high and hard into the ribs. He fell back against the truck. I closed, grabbed his arm, and twisted, until he dropped the knife. I slammed his head against the side of the truck, and his eyes rolled up before he fell to the asphalt. I was winded and had to take a few breaths. In my condition, I was mighty glad I hadn't taken on both of them at once.

They'd parked in a good spot; our little fracas had attracted no attention. The other guy came out of the building, carrying two big white burger bags in one hand, head bowed against the rain. I ducked back around the truck and got a five-dollar bill out of my pocket. I ran around the semi and waited until the guy was past me, then came out behind him, running and panting noisily, flapping my poncho. He spun quickly, his free hand flashing to his belt, where his jacket probably covered a gun. But I stopped short and waved the bill around.

"Hey Mister, I think you dropped this," I said in the squeaky voice. His eyes automatically looked at the bill, enough for me to move in. I punched him hard in the solar plexus, and he slumped backwards to land on his butt, the breath knocked out of him. He gulped for air, clutching his injured middle. The bags of food he'd dropped lay on the ground, with spilled, catsup-covered french fries like bloody fingers.

I took his gun and removed his keys and driver's license from his trucker's wallet. One of the keys opened the truck door. Behind the seats was a tarp, and I had a look underneath. I found a pump-action shotgun, wrapped in an old cloth, and the toolbox. I took out the toolbox, using my handkerchief so I wouldn't leave fingerprints.

The driver was in pain, but still tried to talk. "You're a dead man," he wheezed.

I squatted on the pavement in front of him, with only a twinge from my abused body. "Tell Castle this is payback."

"Who are you?" he groaned.

"An entrepreneur."

"You're crazy."

"Maybe so," I agreed.

# CHAPTER 43

I opened the toolbox, still using the handkerchief to avoid leaving fingerprints. One section was filled with dozens of small plastic vials like the one I'd got from Royce's boat. Another had clear plastic bags with a white powder. These drugs were the proof I needed that Royce and Grossman were involved. Now to shake them up, see if maybe I could find out who killed Ben.

I needed a place to stash the box in safety, so I drove to the Greyhound terminal in Portland. I removed one of the vials, being careful not to leave fingerprints. I put the toolbox in a locker, fed some money in, and removed the key. I drove to Pine Haven, and the parking lot was uncrowded, the now-heavy rain discouraging sightseers.

Royce's car was parked in its usual spot, at the foot of his office, all covered up and protected against the rain. I thought about how he was so proud of that car, and how he had pushed drugs and got people killed so he could have expensive toys. If he got past me, he might try to run for it. So I'd slow him down.

I deflated a tire with my Swiss Army knife, and tore off the car cover. Then I picked up one of the big stones that marked the border of the driveway. The rock smashed through the windshield, mixing rain and glass and mud together on the dark, luxurious interior.

The steps up to Royce's office were slippery from the heavy rain. I went in without knocking.

Royce was on the telephone, and stared at me for a moment. "Let me call you back," he said into the receiver. "Something just came up." He hung up the phone and tried to wither me with a look. "You're dripping on my carpet."

"They don't have carpet where you'll be going." I set the vial on his desk. He saw it, his face going pinched and white. He got that wall-eyed look horses get when they're spooked.

"Tell me who killed Ben," I said, "and you get your toolbox back."

He stared at me a minute, before his eyes narrowed. I guessed what he was going to do, as he reached into his desk drawer and brought out a gun. I was counting on him not shooting me just yet.

"Where is it?" He was making a good effort not to sound panicked.

"I wasn't about to bring it with me." I held up the key. "I'll take you to it."

"Give me that," he snapped. I tossed it on the desk. He turned it over in his hand for a minute, and smiled. "Airport, or bus station?"

If he had a numbered key and had figured Portland, with only two obvious places to check, he didn't need me. He'd probably shoot me right then and there. I smiled back, thinking quickly.

"It was too big for the locker. So I put in my room key. After I changed where I was staying."

He swore under his breath, set down the key, and rubbed his face with his free hand. I could tell he wanted the toolbox more than he wanted to shoot me, and he had to keep me alive a little longer, in case I was telling the truth. He picked up the phone and made a call.

"Going somewhere?" I said. "Maybe a boat ride?"

"How'd you ...?" He looked startled, then shrugged. "That was my pilot's pager. A few minutes up the coast, and I'm gone."

"Life on the run?"

"With the money I've got, I can have a very nice, very long run."

"So why haven't you quit before now, if you've got so much?"

He shook his head. "You can never have enough."

He put the locker key and vial in his pocket, and kept the gun aimed at me, while he went to the safe in the corner. He spun the dial, opened the safe, and took out a gym bag. Trying to close the safe and juggle everything didn't look easy. He set down the bag and draped his suit jacket over the hand that held the gun. He retrieved the bag. "Let's go."

"Should I put my hands up?" I asked.

"Shut up and don't be stupid. Now move."

I opened the door slowly, and stepped out onto the landing. Rain lashed my face.

"Down the stairs."

I went down a couple of steps, and he came out onto the landing, looking annoyed when the rain hit him. He saw I hadn't gone very far.

"Keep going." He waved the gun like an old movie tough guy.

I took a couple more steps. He closed the door, then started down. Three waitresses came out of the side door of the hotel. Now was the time, while they were around. If this didn't work, and Royce killed me, I'd at least have witnesses.

"Hey, Royce, what happened to your car?"

"What?" I gave it a beat and spun around when I heard a gurgling sound. I got a hand under the gun, pushing it up as it went off. The bullet burned past my ear, and the blast made my ears ring. My other hand grabbed his leg behind the ankle, and I pulled. He hit the staircase rail and went over.

255

I ran to the bottom of the stairs and down the drive to the crumpled form on the asphalt. Royce looked like a rag tossed into a corner. I checked his pulse, but there wasn't any. The waitresses stood immobile, three looks of absolute horror.

A gray wave of emotion washed around inside me, but I refused to think about it.

"Is he ...?" One of them whispered. I nodded.

"Oh, God," she moaned.

"Listen to me," I said, standing up. Her eyes were rolling, trying to avoid the body, but drawn to it.

"Do you see that gun?" I said, pointing to it on the ground.

She nodded.

"Royce and Chef Grossman were part of a drug ring. Royce was going to kill me, and he fell. Go call the police. Ask for a Lieutenant McClaren of the Portland police and tell him what happened. Okay?" I snapped my fingers to get her to focus on me.

"Yes," she said slowly. She turned to go, but like Lot's wife, turned back for one final look, like she couldn't believe it. At least she didn't turn into salt. She scurried away, and the other two took off after her.

I took the vial and key from Royce's pocket, and scooped up the gym bag. I tucked the bag behind an ice machine in the hallway, on the way up to the kitchen, and covered it with my poncho.

"Hey Grossman!" I yelled at the top of the stairs. Everybody dropped whatever they were doing to stare at me. It was suddenly very quiet in the huge room. Grossman stood behind the line, glaring at me with narrowed eyes.

"What are you doing here? Get the hell out."

"I don't think so. Your buddy Royce just took a fall, and now it's your turn."

"What are you talking about?" Steam rose around him, as though he was some fat demon from Hell.

"I'm talking about the drugs that you helped distribute. About how it must have been you who poisoned Ben. Ringing any bells?"

He turned even redder. I piled it on.

"The state prison up in Thomaston will be good for you. On the food they serve, you should drop a couple hundred pounds. You know, for someone so ugly, you're also pretty stupid."

He roared out from behind the counter. Too late, I saw the big french knife in his hand, ten inches of professionally sharp-honed steel that could cut through bone, and open me up like a balloon. He struck at me, and I barely moved in time. But I felt something tug at my arm, and knew he hadn't missed completely.

He came forward, slashing with short, quick arcs that kept me from getting to his arm. Despite his bulk, he was fast, and I had trouble getting traction with my wet shoes.

I backed into the door of a walk-in cooler. He saw his chance and lunged, trying to jam the blade through me. I grabbed his arm and twisted, as he threw all his weight forward. There was a look of utter surprise on his face. He stepped back, the handle of the knife protruding from just below the breastbone, all ten inches of steel buried in him. He pawed at the handle, his mouth gaping, but no words came out. He took a wobbly step and crashed to the floor like a felled tree.

I felt wobbly myself. Blood flowed from the foot-long gash in my arm where he'd sliced me. I grabbed a white cloth from a nearby counter, slapped it hard over the wound, and held the arm up over my head.

"The police are on their way," I said. Nobody had moved; nobody spoke. They all looked in stunned silence at the white, bloody body, looking like a slaughtered whale in checkered pants.

"Got a first aid kit?" I asked.

"Yeah," said one of the cooks. It was Brian, the sous-chef. He returned in a moment with the box. He pulled back my cut sleeve, put compresses to the wound, and started taping it down.

He looked at me. "Did he really do what you said? Tried to kill Ben and all that other stuff?"

"Yeah."

"Serves the asshole right, then," he said, looking at the corpse.

# CHAPTER 44

The rain drove down harder as I made my way back to Portland. The police would have to wait, because now I had a lever to move the world. With Royce and Grossman accidentally dead, I needed to draw out Castle's men to find out who had killed Ben. And a toolbox full of drugs was nice bait.

Royce's gym bag was stuffed with money. I stashed it in the locker next to the one holding the toolbox, and mailed the key to Allison, with a note inside. I had Royce's prints on the locker key for the toolbox with the drugs inside, so I mailed that one to Lieutenant McClaren with another note. If I didn't make it, there'd still be some justice.

I sat in my car in the rain, thinking of how to even the odds against a group of armed men. I tried to envision a setting where they'd be at a disadvantage. Someplace unfamiliar, with no other people. Outdoors, then, in the driving rain, with different kinds of ground cover, and close by.

The rain reminded me of something Allison had said. Fort Williams, deserted on a rainy day. It had open vistas, but lots of places to hide. The outdoor noises, with the wind and waves and sound of the storm would do nicely. Castle's men hadn't seemed like the outdoor type. I doubted if any of them had been to a park since they were kids.

The more I thought about it, the more I liked it. I closed my eyes and remembered the layout, figuring out a rough vantage point where I could see everything without being seen, and still move when I had to.

I stopped at a pay phone and made the call. Some efficient soul picked up on the second ring.

"Let me speak to Castle," I said.

"Who's this?"

"The guy who paid the visit the other night."

"You wanna try coming back? You and I got some unfinished business."

"Yeah, he must have chewed your ass pretty good over that one. Listen, I'd love to chat, but I've got a toolbox of his I know he's going to want back. Be a good flunky and go get him, huh?"

"I'm gonna find you someday."

"Can't wait," I said. There was silence on the other end as the master was fetched.

I recognized Tony's voice when he said, "You're a dead man, you know that?"

"Tony, is that any way to greet an old friend? I've got some merchandise of yours I thought you'd want back. I took it from a couple of truck drivers."

"You son-of-a-bitch!"

"Name-calling won't get you your package. One hundred grand will, however. That'll give me enough to get away from here and out of your hair. What do you say?"

"All this for a shakedown?" He sounded disgusted.

"Hey, we all have bills. You interested?"

"We can deal."

"Great. Have the money in an hour. I'll meet you at Fort Williams, out by the lighthouse in South Portland. You know where it is?"

"Yeah."

"As you go in, there's a road off to the left, leads out to a point, with some stone ruins. I'll meet you out front of the ruins there. One hour if you want your merchandise back. No tricks or it's gone."

I hung up. Maybe he'd think I was stupid and greedy enough to expect him to show up with the money. After all, that was the kind of world he lived in. He'd try to kill me, of course, but I planned to get there first and be ready. I took along some duct tape in case I had to tie anyone up.

I parked my rented car and hoofed it in, scouting the territory. The rain came in like silver spikes, and the park was indeed deserted. The bruised color of the sky cast a gloomy, desolate pall over everything. The ocean pounded angrily against the shore, hissing spray driving high over the rocks.

It was a miserable day to be out. Just right for what I had in mind. There was some heavy equipment parked in the field to the left: a backhoe, bulldozer, and dump truck. A dozen huge mounds of dirt stood like pyramids, providing plenty of cover, with plenty of room to lead a chase. In the middle of the park was a stretch of trees, from where I could see everything. I found a spot where the leaves sheltered me, and got the binoculars ready, squinting into the one good lens.

Fifteen minutes later, a big, black Lincoln pulled up to the gate. A man in a camouflaged rain poncho got out and went to the trunk. He pulled out a case, closed the trunk, and jogged toward my area in the trees. I moved back to where I could see him without being seen. He made it to the trees and started working his way forward, down toward the water. When he was near the point where the trees ended and the open space began, he stopped and set down the case. He pulled out a walkie-talkie and spoke into it before setting that down as well. He opened the case and began to take things out of it. I was close now and could see that the pieces were parts of a rifle he was assembling. He was setting up as the sniper, to pick me off when I showed myself. Their insurance policy that I was about to cancel.

The sound of the wind and rain covered my movements, and I got right up behind him. He was attaching the high-powered scope when I deliberately cleared my throat.

The barrel of the rifle came swinging around as he moved. I grabbed the rifle and yanked in the same direction, pulling him off balance. I cracked a fist into his mouth as he stumbled, and twisted the rifle out of his hands. I snapped the butt of the gun back up into his jaw, following with the barrel up against the other side of his head. He crumpled to the ground, out cold. His hat fell off, and it was Castle's bodyguard, the one who'd wanted a rematch.

I pulled the bolt from the rifle and threw it away. I propped him up with his back against a tree, put the rifle lengthwise behind the tree, pulled his arms back, and bound them to the rifle. His head got wrapped to the tree, and I covered his eyes with the tape. I also put some over his mouth, so he couldn't yell to his buddies, although I doubted they'd have heard him.

A sweep with the binoculars showed the Lincoln parked in the lot down below. I ditched everything and jogged to the bulldozer. Using the dirt piles as cover, I moved until I was in the trees on the other side, with my back to the beach and the ruins. There was a steep bank next to the entry road, from where I could launch an attack. My whole grand plan to stop a group of armed men involved a few rocks.

Finally, they left the car and came into view, wearing hats and trenchcoats, walking slowly in the driving rain. Moose and Ray had pump-action shotguns, Slick had some kind of revolver in his good hand, and Speed carried a little submachine-gun, maybe a MAC-10 or an UZI. The only things they were missing were a flamethrower and some grenades.

Moose was point man, Slick and Ray a few paces behind, with Speed bringing up the rear. Ray didn't look happy about being included in the hunting party. He was probably here on punishment detail. From the way he waved the barrel of his shotgun around as he twitched from side to side, there was a good chance he'd accidentally pull the trigger on one of his compatriots and do part of my job for me.

They moved without talking, taking their time. Speed wasn't living up to his name any longer, lumbering along with some difficulty and lagging behind. I stayed down until the first three passed, then quietly hoisted a rock over my head. It was more of a drop than a throw, and I couldn't miss from this distance. Speed heard me at the last second, but couldn't get out of the way, or bring the gun around fast enough. The rock hit his head with a plop and I rolled away as shotgun blasts and bullets tore the hell out of the bushes all around me. As I wriggled backwards, I heard them.

"He killed him. Jesus, look at the blood. That bastard killed him."

"Shut up Ray," Slick said. "He's still breathing."

"We gotta get him to a doctor. We gotta—"

There was the sound of a slap.

"Listen to me, you stupid shit. We're out here to kill a man. You understand that? We'll get the fucking doctor later. You got that?"

"Yeah, but—"

"No buts, Ray. We gotta work fast. Let's get this bastard and get outta here."

So now they were three. Moose put the submachine gun around his thick neck, where it seemed to get in his way. Ray looked close to panic.

Since I wanted to lead them to the point, I ran ahead and broke from the trees where they could see me, sprinting across the grass. Two shotgun blasts boomed, and the revolver cracked, but I was far enough away and moving. They were probably wondering where their sniper had gone.

Once at the ruins, I ducked out of sight. My pursuers came at a fast trot. There were two square rooms up above, where the walls went only halfway up. The roof was only a few feet off the ground at the back, and there was a walkway directly in front of the rooms. Someone would have to come all the way around to the back to see me, and they'd have to be looking in several directions, in case of ambush. There were plenty of places to hide to divert their attention, and room to roll and get some stone between me and their gunfire.

Slick gave orders as they came up. "You go up top. Ray, go to the left, up those stairs. Stay in sight and cover each other."

"Where will you be?"

"Right down here, Ray, to cover your fucking back and keep that shitbird from squirting out the side, or doubling back down along those rocks and getting behind us."

Moose came along the walkway. The rain had made everything slippery. I gripped a rock and got ready. A seagull cried out overhead, so I took it as a cue. I popped up and fired the rock like a pitcher hurling a fastball.

It caught Moose a solid one in the face, and the shotgun went off. Moose hit the walkway rail with the backs of his legs, and was so tall, he kept going over.

Slick was screaming at Ray to cut me off as I dashed to the next room. From one side of the wall, I heard Ray pounding down along the other side. I waited by the end, intending to jump him when he came around. But suddenly Ray stopped. I heard his wheezing breath around the corner, and smelled his cologne, mixed with sweat and fear.

If I could get the gun pointed away from me, I could come around the wall and get him. I lobbed a rock up onto the roof. The shotgun blasted, and I was moving. He saw me and swung the gun back, but too late. I grabbed the barrel in one hand, and punched him with the other. Then I put both hands on the shotgun, twisted, and ripped it away from him. I swung it at him, hitting him hard in the stomach. He collapsed like a popped balloon.

Bullets struck the rock as I ducked back down behind the wall. Slick had come up the other side. On hands and knees, I made it over to the head of the stairs, then burst from cover and raced down, rolling off to the right at the bottom. Two more shots came after me.

Now it was one-on-one, and if I wanted to, I could hide from him in a dozen places. There were tunnels in the walls, dark and deep. Suicidal for a lone man to check out with the threat of ambush. The game was a draw, because he couldn't flush me out by himself, and I couldn't come after him because he had his gun.

"Hey," he yelled to be heard above the noise of the waves and the rain. "You want to know who popped your buddy? It was me. What do you think of that?"

He was trying to sucker me into coming out after him. My throat closed up.

"Want to know how I did it? We got that fat cook out at the resort to set him up. He started talking to him, and I blew his brains out, sitting right next to him. Made a hell of a mess, too."

I didn't answer, but pounded the ground.

"I had to laugh when I did it. Little prick wanted to screw up our operation, so we swatted him like a bug. Nobody even cared. They came and scraped him out of the car and into a plastic bag and threw him out with the rest of the garbage. What do you think of that?"

"I think you're about to suffer," I said, coming out of hiding. Slick's eyes grew wide, but he checked his impulse for a fast shot, letting me get closer, to make sure of his kill.

"How's the arm, Slick?" I said, now playing his game. Rattle the opponent, get them mad, and maybe they miss by a fraction, enough to make the difference.

"Do you remember how it felt when it snapped? I'm going to do the same to your other one. You're going to need someone to feed you and wipe your ass for a long time. And when you get out of the casts up there in state prison, you know what's going to happen?"

He watched me like a snake watches a mouse, calculating the distance and my chance of reaching cover when he started shooting.

"Your organization won't be there to support you, Slick. It'll all be gone. You won't be able to fight with those shattered arms, so you're going to be anybody's bitch. They're going to use you for fun and games. You're going to be lying there in your bunk, wondering when the next guy is going to come for you. You ready for that?"

Through the red mist of my anger, I looked him in the eye as I came toward him, and his grin got wider. He swept the gun up as I ducked and rolled. I felt the bullet tear across the skin of my cheek. I changed the direction of my roll, and the second shot hit empty ground. Then a click. He couldn't believe I was still alive, and on my feet. Shooting with an unfamiliar gun in his off hand had made the difference. Now he had nothing. He opened his mouth to say something, but my punch cut him off. He staggered back, bleeding.

"How come you're not laughing?" I said, hitting him in the stomach. "Isn't this funny now?" I hit him again, watching his eyes as he absorbed the pain.

"You know the worst part?" I was shaking now. "You're not even worth it." One more punch made him fall back against the wall. I snapped out a hard sidekick, but his knees buckled, and the edge of my foot caught him in the throat, instead of in the chest. His eyes bugged out as he clawed at the air. He made a horrible, wet sound through his crushed windpipe, and fell over. His thrashing turned to twitching, and then he lay still.

I stood there, swaying in the rain. The side of my face was numb where the bullet had grazed it. The red mist began to clear from the world. My knees shook, and I tried to walk. After a few steps, I fell down and threw up.

There was no joy in my vengeance, just a hollowness. I sat in the rain, in a place of death, with pain throbbing in my head, and the sour taste of ashes in my mouth.

# CHAPTER 45

Castle was the man in charge, but he hadn't come on the mission. His type stayed safely at home and let the foot soldiers do the grunt work. I wasn't about to take a chance on him using his influence and money to escape justice. I got to my car and headed back toward Falmouth. I made a stop on the way to call the police, to send them to clean up the mess I'd left behind.

The rain continued to pour down as I took my old route over the wall to Castle's property. I stood on his back patio, wondering how to get in without being heard. I couldn't think of anything, so I decided to just bull my way in. There was a big gas grill on the patio, and I smashed it through the French doors, following it in.

There wasn't a sound, an outcry, any noise, but I had the impression the place wasn't deserted. I searched the rooms carefully but quickly, and saw the door to Castle's study wide open. Peering around the corner, I saw Castle himself seated behind his desk. There was a gun on the desk, inches away from his hand.

I came in and let him see me, tensed for a sudden spring if he went for the gun. He seemed twenty years older than

267

the last time I'd seen him, and he looked at me with tired eyes.

"You," he said.

"You're done for," I replied. "The police have your boys, and will get enough to put you away."

Castle made a sound like grinding metal.

"Why?" he said. "Who the fuck are you, come here like a hurricane and blow apart my organization? Who sent you?"

"You killed my friend."

"That cook? Jesus Christ, are you serious? That fat chef didn't leave us no choice. It wasn't personal, just business."

"Just business?" I felt the anger rise again. "You kill a man, and it's just business? Well, you're out of business."

"Don't I know it," he said. He looked at the gun.

"Go ahead," I said. "Do some more shooting, but it won't save you."

"All this," Castle said, looking around the room. "Everything I've worked for, gone because of a couple of fucking cooks."

There was such a note of regret in his voice, I stopped.

"You don't even consider how many lives you've ruined, do you?"

"I got a daughter going to college in a few weeks." He shook his head.

"She know her daddy kills people?"

"I keep my family out of the business," he snarled at me.

"Well, good for you," I said. "What a terrific father. Maybe she can come visit you in prison."

"You still don't get it, do you?"

I stood there thinking as I dripped water. It finally came to me. Castle had been waiting for the news. He hadn't even got up when he heard me crash in. He'd never go to prison.

"The people you work for don't allow failure. And you've got a family."

I heard a siren off in the distance. I wasn't sure if it was coming this way, but I took it as a cue, and backed out of the room.

"Time's up, Tony."

"None of this was supposed to happen," he whined.

"Should have thought of that before you released your dogs. I'd have my friend, and you'd have your empire."

He was looking at the far wall now, and there was nothing more to say. I walked back toward the hole I'd made, and as I left, I heard the single shot ring out.

Dale T. Phillips

# CHAPTER 46

My arm was stitched back together and hurt like hell, the head graze had taken off a chunk of scalp and hair, and the angry blister along my cheek, courtesy of Slick's bullet, stung like the bite of fire ants. They'd brought a meal at some point, which I hadn't touched. I was still loopy from the painkillers when Allison came in.

She didn't look very happy with me as she inspected the new stitches with a critical eye. "What was it this time?"

"I got them. The ones that killed Ben. It's over now."

"How'd this happen?" She pointed to my arm.

"Chef at the resort. Butcher knife."

"God. And this?" She ran a finger along the head bandage.

"They tried to shoot me, too. Didn't work. Maybe they should try hanging."

"How can you joke about this?"

"Nervous reaction. I killed somebody. Never done that before."

She looked at me with horror. "And those other men that were brought in. You did that, too?"

"They tried to kill me."

"You lead a very frightening life."

"Not anymore."

"You're finally going to let the police take over?"

"The guy that killed Ben is dead. The rest are going to jail. Good enough."

"So you'll settle down now?"

"One more thing," I said, thinking of Maureen. "A little trip, it'll take a couple days."

"And then?"

"Depends. Want me around?"

"Maybe," she said. "But we can't have any more of this."

I was about to tell her how I felt, but the door flew open as McClaren charged in. His suit was rumpled, and his face was haggard, as if he'd had a very long and troubled day. He stood by my bed, clenching and unclenching his fists, as he said to Allison. "Excuse me, Ma'am, but I need to talk to this man right now, on police business."

"Are you going to assault him?"

McClaren glowered at me. "I might."

"Good. Smack some sense into him, then."

"Wait," I said, and pointed to the tray of food. "Tell him he can have the Jell-o. Just don't let him hit me."

Allison made a sound and left the room.

McClaren turned on me. "You stupid, sorry, son-of-a-bitch. I've got bodies everywhere."

"Could you stop yelling? My head hurts." I reached up, touching the bandage.

"Your head hurts. You're goddamn lucky to be alive."

"Only because of the wonders of medical science," I said. "Sure you don't want the Jell-o? It's red."

McClaren sighed, pulled over a visitor's chair, and sat down. "When you get done with your comedy routine, maybe you'll tell me what happened. How the hell did you stop five armed men?"

"Split them up and picked them off."

"I'll say you did." McClaren held up a hand and ticked off fingers as he spoke. "One dead, one in a coma, one with a broken back, one with a broken jaw, and the other talking nonstop. Guess I underestimated you. Should have thrown you in a cell the first time I saw you. So talk about Pine Haven."

"Royce had a getaway plan. Private plane. He pulled a gun on me, but slipped on the stairs. Grossman came at me with a knife, fell on it."

"What a mess." McClaren shook his head.

"Get that key?"

"And that. What in the hell were you thinking?"

"Sorry. I was in a hurry. But you wanted to find out about those drugs. I tailed Grossman, and saw him pick up the package from a pulp truck. Somebody up in the woods making this stuff?"

"It came down from Canada. Those guys at the resort set it up so they would take a cut and spread it around."

"Sounds like a big operation," I said.

"The best part is, your buddy Royce left behind a notebook listing all his customers, either for insurance or a little blackmail on the side. Going to keep lawyers from Maine to New York busy for the next few years."

"How did Royce and Grossman get involved?" I asked.

McClaren stood up and went over to the window. He peeked through the blinds, then paced around the room as he spoke. "Royce has a history with big deals. Ski resorts, condo developments, places with people who have too much money. He and Grossman worked together. Grossman was a boozer who liked to beat up women. Royce bailed him out of a couple of bad situations, and from then on, he owned him.

"They were at a West Palm Beach club which was a money-laundering operation for the south Florida crime families. Feds were finally about to get something on the owners, from an accountant who was about to become a very big embarrassment. But he up and died rather suddenly. You'll never guess how."

"Amanita mushrooms."

McClaren nodded. "Bastards walked, that time. But your friend survived," he said. "So they panicked. How'd he get mixed up in this, anyway?"

"Sheer accident. He got in the way, and they killed him."

"I'd say you paid them back."

I looked away. "All of them put together still aren't worth his life."

"Yeah." There was a minute of awkward silence.

"Am I under arrest?" I asked, looking back at him.

"As long as you testify, you probably won't go to jail, although if I had my way ..." He paced back to the window and looked out once more. "Just to let you know, there's reporters swarming all over downtown, and more flying in."

"I'm not much for headlines."

"Good. Keep your mouth shut, and we won't say anything. There's plenty of people willing to take the credit for this one. But I still wish we could have done it by the rules."

"I wish we couldn't have done it at all."

McClaren looked at the food tray.

"Seriously, help yourself," I said.

He gave me a sour look. "I haven't eaten since lunch, and I've been running around cleaning up after you. Right now I'm so hungry I could eat the ass-end out of a moose, but I wouldn't touch that stuff."

"Yeah, I know what you mean."

McClaren sat down again, and ran a hand over his face as if to wash away all the tired. One of my unanswered questions came to mind.

"Which one of them tried to do me with the truck?"

McClaren laughed. "Great detective you are. It wasn't them. You've got plenty of enemies."

"Then who?"

"Guy by the name of William Dobbins."

"Who's that?"

"Hangs around that karate guy Thibodeaux. Nicknamed Chip."

"Christ." I lay back on the pillow. What an idiot I was.

McClaren went on. "Kid thought he was being real smart. Took the truck a whole thirty miles away to get it fixed. It matched the report we'd put out, and the owner called us. Ten minutes of questioning and the kid broke down."

"Did he say why?"

"Apparently you put the mojo on his main man Thibodeaux. Kid says he's not the same since you knocked him on his ass. Figured with you off the scene, Thibodeaux might get the lead back in his pencil or something."

"What's he looking at?"

"Three to five years."

I shook my head. "They'll eat him alive in there."

"He almost killed you, and you feel sorry for him?"

"The kid needs counseling. He's pretty messed up."

"Feel free to go to the sentencing and recommend it."

"What about Beaulier?"

McClaren smiled and leaned back in the chair. "Let me guess. Your humanitarian streak does not extend that far."

"He's the one that should be locked up."

"Oh, he is, never fear. At the hospital, the stupid bastard was caught trying to jimmy the lock where the drugs are kept, while he was still in his hospital gown. And all this while on parole. He'll be taking a three-year trip."

"Good."

McClaren got to his feet. "So if you're through playing sheriff, can I have my badge back?"

"It's all yours. I'm through with this stuff."

"So what are you going to do now?"

I lay back and looked at the ceiling. "I have no idea."

Dale T. Phillips

# CHAPTER 47

The long drive down to Carolina wasn't as bad as it had been coming up from Miami. It gave me time to think, now that I had a life in front of me and no idea of what to do with it. I wasn't going back to Miami, or back to the life of the night people. I'd live in the daytime for a while.

My hope was that Maureen was ready to grab a lifeline and get out. Most people are too afraid of the unknown to do the thing they really need to do. I couldn't make the decision for her, but at least she'd have that chance. Probably her last one.

I slept through the day in a motel, about a half-hour's drive from Maureen's. I was hungry when I got up, but didn't eat anything, as I'd be fighting soon. I stretched slowly and completely, then shadow-boxed until I had the timing. I put my stuff in the car and checked out. Then I drove to yet one more battleground, hopefully my last.

It was early in the evening when I pulled into the yard by the shabby trailer. Bobby Lee sat in a lawn chair, drinking beer, watching me pull in. He picked up his head, an animal in his den sensing trouble.

As I got out, I smelled the same odor of decay and failure hanging in the air as before.

"What you want?" Bobby Lee knew my arrival did not presage anything good, but he hadn't got up yet.

"Is Maureen in?"

"What? What the hell's that to you?"

"Hey, Maureen," I shouted. A curtain twitched, and the door of the trailer opened as Maureen looked out. Bobby Lee was dumbfounded, and swung his head to look back from her to me.

"I'm here, if you'd like to leave," I said, ignoring him. She had a fresh bruise on her cheek. At least it would be her last one from him.

"You been messin' round on me, you no-good bitch?" Bobby Lee crushed his empty beer can, and let it fall to the ground as he heaved himself up out of his chair. "I'll fix you good."

"You're not fixing anything," I said. "Maureen is leaving. Say goodbye."

"She ain't goin' innywhere. You get back inside." He pointed a finger at her. "I'll take care 'a you later."

I shook my head. "Bobby Lee, she is not the reason your life sucks. She doesn't deserve the beatings you give her."

"What the hell you know about my life? And how you know my name?"

He glared at me and snapped his fingers. Then the big pointing finger was aimed at me.

"I know you. You was here before." He nodded. "Prob'ly come by a lot when I'm not here." He shot a glance at Maureen, who still stood in the door of the trailer. "Well I'm gonna take care of lover-boy here. He won't look so good when I get done with him. Then it's your turn, missy."

Maureen could take no more. She closed the door, retreating to the inside. Bobby Lee took this as a surrender, and turned to grin at me. The grin reminded me of Slick, and I felt a sour taste in my mouth.

"I will tell you this one time," I said. "I don't want to fight you, but I will because you want it, and it's the only thing you understand, and it's the only way to make you stop. Remember, you wanted this."

"Oh, I want it all right. I'm gonna break you in half. I boxed for three years in the Navy."

"No shit," I replied.

"I was fleet heavyweight champeen. How you like that, smart boy?"

I didn't like it at all. I wasn't fond of pure boxing, because it was so much better to use your legs in a fight. His size and skill worried me, because he could do some real damage with those big hands. Boxing is a game that favors the bigger, stronger man. If he got his weight behind a good punch, he'd crush me. And he wasn't the type to stop the punishment when an opponent was down. If I lost here, I would be crippled or killed.

But I had to beat him at his own game, so he wouldn't be able to claim foul afterward. He would remember getting beat at what he did best, by a guy who was a good deal smaller.

Bobby Lee went into his stance, hands up, shuffling and snorting as he came toward me. I circled, giving him plenty of room. He fired off several jabs, which I had no trouble avoiding. He was getting back into the old pattern, throwing shots, bobbing and weaving, putting together combinations. I kept circling, changing the distance, making him move.

"Whassa matter, boy? You wouldn't be scared now, would ya?" He huffed out the words. Good. Let him use up his oxygen. He'd be needing it before long. Sweat was already rolling down both of us, and the dust rose in the yard from our scuffling feet. I could smell him from several feet away.

After he bounced a few harmless punches off my shoulders and arms, he rushed me and landed a hard right. It caught me in the head, and staggered me. I dodged and ducked and backpedaled for my life, trying not to let him follow it up. He tried to catch me, but the years of beer and fried chicken and sitting on an old couch had taken their toll, and he was losing his wind.

All the while, I was timing him and getting his pattern. As he tired, he started telegraphing his punches, giving away where he was going to throw by the way he set up. He had a good combination, but he didn't vary it enough. He'd shoot a couple of jabs with his left, follow with a hard right, a left uppercut, and sometimes another right. All of which was great if the opponent stood still, which I wasn't doing. And every thrown punch cost him a little more air. He was gulping for it now, at that stage where you can't get enough to keep everything working. I thumbed the sweat out of my eyes. Bobby Lee looked like he'd been drenched with a bucket of water.

It was time to go on the offensive. When the big right came in, I sidestepped and drove my own right hand into his stomach, and followed with a left hook to the eye. I danced back out before he could retaliate. The hurt showed, and he sucked air for a minute before coming back in.

When he was in range, I dropped my left shoulder for a fake and rocked him with a hard right straight to the nose, a left under the ribs, and followed up with a right to his other eye. He stumbled backwards, bleeding from his now broken nose. His right eye was starting to puff up, and he'd lost a lot of steam, but he wasn't done yet. I'd thrown good, solid punches that connected the way I wanted them to, and the guy was coming back for more. He'd have torn me apart in his prime, or in a ring, where I couldn't get away.

He lunged forward. I blocked his weakened right, drove another shot deep into the belly, and came up with a hard left uppercut that snapped his jaw shut. He backed up again and spit out a mouthful of blood, having bitten his tongue. The broken nose made it hard for him to breathe, and his other eye was puffing and bleeding from a cut over it. He was a mess, and I felt a surge of pity.

"We can stop anytime," I said.

"Thun of a bits," he mumbled, spraying blood. He shook his head to clear it and came in once more. I jabbed at his face to bring his hands up to protect it, and when his belly was exposed, I hammered a pair of shots in. He was a stationary target now, and I hit him four or five more times and backed away. He sank to his knees and dropped onto all fours, panting like a dog. I was breathing hard myself by this time, and gratefully took an oxygen break. Bobby Lee threw up all the beer he'd been drinking. He looked finished, but I kept my eye on him while I crossed to the trailer.

"How you doing Maureen?" I called out. She appeared at the door and saw Bobby Lee down. She went back in. As I stood there, Bobby Lee watched me like a sneaky dog.

I half-turned away, and saw the movement from the corner of my eye as he hurled a rusty gas can. The can bounced off my left arm where I'd been cut, hitting square on my stitches, and hurting like hell. When I looked up, Bobby Lee was standing between me and the car, holding a metal-toothed rake. I sighed, amazed at his capacity for stupidity. Most of all, I was astounded to find I wasn't even angry. It was good to have this much control. I was even willing to give him another chance to quit.

"Up to now, Bobby Lee, you've got off pretty light," I said, though anybody seeing his face would have disagreed. "So if you put down the rake, we'll call it quits and you can go put some ice on that face. Otherwise, you'll be going to the hospital. Your choice."

Bobby Lee gripped the rake defiantly and came at me. He used the rake in the same pattern as he boxed, jabbing with the handle and following it with a vicious overhand slash with the metal teeth. I caught the handle and twisted the rake horizontally between us. I butted my head into his broken nose and kicked him hard in the groin. I slammed the handle against the side of his head, pulled the rake from his grip, and jammed the wooden end into his gut. Throwing the rake aside, I caught his arm as he swiped at me, and broke it at the elbow. He'd never throw that big thundering right again. When I let go, he collapsed in the dirt of the yard.

Maureen appeared once more, with a suitcase in her hand. She followed me to the car, stopping to look at Bobby Lee, who was crying and holding his arm. She hesitated, and looked like she might go to him. I was about to say something, but held my breath. She had to leave under her own power, not under my influence.

Maureen watched him for maybe a minute. She brushed the hair out of her face, and the hand lingered on the bruise there.

She turned away abruptly, and came to the car. "Let's get out of here."

She never looked back as we drove away, and was silent for a long time. My arm throbbed in pain, but it was a small thing compared to being free of the crippling rage. The battles were over, the debts paid, and I didn't have to fight anymore.

Somewhere near the border of Tennessee, it began to rain. Big drops snapped against the windshield, and Maureen started as if she'd woken up from a long sleep.

She looked at me and looked away, bowing her head. "He'd 'a kilt me if I'd stayed."

"Yeah. Not only can't he live with anyone else, he can't live with himself, either."

"I know what it's like, blaming yourself."

Me, too, I thought, though I didn't say it. "What happened to Ben wasn't your fault. Or mine. Other people did it, and they're dead or in jail."

She was quiet, studying me. "You'll tell me about it later."

"Yes."

"It's gonna be tough." She sighed.

I reached over and opened the glove compartment, taking out the manila envelope. I tossed it in her lap. She looked at it, and then at me before opening the flap. She fingered a thick sheaf of hundred-dollar bills, and looked at me with wonder.

"A gift from Ben," I said, and in a way it was. Ben had died for that pile of money, so I viewed it as a kind of death benefit payout.

"Keep it," I said. "He'd want you to start over and be happy."

"I don't know if I can do that."

"The best thing about us is that each day we can choose," I said, thinking of myself as well. "If you can easily forgive someone as bad as Bobby Lee, why can't you forgive yourself?"

She was silent after that for a long while. After a time, I left her in a place in the Midwest I'd found out about, a place where women could go and get away from their past, and get some help to build a future. I drove back to Maine, thinking about a woman, and a dead friend, and wasted years of guilt and pain.

Maybe it was time for me to start living as well.

Dale T. Phillips

# CHAPTER 48

I rang the bell on the big porch. Allison came to the door and let me in. We went into the living room, and I sank into a chair.

She looked me in the eye. "There's something you want to tell me."

"And how do you know that?"

"You wrinkle your brow."

"Oh. I drove down to North Carolina to see Ben's ex-wife, tell her what happened." I knew she'd worry if I told her about Bobby Lee, so I said nothing. Here I was, just starting a relationship, and already I was keeping secrets.

"Nothing dangerous, though, right?" She was frowning.

"Hey, come on, I'm the guy who took on the whole Northeast syndicate, remember?"

"I remember," she said, not smiling. "How's your arm?"

"Still sore, but that's all. Everything else is working a hundred percent." I waggled my eyebrows up and down for suggestive emphasis.

"Uh-huh."

"There's something here I've been missing all my life. You. And a place to belong."

Allison favored me with a fleeting half-smile, and hesitated a moment before asking her question. "Do you think you can forgive yourself now?"

I searched for the words. "There's a line in Coleridge's *Rime of the Ancient Mariner*," I said. "'The man hath penance done, and penance more will do.' I'll remember Tim and Ben, but I can live my life for me now. With your help, I think I can put some of the anger and guilt away. Maybe I can change them into something else."

Allison took my hand in hers and smiled. Her love cut through my inner gloom, and brought light to places where there hadn't been any. She was a healer, all right.

She led me to the bedroom slowly, dancing in a swaying rhythm. She took her time undressing me, kissing each portion of my skin as it was uncovered. Then it was my turn, and I took even longer. Finally we were both naked, touching and tasting hungrily.

Some time later, we lay wrapped in each other. We drifted off to sleep, still clinging to each other, like survivors of a disaster. I finally fell asleep, and saw no ghosts that night.

THE END

## *LIKE MORE ZACK TAYLOR?*

Sign up for my newsletter to get discounts on upcoming titles
   OR- Get a free ebook or audio book
   At http://www.daletphillips.com

## *A FALL FROM GRACE*

*When a small-town single mother is wrongly accused of murder, Zack Taylor must work to clear her name. Not an easy task, as the whole town believes her guilty. Zack finds, however, plenty of people who wanted the victim dead. He discovers that when small-town politics mix with big-time ambition, the combination can be lethal.*

**Read on for the exciting first chapter in *A Fall From Grace*, the second book of the Zack Taylor series.**

## CHAPTER 1

The jailhouse lay before us, an ugly, squat, building full of menace. Pelted by the November sleet, I was unable to make myself move, like a fear-frozen kid on a high-dive board. Allison looked at me, waiting for me to make good on my promise to go inside with her. I had agreed for love's sake, and now had to plunge into a lake of broken glass to help out a stranger.

Allison came to me trembling. She shielded us with the three-dollar umbrella she'd bought at a LaVerdiere's drugstore on the way. It had improbable yellow daisies in defiance of the locale and the weather, and reeked with a sharp smell of bad vinyl. Sleet crackled on its surface.

My arm went around her and I put my head against hers, her scarf tickling my nose.

"I don't want to go in either," she said. "But we have to."

Yeah. So we did. But I was in another jail, on the other side of the country, where I'd been more than a dozen years ago. Flashbacks came in lightning flickers, illuminating painful memories that had lain long buried.

There was no way for her to fathom how close I had come to dying as that piece of my life was torn from me. She could run her fingers over the puckered silver-dollar-sized sunburst mass on my torso like a bad appendectomy, or the jagged red ridge forking off from my eyebrow. But she couldn't conceive of prison's constant assault on the senses, or the life-bludgeoning despair and hate.

I'd like to think that maybe she wouldn't have asked if she had known how much it hurt, but then again, maybe that didn't matter. Family was involved, blood thicker than water and all that. Anyway we were here, and I had to make my feet move, make myself go voluntarily behind bars once again. It felt like digging my own grave.

I breathed deeply, trying to ease the constriction in my chest. With an effort of will, I pushed the ghosts back and looked once more at the buildings and the fences strung with concertina wire. I had got out, I was free. I could walk in here and walk out again this time. Okay.

We went together toward the huge steel doors of the entrance. Twitching like a junkie, with pounding pulse and a dry mouth, I showed my ID, filled out a form, signed Zack Taylor with a trembling hand on the visitor sheet, and passed through a metal detector. Cameras with unblinking red Cyclopean eyes stared down from the walls. The pat-down for contraband made me shudder. It felt too much like being an inmate again.

The faces on the guards were the same as I remembered, as pitiless and immobile as the carved heads of Aztec gods. The only reaction they showed was in the eyes, taking in everything and measuring everyone by level of threat.

My shoulders were hunched and tight. I had to force myself to stand erect and look at faces instead of at shoes. In prison, a straight-on look to anybody is usually taken as a challenge, and you simply don't look a guard in the eye, even when he talks to you.

One of the guards gave me a sharp double take and whispered to a cohort. The other looked over and gave the first an almost imperceptible nod. The first one stepped away. Panic sweat traced the length of my spine. I wanted so badly to run back through the heavy doors to the cold outside air.

The guard came back, and gave a slight shrug, while I pretended not to look. We started moving to the next door, and I started breathing again.

The outer rings of personnel were all males, but as we got deeper in, it was all women, though they had the same stone faces. The hell that I'd been in had smelled of sweat, piss, and misery. This jail smelled of industrial cleaner.

We were taken to a room separated from the prisoners by thick, wired glass. We sat on hard plastic chairs while they brought Bonnie in to the other side. She looked like a terrified mouse, small and pitiful inside the shapeless gray jail outfit. She had a half-moon cut under one eye, with a telltale discolored bruise.

Looking at her, I didn't see a killer. In the many years I'd spent studying people, I'd seen those who had killed, and I could tell. This woman was lost in a nightmare, and she looked at us like a drowning person sees a rescue rope. She picked up the phone on her side, while Allison put her head against mine as I held the one on ours.

289

"Kelly's fine," Allison said. This was just what Bonnie needed, and I saw some of her tension ease. "She's doing well. You'll see her soon. We'll get you out of this."

Bonnie's throat worked as she tried to speak, but she broke down and sobbed. A jail matron came over and handed her a tissue, an act of human kindness I'd not thought possible in this place.

Allison put her hand on the glass and spoke.

"This is Zack, honey, you remember? He grew up on a turkey farm out in California. That's right. Thousands and thousands of turkeys, just like him."

I laughed, and Bonnie half-smiled. I saw more tension drain away. Allison knew her stuff.

I chimed in. "And here we are, close to Thanksgiving. So I'm getting a little edgy. How about you, Bonnie?"

"They think I killed him."

"Yeah," I said. "But hang tight. This is rough, but you'll get through it. When someone's killed, the cops like to arrest someone quickly. So they take the shortest route. But we'll get you a good lawyer, get some lab tests done, prove there are other people they should look at."

She looked stricken. "I ... don't have the money for all that."

Allison jumped in. "Don't worry about that. We'll see that everything is done. We'll get you out."

"It's awful in here. The other women. You can't believe the things they say."

"Yeah, it's what they do for entertainment," I said. I looked at her eye. "Did they give you that cut?"

Bonnie touched the wound. "No, he did this to me, the day he was—"

"Okay," I cut her off. "Instead of thinking about what they say in here, think about what you'll say to your daughter when you see her."

"They said the state would take her away from me."

"Because they want to see your pain. Don't talk to them, don't answer back."

She nodded again, very serious, seeming to absorb what I'd said. She might make it.

"So how's the food?" I asked, trying to gauge what she had left. "Good, huh? That gray stuff is the best. Too bad you won't be in for Thanksgiving. You get a whole spoonful of green mashed potatoes."

She smiled a little and shook her head.

"Actually," I went on, "it's better if you mold it into sculptures. Decorate the cell for everyone, since you'll be out soon. Just think, you can be the Martha Stewart of Cell Block D."

She snorted. Definitely a good sign.

# AFTERWORD

Maine is a wonderful place, a land of mystery, magic, and madness. Driving there from elsewhere in the country requires that you first pass through New Hampshire—some sort of test. Maine is the extreme, almost-forgotten corner of the country, jammed up against Canada. Parts of it are years behind the rest of the country, and going there can be like going back in time, like a Twilight Zone episode about a place that doesn't change.

What happens in a place like that is great fodder for art, especially for writing. It is no accident that Stephen King was raised there, and has based so many disturbing tales in that land. And yet while I have placed the adventures of Zack Taylor in Maine, it is not the Maine of Real Life. No real persons are represented in these pages, and towns exist only as a scenic backdrop to the tale, not as the places they actually are.

While Zack's travails can be read as a ripping action yarn, there are also greater themes represented. "*A Memory of Grief*" is from the Epic of Gilgamesh, one of the most ancient recorded stories of our species. Gilgamesh was a king whose actions caused such a ruckus that the gods sent down a companion, Enkidu. After adventures, Enkidu dies, and the sorrow of Gilgamesh sends him off the rails. Zack is a flawed character, who finds that a life of grief and anger cause one to commit great harm, even while trying to do good. Doing the right thing may not be easy, but it must be done, despite the cost.

And so the story awaits. When you're done, let me know what you thought of this work, if you liked or didn't like it, and whether you would recommend it to your friends. Thank you for being there.

Dale T. Phillips

# ABOUT THE AUTHOR

A lifelong student of mysteries, Maine, and the martial arts, Dale T. Phillips has combined all of these into A Memory of Grief. His travels and background allow him to paint a compelling picture of Zack Taylor, a man with a mission, but one at odds with himself and his new environment.

A longtime follower of mystery fiction, the author has crafted a hero in the mold of Travis McGee, Doc Ford, and John Cain, a moral man at heart who finds himself faced with difficult choices in a dangerous world. But Maine is different from the mean, big-city streets of New York, Boston, or L.A., and Zack must learn quickly if he is to survive.

Dale studied writing with Stephen King, and has published novels, over 30 short stories, collections, as well as poetry, articles, and non-fiction. He has appeared on stage, television, and in an independent feature film, *Throg*. He has also appeared on two nationally televised quiz shows, *Jeopardy* and *Think Twice*. He co-wrote and acted in The Nine, a short political satire film. He has traveled to all 50 states, Mexico, Canada, and through Europe. He enjoys competitive sports, historical re-enactment, and his family.

Connect Online:
Website: http://www.daletphillips.com
Blog: http://daletphillips@blogspot.com
Twitter: DalePhillips2

### *Try these other works by Dale T. Phillips*

*Shadow of the Wendigo* (Supernatural Thriller)

Dale T. Phillips

**The Zack Taylor Mystery Series**
*A Memory of Grief*
*A Fall From Grace*
*A Shadow on the Wall*

**Story Collections**
*Fables and Fantasies* (Fantasy)
*Crooked Paths* (Mystery/Crime)
*Strange Tales* (Magic Realism, Paranormal)
*Apocalypse Tango* (Science Fiction)
*Halls of Horror* (Horror)
*Jumble Sale* (Mixed Genres)
*The Big Book of Genre Stories* (Different Genres)

**Non-fiction Career Help**
*How to Improve Your Interviewing Skills*

**With Other Authors**
*Insanity Tales*
*Rogue Wave: Best New England Crime Stories 2015*

Sign up for my newsletter to get special offers
http://www.daletphillips.com

Made in the USA
Middletown, DE
18 May 2015